ROPING THE COWBOY BILLIONAIRE

A CHAPPELL BROTHERS NOVEL: BLUEGRASS
RANCH ROMANCE BOOK 2

EMMY EUGENE

Blaine Chappell rode along the northernmost fence on the ranch, just him, the June Kentucky sunshine, and his horse Featherweight. There was no traffic out there, as there were no roads that bordered this side of the ranch. Only long, straight, white fences, characteristic of every horse farm in the state.

Emerald green grass waved in the slight breeze, and Blaine wished the wind would pick up a little bit to cool him down. He loved Sunday afternoons like this, with the pastor's words flowing through his mind, his thoughts wandering where they wanted, and only a sense of beauty in front of him.

Today, though, his thoughts seemed a little stickier than usual. Featherweight plodded along, her hooves barely kicking up any dust from the grass that had settled in the last week. Blaine felt more at home in the saddle than anywhere else, and had he been shorter, he'd have been the one riding the horses he and his brothers raised to run in the races.

As it was, he oversaw all the medical care of the horses and other animals at Bluegrass Ranch. He'd left the ranch for a couple of years to get his veterinarian technician license for large animals, but the time to invest in veterinary school was too much. The ranch had a team of vets they called on daily, and Blaine didn't need to get the doctorate degree to work with the animals.

He monitored the cattle, the chickens, the sheep, and the goats, as well as the horses. Their main source of income was the championship horses they raised to win the Kentucky Derby, the Preakness, and the Belmont stakes, but there were dozens of other races with tidy prize pots too.

Blaine scheduled all the breeding, and he had seven studs coming in this week to breed with their mares. He, Spur, Duke, and Cayden named every horse, with a lot of the input coming from Cayden, as he was the public face of the ranch. Whoever bought the horse could and usually did rename them, but for a while there, when the Internet headlines ran about the birth of a possible future champion, it was the name the three of them chose.

"What do you think?" he asked Featherweight. "The ones with three or four words sometimes hit the best."

With a gestation period of eleven months, he had plenty of time to pick out names for any foals they might get. There were races for fillies and mares only, some for colts and geldings, and some where they raced against each other.

His favorite race was the Kentucky Oaks, and while most people hadn't heard of it, there was still over a million dollars to be won. Every time a Bluegrass Ranch horse won a race, their bloodlines became more coveted. They could sell their horses for more money.

Spur managed all of that, and Blaine helped when it came time for breeding. They owned one of the former Derby winners who could stud, and that didn't cost them anything. Getting the other males to come to the ranch cost a pretty penny, and besides advertising their two-year-old sale every spring, that was the bulk of the money the ranch spent.

Ian was the numbers brother on the ranch, and Duke was the one who dealt with procuring all the studs. He'd been preparing for this week for the past month, and Blaine had been right at his side for most of that.

He needed to stop thinking about horses, horses, horses. He woke with horses on his mind, and dreamed of horses. He went to bed with horses in his brain, and sometimes he even counted horses when he couldn't fall asleep.

The problem was, if he wasn't thinking about the ranch, his job on it, or horses, he obsessed over Tamara Lennox.

She was ten times as dangerous to let into his mind,

especially because he couldn't seem to have an innocent thought about her. She stuck around, needling him, making him question the last two decades of his life. He felt like he'd wasted the last five at least, since she'd turned thirty then, and he'd completely forgotten about their agreement.

She'd reminded him of it last week. They'd agreed that when she turned thirty, if neither of them were in a relationship, he'd ask her out and they'd try something romantic. He'd given her a deluxe set of car mats instead.

"Stupid," he muttered to himself. He'd started dating Alex about six months after that, and that had been his last relationship. He'd thought it would be his last relationship ever, but Tam had him thinking again.

He could picture her in his mind without even trying. They'd been friends for a little over twenty years, and there was no one on this Earth that he knew better—not even one of his brothers.

He could feel the way her lips pressed against his, as he'd kissed her last week in some insane moment where he'd told Spur to follow his heart, and then Blaine thought he could follow his. If only his heart hadn't led him down such a twisted path.

"She likes you," he told himself, which seemed surreal and natural at the same time. She had admitted to a crush on him, but Blaine still wasn't sure what zone they were in. They'd argued a lot on their last date—which was over a week old now—and he hadn't kissed her when they'd gotten back to the homestead.

She'd thanked him for dinner, and he'd said he'd call her. She'd rumbled away in her beat-up pickup truck, and he'd somehow made it to his suite in the house without encountering another Chappell.

That alone was a miracle, as he'd expected Trey to be lying in wait, a dozen questions on the tip of his tongue.

Trey hadn't said anything to Blaine about going out with Tam. Not one thing. Red flags existed all over that, but this past week had been exceptionally busy at the ranch. Even Duke and Conrad hadn't seen their girlfriends, and Spur had only spent one evening with Olli.

He'd gotten engaged on Thursday night, so he'd had a really busy week.

Blaine had had to hear all about the engagement from his mother when he'd gone for breakfast on Saturday morning. That was probably why Tam had lodged herself in Blaine's mind and refused to be moved out.

"Let's head back," he said to the horse, and Featherweight seemed to understand English. He barely had to point her in the right direction; he just told her where he wanted to go, and she got him there.

He spent a long time brushing her down and cleaning her tack. Once she was back in her stall with a few extra treats in the form of apples and carrots and oats, Blaine started for the homestead. The ranch was massive, spanning hundreds of acres, and they had row houses, walking circles, a full-size track, administration buildings, selling courts and stadiums, arenas, and parking lots for when the buyers came.

There was always someone around, doing something, but Sunday was their slowest day of the week.

Blaine took a long, deep breath, and held it before pushing it from his lungs. Conrad was the best cook out of all the brothers, but Blaine put Sunday evening meals together more than anyone else. Momma usually fed everyone for lunch after church, but she hadn't today, because she and Daddy had gone to see her mother.

Gramma was getting way up there in years, and she lived in an assisted facility in Dreamsville now. Most of the Chappells lived on the ranch until the day they died, and one of Blaine's favorite places was the cemetery.

They buried people on the east half and animals on the west, and some of his favorite childhood pets had been laid to rest on the patch of land in the far eastern corner of the ranch, where the family cemetery sat.

His phone rang as he went past the homestead, his goal the front shed. He had barbells there he liked to work with in the mornings and evenings, and he wanted to check his schedule for the week.

Tam's name sat on his screen, and his feet froze while his heart flopped. He'd texted her quite a bit the past few days, but he hadn't seen her, and he hadn't spoken to her. He quickly swiped on the call when he realized it had rung three or four times already and lifted the phone to his ear.

Tam was swearing, her voice loud, though he could distinctly hear a hissing sound in the background.

"Tam?" he asked.

"Blaine," she barked. "Some idiot ran a stop sign and hit me. Can you come get me?"

His pulse sprinted now, and he jogged toward the homestead. "Yep. Where are you?"

A man said something Blaine couldn't catch, and Tam yelled, "Yes, I called you an idiot. Stop means stop!"

"Tam," Blaine said. "Focus, Tam. Don't engage with him." He could be anyone, and Blaine's worry for his best friend doubled. Inside, he swiped his keys from the hooks inside the mudroom and retraced his steps.

Tam didn't hear him or didn't care what he had to say, because she said something else to the guy who'd hit her.

"You're obviously okay," Blaine said. "At least your mouth."

"I called nine-one-one," she said. "My back hurts."

"Are you sitting down?" Blaine asked, jogging to his truck now. Half of them sat in front of the homestead, as four of the Chappell brothers lived there. The other four lived in a second house further west, and their parents lived on the road that ran along the front of the ranch.

"Yes," Tam said. "I'm fine, Blaine. I'm not going in the ambulance."

"But an ambulance is on the way, right?"

"They're here already," she said. "The police too."

"Then why are you yelling at that guy?"

"He's a police officer, so his buddies are just letting him go wherever he wants."

"Okay, Tamara," Blaine said, employing the use of her full name as he got behind the wheel and started his truck. "Do not yell at a police officer." Especially some of the obscenities she'd been using. "Please."

"I don't feel good, Blaine," she said, and her voice was half the volume and twice the pitch it had just been.

"I'll be right there." He went down the lane that led to the highway at twice the normal clip. "You never told me where you are."

"The stop sign just down from my shop. I got new leather delivered yesterday."

"Which way from your shop, Tam?" he asked, turning left onto the highway. Her shop was near downtown, so he knew he needed to go that way.

"Uh...I don't know," she said.

"Tam," he said. "What's your middle name?"

"Um, Presley?"

Why was she guessing? "Where are the paramedics?" he asked. "You need to get them. You don't sound good, Tam."

"I don't feel good," she said, her voice ghosting into a whisper by the last word.

"Tam," he said, raising his voice. "Tam, which direction from the shop?" He could probably find her pretty easily once he got to her leather-working shop. The flashing lights and emergency vehicles in a small town wouldn't be hard to find.

"Tam?" he asked when she didn't answer. A loud clunk came through the line, and Blaine's blood turned to ice. "Tam," he yelled.

Other voices came through the line, and he heard a man said, "Ma'am? Ma'am, I need you to wake up."

"Hey," Blaine yelled, hoping to get someone's attention.

"Who's this?" a man asked.

"I'm her boyfriend," Blaine said, wearing the label proudly. "Did she pass out?"

"Yes, sir, she did. We've got a team here working with her."

"She said her back hurt," he said. "She was in a car accident about five years ago with her mother." Blaine could still remember getting that phone call too. His anxiety shot through the top of his skull. "She couldn't tell me where she was, and she guessed at her last name."

"We're at the corner of Leavers and Hoof."

"I'll be there in five minutes," Blaine said. "Or should I meet you at the hospital?"

"We'll still be here in five minutes," the guy said. "I have to go." The line went dead, and Blaine banged his open palm against the steering wheel. He wasn't angry, but frustration looked a lot like anger for Blaine Chappell.

So did worry, and that what was really eating through him.

"I'm coming, Tam," he said under his breath, practically taking a corner on two wheels. "Hang on. I'm coming."

2

*T*amara Lennox opened her eyes at the touch of someone with cool fingers.

"Tam," he said, and she blinked to be able to see Blaine better. He came into focus slowly, and she tried to sit up.

"Shh, no," he said, pressing that large, cool hand against her shoulder to keep her down. "You're in the back of an ambulance, sweetheart, and you're not getting up."

"No," she said, a powerful sense of choking coming over her. She coughed at the suddenly sterile air. "I said I didn't want to go in the ambulance." Her legs thrashed, and she found them tied down. "Blaine," she said, plenty of panic in her voice. "Help."

But he moved, and another man's face filled her vision. "Ma'am," he said. "It's a six-minute drive, and we're already halfway there."

"No," she said again, desperate now. She couldn't be in an ambulance. They were so tiny, and she was fine. Even as she thought it, a wave of pain moved down her back. Tears sprang to her eyes.

"I can give you a mild sedative," the paramedic said.

"No," she said again.

"Tam," Blaine said from somewhere. His voice echoed, but she felt it when he slid his fingers between hers. Her body sighed, and some of the panic inside Tam ebbed away. "There you go, baby. Just calm down. They're helping you, not hurting you."

"I don't like ambulances," she whispered. "They're too small."

"You're okay," Blaine said. "You passed out for a minute there, and they had to do something to stabilize your back and neck."

"I said I was fine."

"You're a liar," Blaine said. A moment passed, and he chuckled. Tam found what he'd said funny too, and to her horror, a very girlish giggle came out of her mouth. Maybe they'd already given her something for the pain in her back. Maybe that was why she couldn't feel it anymore.

Another round of anxiety kicked against her ribs. "Don't give me anything," she said. "I don't like drugs." Her voice slurred on the last sentence, and she knew then that she'd already been given something.

Her brain sloshed from side to side as the ambulance turned, and she closed her eyes as a debilitating round of vertigo hit her. "I hate ambulances," she said over and over.

"I hate you, Blaine, for letting them put me in this ambulance..."

SHE WOKE THE SOUND OF BLAINE'S DEEP, LUXURIOUS VOICE reading to her from her favorite book. "It doesn't happen all at once. You become. It takes a long time. That's why it doesn't happen to people..."

...who break easily, Tam thought, reciting along with him. Or have sharp edges, or have to be carefully kept. Generally, by the time you are real, most of your hair has been—

"Loved off," Tam said, her voice creaky as she opened her eyes. "And your eyes drop out and you get loose in the joints and very shabby."

Blaine stopped reading, and he met Tam's eyes.

"But these things don't matter at all," she continued. "Because once you are real, you can't be ugly, except to people who don't understand."

A smile bloomed on his face while she finished the page, and he closed the book and set it somewhere out of her sight. "Hey, Tamara." He reached out and stroked her hair off her forehead, and he did it with such love, that she hoped he could love her enough to never think she was ugly, when she grew saggy and old.

She realized then that she wanted to grow old with him, and she wasn't sure how to make that a reality. They hadn't talked much about their actual plan to convince Hayes that they were dating. They'd just been dating. Sort of.

Not really at all, Tam thought. You went on one date, and he didn't even kiss you afterward.

"How do you feel?" he asked, pulling his hand away and folding his arms.

"Okay," she said. "How long have I been out?"

"Oh, like, thirty minutes," he said with a slight scoff. "They did some x-rays and an MRI. I told them they'd be glad you were out for that." He smiled like her claustrophobia was a real hoot.

Tam shivered just thinking about being in that confined pod. "Good thing," she said. "I would've gone crazy."

He nodded. "I'm sorry about the ambulance. They had you loaded before I got there, Tam."

She nodded and tried to sit up further in the hospital bed. "Do I have to stay here?"

"Until the doctor comes back," Blaine said. "At least. I can go let them know you're awake." He got up and moved to the door, which slid open. Tam realized she wasn't in a hospital room, but a little cubicle, and there seemed to be plenty of activity beyond the wall of glass separating her from everyone else.

Someone had drawn the curtains over most of it, but

when Blaine stepped out, she heard the chatter, the beeping machines, and the whirring of fans.

Sweat broke out on her forehead, and she flung the blanket off her legs. She wore a hospital gown, and she froze. Someone had undressed her. With fear bumping through her veins, she stared as Blaine came back inside. He slid the door closed and looked at her. "Terrance is coming to check on you."

"Who's Terrance? Where are we? Where are my clothes?"

"Terrance is your nurse," Blaine said without missing a beat. "He's your lead nurse, and nothing gets done unless Terrance says so." He sat back down in the chair he'd been in, a sigh leaking from his mouth. "We're in the ER. Your clothes are in that bag." He indicated a bag on the floor near his feet.

Their eyes met again, and Tam didn't dare ask if he'd seen her undressed. Those milk chocolate eyes buzzed with energy though, like he knew exactly what she was worried about. He said nothing and cocked his head instead.

"Where's your cowboy hat?" she asked.

Blaine reached up and touched his hair, as if he hadn't realized he wasn't wearing a cowboy hat. "I don't know," he said. "I must've lost it somewhere along the way."

"I'm not paying for a replacement," she said automatically. "You have more money than anyone. You cowboy billionaires can buy your own hats."

He laughed, and Tam smiled at the good thing she'd done. "I have plenty of hats, Tam."

"I'm sure you do."

He scooted closer to her and took both of her hands in his. "You sure you're okay? Not feeling dizzy or sick?"

"No," she said.

"Your head doesn't hurt?"

"No," Tam said. "My back either. They gave me something though. I know they did."

"Just a very light sedative," he said. "No painkillers."

"Are you sure?"

"That's what they told me."

Tam wasn't sure if she believed what the doctors told people. When she and her mother had been hit by the twenty-something who'd been texting instead of paying attention to the road, they'd said her mother would make a full recovery. Five years had passed, and she still limped, and she still suffered from neck pack nearly all the time, and her back still went out at least once a week.

She'd been going to the chiropractor religiously every week for years, and Tam didn't think that was a full recovery.

"I just want to go home," she said.

"I'll get you there," he said. "I promise."

"What shape was my truck in?" She watched his reaction, and when he ducked his head, she knew it wasn't good. "You can't hide behind that hat," she teased.

"It's got to be totaled," he said. "The whole front end was smashed up."

"He came out of nowhere," Tam said. "He was going way too fast, and he didn't even slow down for the stop sign." Her blood started to heat. "He's a cop, and I just know he's going to get off with nothing."

"Was he in a police car?"

"No," Tam said. "No lights, no siren, no nothing." She blinked, her thoughts flying through possibilities. "If they say he was, and that the accident was my fault, I won't get insurance money."

"Sure, you will," he said. "You just might have a fee or something."

"Do you know the fee for not yielding to a police officer who has his lights and siren on?" she challenged.

Blaine did not know, and Tam had made her point. "They're not going to do that," he said. "They were taking pictures and stuff when I got there."

"Evidence can be tampered with," she said.

"Okay, Tam," he said with a smile. "This isn't one of your crime dramas."

He hadn't dealt with insurance companies that only wanted to pay the minimum, or who wanted to somehow make a texting college student out to be her mother's fault. She didn't say anything, because she was tired of arguing with Blaine. When they were best friends, it was fun, witty banter. Now that she wanted him to be her boyfriend, the arguments were just annoying.

"Thank you for coming," she said, leaning back into the bed.

He released her hands so he didn't have to lean so far forward. "I will always come when you call, Tam."

Their eyes met, and Blaine rose to his feet slowly. Sparks practically shot out of his eyes, and Tam felt them moving up her arms and into her neck. "I've missed you this week," he said huskily. "We've been so busy on the ranch, and I hate not seeing you." He bent down as if he'd kiss her right there in the emergency room, where the AC clearly wasn't working and she was wearing a white gown with faded, blue flowers on it.

"All right," a man said, his voice easily being broadcast through a microphone. She jumped and looked toward the door while Blaine backed up against the wall. Her heart pounded in her throat and ears as she watched a very large African-American man look up from a clipboard. "Tamara, it's so good to meet you. I'm Terrance."

She had never heard a voice so deep or seen hands so big. She managed to shake his and answer a few questions. He took her temperature and blood pressure, never reporting on what his instruments told him.

He scrawled things on the clipboard and finally looked up. "Are you ready to go home?"

"Yes, please," she said, her voice sounding tinny and quiet.

Lawrence grinned and nodded. "I'll get Doctor Millstone in here to sign you out. Then your boyfriend can take you home and make you comfortable." He turned to Blaine. "She shouldn't be alone tonight. She might have a pretty bad headache, and someone should be there if she starts vomiting or in case she passes out."

"Will she do that?" Blaine asked. "Does she have a concussion?"

"I'll have Doctor Millstone go over the films," Terrance said like the doctor would be handing out brownies. "Her temp is a little elevated, but everyone's is because of the darn air conditioner being out."

Tam knew there'd been a problem with the AC, and for some reason, she felt so proud of herself.

"Otherwise," Terrance said. "She's good." He turned back to her. "Any pain in your head or back? Your neck? Anywhere?"

"Not much," Tam said. "Nothing I'd even take pills for."

"I'm still going to recommend that you go home with something," he said. "Sometimes our adrenaline covers up pain, and we can't feel it until later." He smiled again, nodded, and left the pod.

Tam looked at Blaine, who looked steadily back. "I'm staying with you tonight," he said.

"I can call my sister."

He grunted, a look of displeasure crossing his face. "I'll have Trey bring me some clothes."

"Yeah, because I'm not going to have anything that fits you."

"Are you calling me fat?" he teased, and a genuine smile flitted across Tam's face.

"You have been eating a lot of peanut butter sandwiches lately."

"It's not the sandwiches that are the problem," Blaine said. "It's all the ice cream I can't stay away from in the evening."

"I have ice cream," Tam said.

"That's why I'm staying with you and not Stacy," he said, grinning at her. He stepped closer again and straightened the chair that he'd knocked sideways when he'd moved away from her. "Do you really hate me, Tam?"

"Did I say that?"

"In the ambulance," he said. "You said you hated me for letting them put you in there."

She looked up at him, and he wore such a vulnerable look on his face. She shook her head. "I could never hate you."

"Never?" His eyebrows went up. "Maybe a real relationship won't ruin our friendship then."

Tam didn't know what to say to that. She knew he'd been worrying about that for a couple of weeks now. Truth be told, so had she. She couldn't lose Blaine. She'd rather not have him as a boyfriend than lose him completely.

As neither of them had ever had a relationship work out, the likelihood of them remaining friends after all of this was very low. Yet Tam wanted to take the risk. She reached up and cradled his face in the palm of her hand. How could she say everything she felt in her heart and all she thought in her mind?

Turned out, she didn't need to. Blaine leaned down and pressed his lips to hers, and they both said enough with one amazing kiss.

3

---

*B*laine could not believe that he had kissed Tam again. He was honestly just doing whatever came naturally to him, and seeing her in that bed and watching as she woke up had tugged on his heartstrings in a way they had never been pulled before.

He cared about her, and he wanted her to know it.

He wasn't sure if deepening the kiss showed he cared or that he just had hormones, but that happened too. Her fingers ran through his hair—at least until she groaned and jerked her hand away.

Blaine pulled back and straightened, the air in the tiny hospital cubicle suddenly so dang hot. Terrance had said the air conditioner was out, but Blaine knew the heat coursing through his body had more attributing to it than that.

"Sorry," he said, wondering if he'd ever be able to kiss her without apologizing afterward.

"It's just this stupid IV," Tam said, and to his horror, she plucked it right out of her wrist.

"Tam," he said, turning away quickly to search for something to press against the bead of blood that had bloomed up quickly. "You can't just do that." He grabbed a couple of paper towels from the dispenser by the sink and returned to her side.

She simply stared at her blood as it continued to weep from the wound the IV had left behind. He pressed the paper towels to her wrist, and she flinched. It also broke the spell she'd fallen into, and she raised her eyes to his. "I want to go home."

"I know that, baby," he said. "But you can't go ripping out IVs." He glanced at the machines monitoring her vital signs, but he had no idea which one was connected to the IV. A moment later, three nurses entered the room.

Terrance led them, and he said, "We've got an alarm going off in here." He scanned the situation quickly and took Blaine's place at Tam's side.

"It was bothering me," Tam said, not an ounce of apology in her voice. "When is the doctor going to be here? I'm fine, and I want to go home."

Blaine actually liked her spunk, though sometimes her sass could be a little much. She needed to learn that she sometimes could get more with honey than vinegar. He said nothing, though, because he really wanted to stay with her tonight. If he argued with her, she'd call her sister.

Cara lived in nearby Lexington, just on the other side of town. While Dreamsville ran along the rolling hills north of the city, Borderville hugged the southern side. It was still only a half an hour drive Cara could make easily.

He should probably offer to call her sister, and then he needed to call Spur and Cayden. They could get all the information to Duke about the breeding. He should call his mother too, because Blaine knew not many of her sons went out to visit her—Spur was really the only one who made any effort to do that. He went from time to time, but Blaine called her a lot. At least five times a week.

His thoughts lingered on his parents and the lecture Spur had given the brothers a little over a week ago.

They need us, Spur had said. *We owe everything to them. So whatever it is keeping you from going to see your own mother when she lives five minutes down the road, get over it. Figure it out. Make peace with it—and then go make peace with her.*

His eyes had blazed like the depths of the ocean— unrelenting and absolutely lethal. All of the brothers had hung their heads and murmured their assent. Blaine was still trying to figure out how to show up at his mother's doorstep and tell her all of the things that sat between them.

He knew the biggest one: Alexandra Alloy.

She came from a family of Southern socialites, and

that meant she'd been perfect for one of the Chappells. His mother had paired Blaine with Alex for a fundraising dinner they'd hosted at Bluegrass Ranch, and the rest was history.

They'd started dating. Blaine had fallen hopelessly in love with her. He'd thought she was hopelessly in love with him. Then he'd learned she'd been stepping out on him with other men.

Even then, he hadn't broken up with her. That had taken an extreme amount of courage, and Blaine had taken almost a month to store up enough to be able to do it.

His mother had been livid. Absolutely irate, and she still didn't know the real reason Blaine had called off the wedding and asked for his very expensive diamond ring back.

Alex hadn't given it to him, though. He hadn't fought her for it, and as far as he knew, she still had it. More likely, though, she'd sold it for as much as she could get. Her family might have money, but Alex was the type of woman who would never have enough.

He blinked as another man came into the room, making the small space very crowded. Blaine shifted back over to the chair he'd been sitting in earlier and picked up the bag with Tam's clothes in it.

"I'm Doctor Millstone," he said, extending his hand to Tam. She took it and shook it, all with that blood smeared on her arm. "I understand you're ready to go." He took the clipboard from Terrance, who cocked his eyebrows at Tam.

She had the decency to look somewhat ashamed as she dabbed at her wrist again.

"Your vitals do look good," Dr. Millstone said. "Look here." He held up a light and shone it in Tam's eyes. "Good response. I don't think you have a concussion, Miss Lennox." He looked in her ears and then listened to her heart.

"If she starts to act strange, or sleeps too long, she needs to come back in." He spoke to Blaine as he wore his stethoscope.

"You got it," Blaine said, though he thought it would take an act of God to get Tam back in this hospital.

"Throwing up, disorientation, dizziness. Vertigo." The doctor continued to lecture Tam about symptoms to watch for, but Blaine knew she wasn't even listening. She was like a caged tiger, on the edge of breaking free. She'd agree to anything just to get out of there.

Finally, the doctor handed some papers to Blaine and said, "All right. I'll send in Catrina with the discharge papers. You just have to sign those, Miss Lennox, and you're free to go."

"Thank you," she said with a smile, and Blaine saw that honey-coated version of his best friend. He waited until everyone had left, and then he shook his head at her.

"What?" she asked.

"You ripped that out on purpose," he said.

"Of course I ripped it out on purpose," she said.

"I'm not even sure it hurt."

"It did," she insisted, her blue eyes so bright.

Blaine chuckled and handed her the bag of clothes. "Do you need help changing?" he teased.

"Get out," she said with a laugh. "And we're driving through somewhere on the way back to my house. I'm starving. Plus, I've got to get these drugs out of my system."

"I'll check with the doctor," Blaine said. "Maybe you're supposed to drink clear fluids or something."

"I don't care what he says," Tam said as Blaine left the cubicle.

"I know that," he muttered. Tam was fiercely independent. Blaine actually really liked that about her. He liked that she wasn't afraid of a challenge, and she wasn't afraid to get hurt. He'd seen her ride in a barrel racing final with a fractured collarbone, refuse to ride in the ambulance, and only go to the hospital when her trainer threatened to pull her from the next rodeo.

As he thought about that, Blaine realized that she was far more ready to take their relationship out of the friend zone than he was. "She's not afraid of a challenge," he mused. Transitioning from best friends to lovers would definitely be a challenge.

"She's not afraid to get hurt," he added. At the same time, she'd told him she *was* afraid to lose him. Apparently, she did have boundaries, and she did experience fear.

He paced toward the nurse's station, his mind on overload again. He hated feeling this stuffed with thoughts and not being able to grab onto a single one.

"Bottom line," he told himself. It was an exercise to get him to focus. "The bottom line is...she asked you to pretend to be her boyfriend while Hayes is in town. It's a yes or no question."

He turned back to Tam's cubicle just as she walked out of it. Their eyes met, and he hurried toward her. "Yes," he said.

"Yes what?" she asked.

"You asked if I'd be your fake boyfriend when Hayes is in town. I'm saying yes."

Tam smiled up at him. "I thought we already established that."

"I'm starting from the bottom," he said.

"Oh, bottom line," she said. "You think too hard sometimes, Blaine." She led him to the nurse's station and asked for the discharge paperwork.

"Oh, I'm sorry," the woman there said. "It's not ready yet."

"Not ready?" Tam asked. "What does it take to get ready?"

"Well, we have to print some stuff, and it takes a few minutes for our system to update with the doctor's orders," the nurse started to explain. "So your form hasn't been unlocked yet."

Blaine slipped his fingers into Tam's and squeezed. She looked at him and then back to the nurse. She drew in a deep breath. "How long?" she asked, her voice pitched up slightly.

"Should be soon," the nurse said with a smile.

"Can we wait in the waiting room?" Blaine asked.

"I'm sorry," she said, and she had a very good apologetic face. "You'll have to wait in your assigned room."

"I'm not—"

"Okay," Blaine said over Tam. He tugged on her hand to get her to go with him.

"That room is tiny," she hissed at him. "And it's so dang hot in here."

"It's okay," Blaine said. "Besides, then we can figure out the next step above me saying yes to be your fake boyfriend."

"The wedding," Tam said. "You promised you'd go to the wedding."

"Can I go with you?" Blaine stepped into the small room and had to pull extra hard to get Tam to come with him.

"No," she said. "It's my friend Nita that needs a date. She's the same age as you, and you guys will get along great. Remember, there's lobster and steak..."

"Who are you going with?" he asked.

"No one," Tam said. "I don't care if I have a date for the

wedding. It's Nita who cares. She dated the groom, Blaine. She has to show him she's over him."

"So I'm going to be her fake boyfriend too."

"Hey, it might be good practice for us." Tam smiled at him and sat in the chair he'd used earlier. "Although, with the way you keep kissing me, I think we've got the essentials in the bag." She gave him a knowing look, one that was also laced with a lot of questions.

"Yeah," Blaine said, because he didn't know what else to say. He needed a new bottom line.

Bottom line, he thought. *You like Tam and don't want this to be fake.* He opened his mouth to tell her that—again, as he'd said it once before—but the nurse walked into the room.

"All right, Miss Lennox," she said. "You sign this, and you're free to go."

Tam signed so fast, Blaine barely had time to breathe.

HOURS LATER, HE LAY ON THE COUCH WITH HER IN HIS ARMS. They'd watched dozens and dozens of movies together over the years. He was a very touchy-feely person, and with the right person, so was Tam.

He was, apparently, the right person.

She'd fallen asleep after eating a double cheeseburger and fries, and Blaine had been awake, thinking and trying to get his pulse to play nice.

The movie ended, and yet he didn't move. He didn't want to move. He wanted to be the rock Tam needed in her life. He wanted to be the one she came to for help, just like she had tonight. He wanted to be her best friend and her boyfriend.

He was going to fully commit. He'd realized about the time her breathing had deepened that he hadn't fully committed to taking the step from friend to boyfriend. He may have said he wanted that. He may have acted irrationally, and said some whack things, and kissed her a couple of times.

He'd sent mixed messages about the rules, and that he needed them, then he didn't.

All of it was because Blaine was very, very good at waffling.

No wonder it took you a month to break-up with a woman who was cheating on you, he thought.

In some aspects of his life, he was very good at making decisions. Big decisions too, like which breeder to call to get a stud scheduled. Which transport company to use. If he should call the vet for a horse or not. All of those seemed so much easier than the step he was about to take.

But if he could commit to being Tam's real boyfriend, he could stop thinking so hard about whether he *should* or not. He'd call her when he said he would. He'd ask her out, and they'd *go* to dinner and movies and community events.

He'd kiss her without apologizing, and he'd find out if his scarred heart could love again.

"Dear Lord," he said as a vein of fear struck right next to his heart. "Please help me." He didn't want to hurt Tam —or lose her in any way—and he certainly couldn't take another lash on his heart.

"If this doesn't work out, I've lost another girlfriend *and* my best friend," he whispered. "How will I ever recover from that?"

The only reason he'd survived his break-up with Alex was because of Tam. If he didn't have her...

He didn't even want to think about it, and his arms around her instinctively tightened. She moaned in her sleep, and Blaine eased his hold on her.

He couldn't lose her. He just couldn't.

4

Tam's muscles ached, though she worked very hard not to show it. If she so much as hitched her step even the littlest bit, Blaine would be all over her, demanding to know if her head hurt or when the last time she'd taken medication had been.

She cut a glance toward the man, her heartbeat doing the same thing it's been doing for a couple of months now. Stuttering.

He was far too handsome to be out in the dust and dirt working. A man like him should wear designer suits and strike poses for the best photographers in the world. Blaine didn't even seem to know how good-looking he was. How kind his heart was. Or how his smile could light Tam's world for days.

He looked her way, a question in his eyes. Tam quickly looked back toward the truck coming down the road. The huge one-ton vehicle had a horse trailer hitched to it, and it was her turn to greet the owners.

She put a smile on her face—none of her "attitude" in sight. Blaine had told her after the first day of breeding that if she even so much as showed one ounce of that attitude, he wouldn't let her come back.

Tam adored Bluegrass Ranch, and she couldn't imagine not being able to come here. Therefore, she'd shelved her attitude and only gave it to him in the evenings, when he tried to come sleep on her couch.

She'd let him for the first two nights, but last night, she'd insisted she was okay. She was. She didn't need a babysitter, especially one as tall, and as tan, and as tantalizing at Blaine Chappell.

He'd said he'd be her fake boyfriend at the hospital, and Tam had no idea what was going on. He'd refused her at first. Then driven over to say she'd forgotten him at the ranch—and then he'd kissed her.

Then he'd stood her up for dinner. Let a week go by. Said he didn't need rules—especially ones about kissing. Gotten mad when she'd come to pick him up for their second date-slash-meeting. Let a few more days go by. Then he'd come to help her after her car accident.

She had no idea what was going on beneath that sexy cowboy hat, and she glanced at him as she approached the driver's door, her smile still stuck in place.

A cowboy got out, and she said, "Welcome to Bluegrass, Mister Harvey. I'm Tamara Lennox, and I'll be escorting you to the breeding pens today." She stuck out her hand, and Wayne Harvey shook it.

"Mornin'," he said pleasantly. "Will I see Spur or Duke inside?"

"Yes, sir," Tam drawled. "I'm just here if you need anything. Can I get you somethin' to drink? Sweet tea? Lemonade? Water?"

"I'll take some water," he said, starting toward the horse trailer.

Tam grabbed a bottle from the cooler at her feet and followed him. She handed it to him and said, "I'll be takin' the vitals on Barely Audible too. Mister Chappell is here to assist with your horse during the covering." She indicated Blaine, who also wore a smile on his face. He should, too, because getting Barely Audible to stud was a huge feat.

He'd won the Triple Crown only three years ago, and Tam suspected he covered a lot of mares in the spring and summer.

"Blaine," Wayne said, grinning for all he was worth now. He shook Blaine's hand heartily and even pulled him into a quick embrace, clapping him twice on the back. "How are you?"

"Great, Wayne," Blaine said. "How's your father?"

"Oh, he's still kickin'. Yours?"

"About the same," Blaine said. "We're going to take Audible to the breeding shed and do the tease," he said. "We've got Brand Spanking New who's looking great from our ultrasounds waiting, and we'll see how they like each other."

"Too bad Never Going Home isn't in heat," Wayne said. "I know Audible likes her."

Blaine chuckled, and the two of them opened the horse trailer. "She'll probably be ready next week," he said. "But you've got quite a busy schedule with him."

"I swear, all we do is drive and cover. Drive and cover."

Tam rolled her eyes, thankful no one could see her, as the two cowboys had stepped inside the trailer. Wayne wasn't just driving and covering. The horse did all the work during the covering anyway. He was certainly taking some money to the bank in between all of that.

All for something that literally took less than a minute.

Still, when Blaine emerged from the trailer with the tall, dark bay, Tam's breath caught in her throat. Barely Audible was a stunning specimen of a thoroughbred horse, and he definitely knew it.

He looked at her as he walked by, already tossing his head. He knew exactly why he was here, and she hoped he liked Brand Spanking New. She was a bit of a fussy horse, and when Tam met Duke at the door of the breeding shed, he looked up from his brood mare notebook. "She's ready. Let's have him go in on the side. We'll just see how she reacts to him."

Tam gestured for Blaine to take the stud to the side

entrance, and she peered past Duke. "Is she being difficult?"

"A bit," Duke said lightly. "She didn't like Gravestone, which is odd, because they've mated before." He looked back at his notebook. "If she doesn't take to Audible, we can bring over The Mayflower." He frowned at his book, which had a variety of letters and symbols in it that only he understood. "I'm ninety percent certain she'll ovulate in the next forty-eight hours."

"You had Brand New scanned, though," Tam said. "And she won the Belmont. Mayflower only won the Oaks."

"I know," Duke murmured. He turned back to the beautiful gray horse in the shed. "All right, New. You've got this one, okay? He's a great horse, and you be good now."

Brand Spanking New just eyed Duke like he'd told her she'd have to eat something rotten. Definitely difficult.

Audible entered the shed on the side, and he lifted his head instantly. His upper lip came back, revealing his teeth, and Duke grinned. "He's ready."

The horse went all the way to the six-foot wall that kept him away from the mare. She tossed her head too, and Spur murmured something to her and held her in place. She nickered, and he said something else to her.

Duke rounded the horse to stand next to Spur, and Tam just enjoyed being there. Blaine looked anxious, as usual, and she really wished he'd learn how to relax. This covering was going to go fine; Tam could tell already.

They'd already covered two other mares that morning, and after this, they'd all get a break. Audible stretched toward Brand New, trying to bite her. Everyone let him, because that was classic breeding behavior for a horse.

Brand New turned her back on him, squatted, and urinated. Spur grinned, and Duke clapped his hand against his clipboard.

Even Tam smiled, because Brand Spanking New had just told Barely Audible she liked him and he could come on over and get the job done. Maybe she wasn't so fussy after all. They still moved slowly, waiting until Brand New lifted her tail before Spur nodded at Blaine to bring the stud around.

He did, and with Duke, Spur, and Blaine there to hold reins and make sure everything went smoothly, Barely Audible covered Brand New. The whole escapade took about five minutes, and Tam wondered how much Wayne Harvey made from that exchange.

He walked back to the horse trailer with Blaine, the two of them talking and laughing. Tam stepped over to Brand Spanking New and ran her hand down the side of the horse's neck. "That was great, New," she said. "Maybe you'll get a fast foal from him."

She smiled at Spur and Duke, and then she followed Blaine back to the horse trailer.

"...thanks so much," Blaine said. "We'll call you again."

"Always," Wayne said. "I've got Black Pepper Spray as well, and he's a fine stud horse."

"Yep." Blaine tipped his hat, and Wayne Harvey rumbled away in his gigantic truck. He looked at Tam. "Three for three."

She smiled back at him. "You Chappells seem to draw all the luck."

He put his arm around her and scoffed. "Luck? You're joking, right? We've *planned* this breeding week down to the minute."

"You're certainly lucky to get Barely Audible."

"That *was* a bit of luck," Blaine said. "But Wayne and I go way back, and I'll call him next week to schedule for next year. He gives me a date, and we cover whoever we have in heat."

"How much does he get paid?" Tam asked as they started toward the homestead.

Blaine looked at her, and Tam just shrugged. "What? I want to know what that foal cost you."

"You've never wanted to know before."

"Yeah, well, we're dating now, and I want to know. I want to know how much of this ranch you own too. And how much of it you'll inherit, if any. I want to know what I'm dealing with...with...you."

His eyebrows went up, and he dropped his arm. "Dealing with with me?"

"Yeah," she said. "Say it was you who got in a car accident and had to go get a new truck tonight. Which you're still coming with me, right?"

"Of course," he said. "I can't let you come home with another rust bucket."

She just rolled her eyes. He'd hated her old truck, but Tam had loved it. Maybe it growled a little when it should've purred. It got the job done, and it had once been her father's, which made its loss all the harder.

"What would your budget be? Would you be financing this truck or buying it with cash?" Tam wasn't going to let this drop. Besides, a girlfriend should know the financial situation of her boyfriend.

She noted that he had not objected to nor corrected her when she'd said they were dating. She wasn't sure what to make of that, but when he slipped his hand into hers, it didn't matter.

"Oh," she said softly, and Blaine's fingers in hers tightened.

"Is this okay?"

"It's fine," she said, clearing her throat. It was far more than fine. It was downright wonderful.

"We paid Wayne one-seventy-five as a stud fee. And that's cheap. His fee is private, Tam, and we don't—*can't*—announce it."

Tam nodded, her movements tight and sharp. That was more money than she could even fathom. "And you? What do you make every year?"

"Well, I'm no Triple Crown stud," he said, his eyes lighting up.

Tam couldn't help laughing, because that really was

funny. Blaine joined in with her, and it was moments like these that she really started to fall for him. Sometimes they argued. Sometimes they disagreed. The last few weeks had been stressful, but all of that washed away as they laughed together.

He took her to the front shed where he kept an office of sorts, and he pulled a couple of sandwiches out of a mini fridge. "Coke?" he asked, handing her a can without waiting for her to answer. He sighed and groaned as he sat down, and Tam laughed again.

"You sound like you're seventy," she said. "Not thirty-eight." Her back twinged a little bit, but she would take that knowledge to the grave. She wanted to stay at Blue-grass, and not just because they were paying her three hundred dollars a day to get bottled water out of a cooler for a horse owner.

"Sleeping on your couch has kinked my back," he said.

"So it's my fault."

"Yes." He passed her a sandwich. "I'll come tonight, though. You sure you don't need me?"

Tam looked at him, and the moment between them sobered. "You know what? You can come if you want. I don't think it's necessary, but..." She shrugged and focused on her sandwich as she started to unwrap it. She didn't know how to say she liked having Blaine in the house with her. She'd told him a couple of weeks ago that she was tired of going home to no one, but she hadn't exactly used the word *lonely*.

It stung her tongue, and she couldn't say it now either. She picked up her sandwich and took a bite, finally looking up at Blaine. He hadn't moved at all, and he kept his head down.

"I inherited five billion dollars when I turned twenty-five," he said, looking up at her. "That's the deal. You turn twenty-five and you commit to working the ranch? You get the five billion. It's yours, free and clear. We all pull a salary from the ranch too, but it's not much."

Tam stared, the food in her mouth forgotten.

"Stop it," Blaine said, looking away.

"Your parents have forty billion dollars?" she blurted out. She quickly chewed her food and swallowed it, waiting for him to confirm that.

"We sell over three hundred horses a year," he said quietly, his fingers moving slowly as he peeled back the paper on his sandwich. "A lot of them for seven figures. We collect three times that much in stabling fees and trainer fees. We rent the track for an astronomical amount. We have coveted studs too. The ranch sustains itself quite nicely. The rest comes from smart investing and generations of Chappells living here and running this ranch."

He looked up at her. "Tell me this isn't going to change anything between us."

Tam shook her head, though her mind was buzzing. "Why would it change anything?"

"Because I can see the way you're looking at me," he said. "And it's changing things."

She looked away, using her cowgirl hat to hide her face the way so many cowboys did. "I've always known you were rich."

"You didn't know how rich, though," he said miserably.

"I do now," she said, glad her voice had turned lighter. "I suppose you wouldn't have a budget for a new truck, and you'd be writing a check."

"Don't be ridiculous," Blaine said, and Tam whipped her attention back to him. He grinned at her, so radiantly perfect in that moment. "I'd use my miles card, obviously. There are rewards you can get for spending that much money, I'll have you know." He lifted his sandwich and took a bite, his smile still wolfishly on his face.

She rolled her eyes and laughed, but the numbers still swam through her head. Maybe having him come with her that night would be a mistake. She definitely had a budget, and she didn't want to haggle with the salesman to make sure her payment was under four hundred a month. Maybe she could say he should stay home and rest his back. Or maybe she could ask him to run out to Chicken Little's for their fried chicken and biscuits while she bought her truck.

"I can see what you're thinking," Blaine said.

"Oh, yeah?"

"Yeah, and it's not going to work." He met her gaze

with a very solid one of his own. "I'm coming with you to buy that truck, *and* I'm going to sleep on your couch again tonight too."

Tam secretly rejoiced, though a skiff of anxiety skipped through her too. "Fine," she said. "Just don't complain to me about your back." She pointed one finger at him. "I also want fried chicken for dinner, and guess what, Mister Money Bags? You're buying."

He burst out laughing, though Tam wasn't sure what was so funny. She'd called him names like that for years. Decades.

He shook his head as he quieted, and when he looked at her again, his expression was soft and kind and all of the things that made Blaine so utterly perfect in Tam's eyes. He reached across the desk and took her hand in his, slowly bringing it to his lips.

Her skin buzzed, and her stomach quaked. Her crush on Blaine had morphed into something else she couldn't identify, but that she hoped would continue to mature.

"I like you, Tam," he said, and those were the best words in the world in that moment.

"Good," she said. "Because I like you too, and we need to get a few things straight about what's happening here."

5

*B*laine swallowed nervously, but he knew exactly what Tam was talking about. "I've been giving off weird signals, right?"

"More like *scrambled* signals," she said.

"Yeah." He took another bite of his sandwich to give himself a minute to organize everything in his head. When he did, he swallowed and said, "I just needed some time to commit. But I'm ready to do that now."

"Commit to what?"

"To taking our friendship to the next level."

Tam's eyebrows went up, though Blaine didn't understand why she was surprised.

"You know how I am," he said. "I have to go back and forth a thousand times before I take the first step."

"Boy, do I know that," Tam said dryly.

"Then you should know that once I've taken that step, there's no going back."

"I know," she said, much quieter this time.

"Tam." He waited for her to look fully at him, none of this flitting around thing she did with her eyes sometimes. "I've taken the step. I'm fully committed. I'm not going to go back and forth anymore."

She nodded, though a healthy portion of fear rode in her eyes. He felt it stinging way down in his soul, and he had the sudden urge to offer up another prayer. Instead, her phone rang, a shrieking, piercing sound that made them both jump.

Her phone sat on the desk in front of her, and he looked at the screen. He saw Hayes's name there about the same time Tam did. Her gaze flew back to his, and time froze.

Blaine wondered if she'd have ever confessed her feelings for him if her ex-boyfriend hadn't been coming back into town. Would he have ever recognized his feelings for her? Would he have ever acted on them even if he had?

Her mouth moved, and he blinked. Time moved forward again. "Should I answer it?" she asked.

"Sure," Blaine said. "You didn't last time, so maybe see what he has to say." Blaine already knew what Hayes Powell would say. He'd tell Tam how much he missed her, and that he was sorry. He'd talk her ear off about his amazing job in California, and in some strange way, he'd get into her good graces again, and ask her to dinner.

In less than ten minutes, Blaine thought. *You wait and see. Ten bucks says he asks her out in under ten minutes.*

He couldn't really bet against himself, and he took another bite of his sandwich as she swiped on the call. Anything to make it look like he didn't care that she spoke to her ex-fiancé.

"Hayes," she said, plenty of venom in her voice. Maybe he'd lose his own bet.

His heart boomed in his chest in a strange way, because he'd just told her he was ready to take the first step to take their friendship to the next level. The very next thing she'd done was answer the call from Hayes.

"No," she said, turning away from Blaine in such a familiar gesture that his chest squeezed. Someone had wrapped him in a rubber band and was twisting it tighter and tighter.

Tam reached up and tucked her hair, and though Blaine couldn't see the smile on her face, he knew it sat there. He'd seen her duck her head, tuck her hair, and giggle whenever Hayes called so many times he'd lost count.

"Ten seconds," Blaine muttered to himself. Whatever magic powder Hayes Powell had been dipped in couldn't be sold at stores. If it could, Blaine would've bought some a long time ago.

Some people just had charisma. Cayden was like that. Trey sometimes too, especially if he was in a good mood. There was a reason they did a lot of the work around the ranch that required them to deal with other people. They were very, very good with people—and Hayes was just like that.

Tam paced away from Blaine, and though the shed wasn't that big, he couldn't hear what she was saying. He felt like a fool, sitting there listening to the woman he'd kissed twice in the past couple of weeks talking to her ex.

You're thirty-eight, he told himself. *Do something.*

He was tired of sitting around, waiting for life to happen to him. Maybe it was time for him to *do something*.

Blaine shoved the last of his sandwich in his mouth and stood up. He wiped his hands, finished eating, and started toward Tam.

"...that's all I'm saying," she said, her voice low. He wasn't sure if it was flirty or not, because he could hardly hear much past the beating of his blood through his veins. "Yeah, I think—"

"Hey there, sugar," Blaine said in a loud voice, taking the phone from her with a single swipe of his hand. "Who you talkin' to?" He put the phone to his ear as if he'd just come upon Tam.

He stared into her shocked, wide eyes as he said, "Who's this?" He sounded happy, but he was decidedly not as confusion and frustration swirled within him.

"Blaine," Tam said, and he couldn't tell if she was happy about what he'd done or not.

"Who is this?" Hayes asked, his arrogance thick even from a thousand miles away.

"Oh, I asked you first," Blaine said though he was too old to play games. "Tam looked a little upset, and I thought I'd take over."

Hayes said nothing, and Blaine's nerves rattled through his bones. "The screen says Hayes," he said. "Are you seriously calling the woman you ditched over a year ago?"

"Who are you?" Hayes asked again, but Blaine wasn't going to give him the satisfaction of telling him. If he did, Hayes would know Tam was just hanging out with her best friend.

"I'm her boyfriend," he said, making his voice hard. "I'd really appreciate it if you deleted her number from your phone and stopped calling."

"I don't—"

"Goodbye." Blaine pulled the phone away from his ear so he couldn't hear what else Hayes might say. He jabbed at the screen to get the call to end, and he started swiping. "You should block him, Tam."

"Can I have my phone back, please?"

Blaine looked up, and their eyes met. She held out her hand, and Blaine handed over her device.

"You're right," she said. "I should block him." She tapped and swiped, an adorable pucker appearing between her eyes. She stepped to his side and tilted the phone toward him. "Can you help me figure out how to do it?" She looked up at him, and he took a deep breath, getting a lot of horse and leather from her, but also just a hint of strawberry.

The scent came from her shampoo; he knew, because he'd been in her bathroom and seen the bottles.

A tender moment passed between them, and Blaine focused on the phone. He wanted to kiss her, but he also wanted this relationship to progress normally. He didn't drive to a woman's house and kiss her before they'd even gone out. He wouldn't normally kiss a woman in a hospital bed either.

He wanted to take Tam to dinner and go horseback riding with her. He wanted to hold her hand as they strolled down the street on a summer evening, laughing and talking as they got to know one another. He wanted to start falling in love with her, as he knew what a profound and special experience that was.

Then—and only then—would he kiss her.

"Yeah," he said, his voice grinding in his throat. "It's just right there. Tap on his name."

She did, and he guided her through the rest of the steps to block Hayes's number.

"So now if he calls or texts, I just won't get it?" She looked up at him again, such innocence in her eyes.

"That's right," Blaine said. He put his hand on the small of her back. "Finish eating, Tam." They moved back across the shed to his desk, and Tam sat down. He crouched next to her and asked, "Will you go to dinner with me tonight?"

A smile stamped itself on her face. "I'd like that."

"Before the dealership?" he asked. "Or after?"

"Have you ever bought a truck, Blaine? It takes hours."

"Maybe we can just look tonight." He ran his fingertips up and down her forearm, his eyes trained on them instead of her beautiful face.

"You'll have to drive me back and forth again," she said.

"I'm okay with that," he said.

"Okay," she said. "Let's look for trucks—just look. Then we can go to dinner."

Blaine smiled, thinking this was a good first step down a path he was very uncertain about.

Tam put her hand under his chin and lifted his face to hers. "Hey," she said softly. "It's just me."

"Yeah," Blaine said, standing and taking his place behind the desk again. "I know." He gave her a smile, but that was exactly the problem. It was her, and he was terrified of the outcome of this new, official relationship.

BLAINE WHISTLED AS HE PARKED IN TAM'S DRIVEWAY AND got out of his truck. He'd picked up his whistling skill from his grandfather, a man who'd taught Blaine a lot of tricks around the ranch.

"Love you, Granddaddy," he said, looking up into the cloudless sky. He liked to think of his granddaddy sipping lemonade and whistling like the birds up in heaven.

"Would be nice if it wasn't so humid though." He cocked an eyebrow at the sky, as if the Lord cared that it was downright oppressive in Kentucky tonight.

He went up Tam's front steps, his heartbeat knocking through his body now. He knocked loudly and tucked his hands in his pockets, glad he'd kept one eye on Spur the last couple of weeks. He now knew that women liked a man in a clean pair of boots—ones that had never seen work on the ranch. A cowboy hat he hadn't been sweating in all day. And a little cologne Blaine had swiped from Spur's dresser—aptly named after him.

Tam opened the door, and Blaine opened his mouth to say hi. Everything froze at the glorious sight of her standing there in that peaches-and-cream-colored dress. He scanned her down to her genuine leather boots— probably made from the finest leather she could find. They were dark brown and made her look country chic.

She'd put a curl in her hair and something red on her lips, and Blaine could barely breathe.

"What do you think?" she asked, grabbing onto a fistful of the fabric in her skirt.

Blaine blinked, closed his mouth, and cleared his throat. "I think." He had to grind the emotion out again. "I think you look like a million bucks."

She smiled and ducked her head, the hint of a blush creeping into her fair-skinned face.

"You ready?" he asked. "I could come in."

"I'm ready." She grabbed a purse that was clearly

hanging by the door and stepped onto the front porch with him. "Are you really staying tonight?"

"I brought a camp cot," he said. "Sleeping bag. It's all in the back of my truck."

"I really don't need you to," she said, glancing at him as they walked toward the stairs leading to the sidewalk.

Feeling flirtatious and bold, Blaine swept his hand along her waist before he took her hand in his. "Sometimes we don't get what we want, you know?"

Tam looked at him, some anxiousness in her blue eyes. The makeup she'd put on somehow made them bluer, and Blaine hadn't thought that possible. "My back did twinge a little today," she admitted.

"I know," Blaine said, looking out over the glorious Kentucky landscape in front of her house. She only lived maybe three-quarters of a mile from the ranch, but he had to go all the way down the road and back up a curve and past a couple of fields to get to her place. "I saw you limping on that last horse."

Next to him, Tam stiffened, but her stride didn't break. "I'm okay, Blaine," she said.

"Don't worry, baby," he said easily. "I'm not going to take you back to the hospital." He opened the passenger door for her and let her step past him. Her dress looked like it was made from crinkly cotton, and it had ruffles down the front of it. He wanted to know how that fabric felt against his skin, and after Tam had settled onto her seat, he reached out and gathered a handful of her skirt in his hand.

She said nothing, and he enjoyed the rougher texture of the fabric. "I really like this dress, Tam," he said, lifting his gaze to meet hers.

"Do you?" she asked, her smile quick and filled with white teeth. "I'm glad. I bought it online and haven't worn it yet."

"Mm." He backed up and closed her door. He'd already known she hadn't worn the dress yet. He saw her at church—the only time Tam wore skirts or dresses—and he'd never seen that dress. As he rounded the tailgate, he wondered if she'd worn that dress to church, would he have realized his romantic feelings for her?

He got behind the wheel and looked at her. "It's Wednesday, and that means Italian night at Six Spurs. I don't really want that, and you can't really dance anyway."

"Plus, you're not Spur when it comes to a dance floor," she teased.

"Hey," Blaine said, putting the truck in reverse. "I know how to dance."

"Yeah, but you're at least...what? Fifth in the family as far as actual dance-power goes."

"Dance-power?" he repeated. "Fifth?"

"Spur's the best dancer," she said.

"I think Trey's better than Spur," Blaine argued. "But go on."

"I would've put Trey second," Tam said. "Then Duke, because he's got moves when the fast songs come on."

"Oh, please," Blaine said, though he was enjoying this conversation. "He watched a couple of YouTube videos on hip hop. He's no dance-master."

Tam pealed out a string of laughter that made Blaine's heart feel ten times lighter. "Fair enough. But he's still third. Cayden's fourth. You're fifth. Conrad can't keep a beat to save his life, but he's marginally better than Lawrence."

"Ian's last?" Blaine asked. "I thought he did a decent job at his wedding." Out of the Chappell brothers, only Ian and Spur had been married. He and Trey had both been engaged once-upon-a-time. Spur was again for the second time, while everyone else remained single.

"That's swaying back and forth," Tam said. "That's not actually dancing."

"We're not actually dancing tonight either," Blaine said, glancing at her. "I was thinking of going to Cattleman's." He watched her for her reaction, something he could do on this relatively straight stretch of road.

Surprise flitted across her face, but it dissolved quickly. "Oh, I see what's happening. You're going to flash around some fancy diamond card or something." She grinned at him, clearly teasing.

"I want good food tonight," he said.

"Mindie's is good."

"We always go to Mindie's," he said, shifting in his

seat. "It's like, what we did as friends." He kept his focus on the road, because he didn't want to see Tam's reaction this time.

"Ah, I see," she said.

He wanted to ask her what she saw, but he decided to keep the question for now. They drove to the dealership on the outskirts of Lexington, which was also where Cattleman's was. It was an expensive, upscale restaurant that served only grass-fed beef and farm-raised produce. The chef and owner had a twenty-acre farm west of the city where she sourced everything that went on her menu.

Blaine liked the food there, and he liked that he could support a local business and a Kentucky farm all at the same time.

In the lot at the dealership, about a dozen men worked near a whole fleet of new trucks. "Looks like you're in luck," he said. "They just got in new inventory."

Tam laughed, and Blaine looked at her as he parked in one of the spots in front of the indoor showroom. She shook her head as he twisted to look at her. "What?"

"Those are sixty-thousand-dollar trucks, Blaine. They're brand new."

"Ah, I see." He grinned at her, held up one palm, and got out to hurry around to help her out. She waited for him, which was a relief. He'd never bothered with opening her door for her when they were best friends, and as a rush of foolishness ran through him, he reminded himself that they were more than that now. He *wanted* to be more than that now.

"What can I help you folks find?" an older gentleman asked, his voice raspy and weathered.

Blaine smiled at the old-timer, recognizing him a moment later. "Darren?"

"Good to see you, Blaine." The old man shook his hand, his grip just as strong as it had always been, despite his health issues.

"What are you doin' here?" Blaine asked, his stomach painfully tight. "I thought you retired."

"Just showin' my son the ropes," he said, and Blaine's whole world started falling apart piece by piece. He had enough sense to step next to Tam again and take her hand in his, though. Maybe he'd done it to ground himself. Maybe he knew what was coming next. Maybe he just wanted to hold her hand for as long as she'd let him.

Darren stepped to the side, and none other than Hayes Powell stood there. He wore a bright smile that disappeared the moment he laid eyes on Blaine.

"You remember my son, Hayes?" Darren beamed at the man like he was indeed the greatest thing since sliced bread.

Hayes wore a cold look now, and he scanned Blaine and Tam standing there in their clean clothes, their hands clenched together.

No one said a word.

6

*T*am could not believe this was happening, and on her and Blaine's first real date too. She told herself this would not ruin their night. It would not. She'd simply ask for a different salesman. There had to be someone else who could walk her around the lot and show her used trucks.

Blaine's hand in hers squeezed painfully tight, and he said, "Yes, sure, I remember Hayes."

Hayes stood there like a blasted statue, a horrible scowl on his face. He knew who'd been on the other end of the line this afternoon now. Tam found she didn't care. She hadn't told Blaine what Hayes had been saying, and she hadn't dared to admit that he'd started to reel her back in with the simple sound of his voice.

Looking at him, though... That was different. She remembered all the awful things he'd said to her, and she remembered how long it had taken her to shake off the chains of his lies and abandonment. She was not going back to him.

"Yes," she finally said. "I remember him, too. Darren, I'm Tamara Lennox. Your son broke off our engagement two months before the wedding, remember?"

Darren Powell looked at Tam, his eyes lighting up when he finally recognized her. "Oh, uh—"

"I think it's best if someone else shows us some trucks," Blaine said, his voice highly political. It actually bordered on kindness, and Tam wondered how he did that. She wanted to lunge at Hayes and rip that perfect cowboy hat from his head and stomp it into dust as she told him all the ways he'd hurt her.

She hadn't seen him in the flesh since the night he'd broken up with her, and she realized she had so many more storms that needed to blow themselves out of her soul before she could truly be rid of him.

"Of course," Darren said. "Let me get Keith. He's an excellent salesman, and he can help you with whatever you need." He tossed a look at Hayes, who hadn't moved or spoken. He didn't do either now as Darren led her and Blaine inside.

She finally faced forward when she couldn't keep glaring at him. Once free from his intense glare, Tam's chest heaved as she sucked in breath after breath. Beside her, Blaine kept a firm hold on her hand and said something. She heard his voice, but it echoed through her ears and brain.

Darren walked away, and Blaine stepped in front of her. "Hey," he said, reaching up with both hands and brushing her hair back. The heat from his hands raced through her skin, and she looked into his eyes.

He smelled like every woman's dream, and she wanted to step into his strong embrace and hold onto him until she felt like she wasn't about to splinter into a thousand shards. Sometimes, Blaine seemed to know exactly what she needed, and right now, he folded her into his chest and whispered, "Don't cry, Tam. Whatever you do, don't cry."

She wasn't going to cry. She was more worried about punching something—or someone. Namely, Hayes Powell.

"Let's just go," she said into his chest, though she was right where she wanted to be. She took a deep breath of his shirt, getting something clean and crisp, as well as a leathery scent she knew well.

"No," he said firmly, and she liked that he could be strong when she felt weak. Sometimes that role reversed, and she liked being there for him too. "We're staying. We're not letting Hayes-Franking-Powell scare us away."

Tam burst out laughing, utterly charmed when Blaine joined her. He stepped back and tucked her hair again, leaning down to look right into her eyes. "Okay, Tam? He's the jerkface here."

Tam giggled again and wiped her hand down her face, though she had not even come close to crying. "You're too old to use words like jerkface."

"Am I?" Blaine asked, looking toward the wall of windows that showed the car lot beyond them. "I don't care. That's what he is."

Tam smiled up at him and took his face in both of her hands. He refocused on her, surprise and desire evident in his eyes. Tam could look at him look at her like that for hours, and a smile started way down deep in her stomach.

"I really liked how you used his middle name in there like a curse word," she said, a laugh immediately following.

Blaine smiled too, the gesture spreading slowly across his face. "I have a few rare moments," he said.

She wanted to tell him he had a few rare moments where he *wasn't* sexy or handsome, perfect, or approachable. Before she could, Keith arrived, a smile as wide as the Mississippi on his face and a voice as loud as thunder.

"What can I help you find, Miss Lennox?" he boomed, and Tam looked at Blaine, almost ready to tell him that this guy was no better.

Blaine kept his smile in place, and that helped Tam retain hers too. "I need a new truck," she said. "Used, because some of us aren't billionaires." She cut a look in Blaine's direction, and he just shook his head, his grin slipping a little.

"We're the largest used truck dealer within five

hundred miles," Keith said, his voice carrying all the way to the rafters. "I'm sure we'll have somethin' you want." He started toward the doors they'd entered through. "Do you have a budget?"

"Yes, sir," Tam said. She was not going to be embarrassed about her financial situation. "I'm looking for a payment under four hundred a month. I'm thinking that's about twenty-five thousand?"

Keith nodded as he held the door for her. "We do in-house financing, so we can offer the lowest rates. Down payment?"

Tam stepped back out into the heat and humidity, glad for her lightweight dress. Blaine sure had liked it too, and a bushelful of happiness filled her soul. "I have the money from my accident," she said. "My truck was totaled, and the insurance is giving me a little over five thousand dollars."

"They gave you five grand for that thing?" Blaine asked.

Tam ignored him and followed Keith, her fingers slipping away from Blaine's. He caught up to them quickly, looked at her, and apologized without having to say a single thing. Tam accepted the apology in half a breath and increased her pace to keep up with the tall cowboy-salesman who would be disappointed she wasn't going to be buying tonight.

~

"I really think you should go with that blue one," Blaine said.

"The F-150?" Tam scooped up another bite of her salad, wishing Blaine had ordered an appetizer so she wasn't the only one eating. She'd never cared about that before, but she did now. Her life had been split in half suddenly, and she was operating on a side of the line she'd never been on before.

"No, that one was navy," he said. "The blue one."

"I'm *not* buying an electric blue Velociraptor." Tam put together a bite of lettuce, tomato, and bacon, swiped it through the ranch and the balsamic reduction, and offered it to Blaine.

He took her fork and ate the bite. "I'm telling you," he said around the BLT bite. "That truck has your name written all over it."

"I'm way too short for it," she said.

"You wouldn't even drive it," he argued back. "You don't even know if you're too short for it."

"It's too big," she said.

"It's classified as a midsize truck."

Tam loved the back and forth between her and Blaine. She could say anything to him, and he wouldn't judge her. She'd been her worst self and her best self in front of him, and she found herself wanting to be better just to be with him.

"Since you told me all about your money situation," she said. "I think it's only fair I share with you."

"You don't have to," Blaine said, but he looked at her with keen interest from underneath the brim of that super-sexy cowboy hat.

"I want to." Tam finished her salad and pushed the plate to the edge of the table so the waiter could take it. "I don't do too bad, actually. I'll hit a million dollars in revenue in the next month or so, if sales keep up as they have so far this year."

Blaine didn't look one ounce surprised. "Of course you will."

"I spend a lot on supplies and stuff," she said. "But it's a good income on top of that." Her smile faltered, as an intense sadness hit her out of nowhere.

"Hey," Blaine said, reaching for her hand. "What just happened inside your head?"

Tam put on a brave smile, because she didn't cry over just anything. Very few things, actually. "I just suddenly thought of Gran." She shook her head, her curls flopping against her shoulders. She hated curling her hair, but it was what women who went out with handsome men did, so Tam had done it.

"I live in her house," she said. "I don't have a mortgage. She gave it to me when she passed away." Those darn emotions choked her again, and Tam reached for her glass of fizzy cola. Blaine released her hand and let her hide behind drinking for a moment, and she appreciated that.

"You're much farther ahead than I am," Blaine said.

"How do you mean?" she asked.

"I live with three of my brothers," he said. "Sometimes I wonder what it would be like to live alone."

"It's not that great," Tam said before she could stop herself.

She looked up as the waiter arrived, thankfully bringing them another basket of bread and taking her salad plate with, "Your food is coming up right now. Be right back."

"You've wanted to get married for a long time," Blaine said.

Tam whipped her attention back to him, her eyes wide. "That wasn't even a question."

"Should it have been?" He calmly reached for his drink too, but he'd opted for no carbonation. He hadn't lectured her about the negative effects of soda either, and Tam was counting that as a win.

"I guess not," she said, mildly annoyed. "I don't know about this dating-your-best-friend thing."

Blaine looked like she'd thrown her cola in his face. "What does that mean?"

Tam's desperation rose up, and she leaned forward. She reached across the table and took his hand in hers. A thrill ran down her spine when she initiated the contact, as he usually touched her first.

"I just mean...you already know all this stuff about me. All my hopes and dreams and just...everything. What are we supposed to talk about?"

"We've never had a problem finding things to talk about," he said.

"You're not worried about it even a little bit?"

"No," he said. "Not even a little bit." He squeezed her hand and smiled at her. "Now, you want to get married."

"Yes," she said in a deadpan.

"You have a plan for it?"

"Define plan."

"Where you want to have it, the colors of the brides-maids' dresses. All of that."

"I mean, who doesn't?"

He smiled at her in such a genuine way that Tam didn't feel stupid for having a file folder with all of her wedding plans in it. Every once in a while, she leafed through a bridal magazine and ripped out pictures of the dresses she liked.

She'd been putting together her dream wedding when Hayes had pulled the plug on the engagement, and she'd destroyed her entire drawer of wedding planning papers, guides, and ideas.

"Do you...is it the same wedding as what you would've had with Hayes?" he asked, and Tam saw the vulnerability in his eyes.

Tam shook her head. "I burned everything the day after he left," she said.

"Tamara," Blaine said, his face lighting up. "You told me that fire was for the dead brush along your fence."

"Sue me," she said. "I lied."

They laughed together, and Tam realized she'd been worried about nothing. Their food arrived, and Blaine got the biggest steak Tam had ever seen. She looked at her French onion chicken, her mouth watering.

She told him how her dreams for her wedding had changed in the moment she'd literally watched what she'd been planning go up in smoke.

"So now what?" he asked, taking one last bite of his steak.

"Now," she said with a sigh. "Well, now, I'm just gathering things I like, and I think if someone ever asks me to marry him, we'll plan our dream wedding together."

Blaine's eyes shone like golden diamonds, and he nodded. "I like that plan, Tam. Seems safe."

"Yes, well, I do everything on the safe side these days, don't I?"

Blaine smiled, but he shook his head. "I don't think so, Tam, or you wouldn't be here with me. On a date."

She swallowed, because he was absolutely right. She hadn't walked on the wild side since her days in the rodeo. She'd dang near broken her back, and she didn't want to be a cripple for the rest of her life.

She did enjoy an adrenaline rush from time to time, and she'd planned out specific things in her life, like who she'd marry, how the wedding would be, and where they'd live.

Now, though, she couldn't imagine living anywhere

but in Gran's house, and she'd realized that a man could be part of a wedding too.

She didn't argue with Blaine's assessment that their relationship was a bit dangerous, but she pushed the idea out of her head. She couldn't think too hard about it, or she'd end things tonight. She didn't want to do that.

You like him, she told herself as he paid the bill and they got up to leave. *You've liked him for so long. Be brave. One step at a time.*

She took that step, took Blaine's hand, and decided that a romantic relationship with him was absolutely worth risking their friendship for.

7

*B*laine pulled up to his mother's house on the ATV, the sky just beginning to lighten. Julie Chappell would be up, because Julie Chappell never slept past six a.m. At least she never had when Blaine was a boy, and she'd come over the speaker system at the homestead at an ungodly hour every Saturday morning when he and his brothers were teenagers.

He could still hear her singing. *Oh, what a beautiful morning! Oh, what a beautiful day.*

Mom ran five miles five days a week, and she had until age fifty-six, when she'd had to have both of her knees replaced. She didn't carry a single ounce of extra body fat, and she didn't understand anyone who didn't know exactly what they wanted and exactly how to get it.

Blaine had failed her in so many ways.

He took a moment to watch the sun finish coming up,

the sky lightening quickly through the navies, purples, pinks, and oranges until it settled into a golden-hued blue. Kentucky and much of the Southeast was in the middle of a week-long heat wave, and Blaine touched the brim of his hat as he said, "Thank you, Lord, that we got the breeding done last week."

They'd have another break for a couple of weeks, and then Duke had more studs coming to the ranch. With a gestation period of eleven months, having foals in spring and early summer was good for their health. They got a long summer of eating fresh grass and learning how to be horses before their training began.

Blaine had scheduled the vet back at the same time the new round of breeding would begin. That way, he could check the thirty-four mares they'd covered last week, and monitor a couple of their other prize-winners to see if they had viable follicles.

Blaine really needed something else to think about besides the horse reproduction on the ranch. He looked toward the house, this breakfast something he'd initiated. When he'd texted his mother over the weekend about getting together for breakfast, she'd been quick to respond with an enthusiastic, *Yes! Come any day next week.*

Blaine had chosen Wednesday, because that gave him some time to gather together his thoughts. He'd sat in Spur's suite last night, and the two of them had gone over a plan for how Blaine could tell Mom about his failed engagement.

"Just be honest with her," he said, repeating something Spur had said. To his knowledge, none of the other brothers had acted on Spur's message about how their parents needed them. Blaine's heart hadn't stopped hurting that they felt abandoned and cast aside, especially Daddy.

He'd worked right alongside all of his sons and all of his men and women for many long years. So many, Blaine wasn't even sure how to number them all. All the Chappells—male or female—learned to work around the ranch from a very young age. One of Blaine's earliest memories was of him toddling after Spur, the end of a rope in his hand while his oldest brother led a horse to a training ring.

Before he went in, Blaine dropped to the ground right there in the front yard and swept his cowboy hat from his head. "Lord, I want to mend this rift between my mother and I. I don't know how to do it, but I believe You do. If You'll guide me, I'll follow."

Satisfied that his prayer was on its way to heaven, Blaine stood and adjusted his jeans. Turning toward the house, he caught the scent of bacon and maple syrup, and his taste buds started to cry loudly for whatever his mother had made for breakfast.

If he was a betting man, Blaine would put money on cinnamon French toast. No matter what he'd find in the kitchen, there would be enough to feed two dozen men, and Mom would probably make him take the food with him for his brothers.

He stepped to the door and rapped lightly as he entered. Mom had warned him that Daddy had been sleeping later than he usually did, due to his recent hip replacement surgery. It had been a little over a month now, but Daddy was still slow and still in some pain almost all the time.

Mom was very good at taking care of a sick man, and whenever Blaine even got so much as a sniffle, he came running to his mother for her herbal tea with lemon and honey.

"Mom," he called as he entered the house. He closed the door behind him quietly and went past all the designer furniture and into the kitchen, where she stood at the twelve-foot island, peeling apples.

"Morning, Blaine," she said with a pleasant smile.

He looked at the stovetop to her right, which had a griddle on it with nine pieces of nearly-done French toast. Grinning, he put his arms around his mother and hugged her. "Hey, Mom." He closed his eyes and took a deep breath of her.

She smelled like comfort in the form of some sort of cleanser. Good food in the form of vanilla. Tartness from the apples.

He smiled down at her as he pulled back. "How long have you been up?"

"Oh, Joey had to go out at four," she said, like that was

a normal time for a woman her age to be awake. "I couldn't go back to sleep, so I just got up." She glanced at him, and Blaine didn't buy it for a reason.

She didn't sleep for a reason, and he suddenly found himself wanting to know why. "Mom," he said slowly. "Have you always been an insomniac?"

"Yes," she said with a sigh. "Every few weeks, I just can't stand being awake all the time, and I'll take some pills." She reached up and brushed her bangs off her forehead with the back of her hand. The knife swooped through the air as she returned to peeling the apples. "Just a couple, and I sleep for eight or ten hours. It's glorious."

A sad smile accompanied her speech, and Blaine's heart went out to her. "Must be why Trey has such a hard time sleeping," he said.

"It's a curse," Mom agreed. "But look, I'm almost done with this apple pie, and it'll bake while we eat. You can take it home for you and the boys."

Blaine watched her finish an apple, and he picked up the skin. It came up in one, long, curled string, and he marveled at the skills his mother had with a paring knife. "Can I just have the pie to myself?" he asked.

"You can do whatever you want with it, baby," she said, moving on to coring the fruit.

"I think I'll take it to Tam's tonight," Blaine said. "She'll buy ice cream, and we'll have ourselves a feast."

Mom smiled at him. "That sounds nice. How is Tam? She's been around the ranch quite a bit lately, I hear."

"She helped every day last week with the breeding," he said, nodding. His heart twitched in his chest, and he wondered how to tell his mother about the next level he and Tam had reached. "She hung out at the homestead on Saturday. I, uh, sat by her and her mother at church on Sunday. I see her every day."

He had seen her every day. He'd held her hand every day. They'd talked, and laughed, and shared things old and new with one another. He had not kissed her again, because it hadn't felt like the right time to do so.

"I stayed with her for a few nights after the accident too." Blaine stepped around his mother and picked up the spatula sitting next to the stovetop. "Is this done?"

"The fire is off," she said. "I just want to get this pie in the oven, and I'll get everything together." She looked at him. "Go sit, go sit."

Blaine knew better than to get in Mom's way in the kitchen. He did what she said and sat at the bar in front of one of the places she'd set. "Mom," he said, and he waited until she'd looked up from slicing apples.

"Yes?" She paused too, obviously sensing that he was about to say something important. He wasn't sure what was going to come out of his mouth, but he believed the right thing would.

"I broke up with Alex all those years ago, because she was cheating on me with two other men." He refused to duck his head, as if he were the one who should be ashamed. He wasn't—at least not anymore.

In the beginning, he'd felt like such a failure. Such a loser. Such a weakling.

"I knew for almost a month before I canceled the wedding. She never apologized, and she never gave the ring back." There, that was it. The words he'd been hiding inside were gone now, and he didn't need to go on and on. He wasn't going to bad-mouth Alex. Mom could do what she wanted with the information; the important part was that she now knew it, and that it no longer seethed inside Blaine's heart, mind, and chest.

"It's been a long five years," he said. "I'm not one-hundred percent sure if I'm ready to date again, but I've started seeing someone new."

Mom's eyebrows went up, the apple pie completely forgotten now. She still held the paring knife in the ready position, but she hadn't so much as twitched since he'd said Alex's name.

"It's Tam," Blaine said, wondering when she'd say something and save him from his own babbling. "She loves apple pie, and if I take that to her, I'm going to win some major boyfriend cred." He grinned, told himself to stop talking, and looked from the half-done pie to his mother's still-stunned face.

Like flipping a switch, her shock disappeared, and anger took its place. "That woman," she spat. "I should march right down to that hoity toity little office of hers and dig around in that desk until I find that ring."

"Mom," Blaine said, shaking his head.

"She has no right to treat you like that." She picked up the apple she'd been slicing and started hacking at it. "How dare she? Who does she think she is? Little Miss Rich and Famous?" She scoffed and dumped the unevenly sliced apples into the bowl with the others. "Please. That commercial she was in wasn't even that good."

She pinned Blaine with the sharpest look he'd ever seen—and Mom had been plenty upset when she'd found out Blaine had broken up with Alex in the first place.

"Tell me I'm wrong."

Blaine shook his head. "You're not wrong, but Mom—"

"I can't believe her. And all this time, she said nothing to me about it. Did you know I sat beside her just three months ago at that equestrian military event? She even had the audacity to ask about you. If I'd have known, I'd have shoved that flute of champagne right down her throat."

"Mother," Blaine said, somewhat surprised, but not really. His mother carried fire in her spirit, and no one crossed her. "I've wanted to shove stuff down her throat too, I guess."

She met his eye, and the two of them burst out laughing. As quickly as that started, her laughter morphed into tears and sobs, and Blaine stared at her in horror.

"I'm so sorry," she said, gasping for breath. She rounded the island, and he stood to embrace her. She was easily a foot shorter than him, maybe fifteen or sixteen inches. But she carried such strength in her frame, and she held him with such love that Blaine's eyes pricked with tears as his heart opened to his mom again.

"I should've asked you what was really going on," she said. "I should've listened to you more. You're a good man, Blaine, and even if she hadn't cheated, and you just didn't feel right about marrying her, that's valid."

Her shoulders shook for several long seconds, until she calmed and stepped away. She wiped at her eyes, and everything in Blaine's head felt too hot.

"You're smart, and you're handsome." She cradled his face in her hands and smiled fondly at him, her eyes watery again. "Out of that mess of boys, God gave me a son with a heart of gold, and a mind to know how to use it."

"Mom," Blaine said, because he sometimes hated his heart of gold. "I love you."

Tears spilled down her face again, and her voice sounded pinched and tinny as she said, "I love you too, my precious boy." She hugged him tightly again, and Blaine stood in her arms though he was much bigger than her, and felt all the cracked and jagged pieces inside him start to mend.

After another several seconds, she stepped past him and went to the sink. She washed her hands and splashed cold water on her face. She covered her face as she dried it with a towel, and then took deliberate seconds to dry between each finger.

With a big sigh, she turned to face him again. "Let me

get the pie in, and then we can talk more about you and Tam."

"I don't want to talk about it," Blaine said, though he sort of did. He hadn't mentioned the relationship to anyone but Spur, but everyone had to know. Maybe they didn't, though, as Blaine had dropped things in his life to go help Tam in the past.

"Okay," Mom said, her voice pitched too high. "You can talk about whatever you want." She finished the pie, and Blaine just watched as she laid the top pie crust she'd already prepared over the filling she'd mixed with butter, sugar, cinnamon, and salt.

With that in the oven, she took out a pan of sausage links, and one full of bacon. "Should I go see if Daddy can get up and join us?" She looked at Blaine for permission, and he gave it. She bustled off to do that, and Blaine snuck three or four pieces of bacon while she was gone.

Her phone started to ring just as he heard Daddy's slow, thudding footsteps start to come down the hall.

Alex's name sat on the screen, and shock traveled through Blaine. Had his mother texted her when he wasn't looking? He dismissed the idea. He'd been watching her the whole time.

"Who is that, dear?" she called from the mouth of the hallway. She did not let go of Daddy, though, her devotion to him pure and strong. Blaine watched them for a step, then two, his desire to have a good, strong woman at his side when he was seventy-six-years-old growing and growing.

"It's Alex," he said, and Mom looked up quickly, her eyes widening.

"Don't answer it," she said as the last ring died.

"I wasn't going to."

"When I call her back..." Mom clicked her tongue and shook her head. "She better start prayin' right now."

"What's this about?" Daddy asked, looking from Blaine to Mom.

"I can't tell it again," Blaine said. "Mom will fill you in." He went around the island and retrieved the spatula again. "How many pieces of toast do you want, Daddy?"

BLAINE PULLED HIS PHONE FROM HIS BACK POCKET AS IT started to ring. Cayden's name sat on the screen, and Blaine resisted the urge to break into a jog. "I know," he said instead of hello. "I'm literally on my way."

"Just wondering," Cayden said. "I don't care, but you should see Spur." He was whispering by the time he finished speaking. "He's pacing like a hungry lion."

"He's just nervous," Blaine said. "Trey's there, right?" As the four eldest brothers, Spur, Cayden, Trey, and Blaine got along really well.

"No," Cayden said. "He's late too. TJ was in the hay loft of the southeast barn."

"Again?" Blaine asked, sighing. "He'll be over at Beth's forever, then."

"Probably," Cayden said. "I've got Spur. It's fine. If you're—"

"I'm on my way," Blaine said, reaching his truck. "I'm getting in the truck. I'll be there in ten minutes." It was a fifteen-minute drive to the men's wear store where Spur was trying on tuxedos for his wedding, but Blaine knew how to shave off a few minutes.

Spur and Olli had set a date for an August wedding, and that meant they only had nine weeks to get everything together. Spur had shoulders that didn't fit into a normal shirt or suit coat, and that meant time in tailoring. A second fitting, and possibly a third.

The call with Cayden ended, and Blaine had the thought to call Trey and see if he needed a ride. If he'd found TJ in the barn, he'd likely walked the little boy home.

He pushed the button on the back of his steering wheel and waited for the beep to come through the speakers. "Call Trey," he said loudly.

Another pause, and then the truck said, "Calling Trey."

The line rang, and Blaine slowed as he neared the end of the dirt lane that was their driveway. He came to a stop and waited for his brother to pick up. He didn't, and his voicemail kicked on.

Blaine hung up, because he didn't need to leave a

message. Trey would see he'd called, and he'd either call back or he wouldn't. Blaine hesitated for a moment, looking left. He had to go that way to get to town, and Bethany Dixon's farm sat that way too. Her husband had passed away a little over two years ago, and Blaine had organized a team of Bluegrass Ranch cowboys to go help her for the few months following his death.

Since then, he'd reached out to her a few times, as had Spur, to see if she needed anything. Beth always said no, and Blaine had the distinct impression that he shouldn't ask. He should show up with a dozen cowboys and see what needed to be done. Then get it done.

His truck beeped at him, and he glanced at the screen. Trey had texted. *Can't talk right now. Taking TJ home, so I'll be about thirty minutes late. Sorry, Spur.*

"Text Trey."

"Texting Trey."

"Do you want me to wait for you? I'm just leaving the ranch too." He waited a moment. "Send."

The text sent, and Trey called him. Blaine tapped the green icon on his radio and waited for it to connect. "Hey," he said. "I'm literally coming up to Beth's place right now." The Dixon farm sported the classic white fences that most horse farms in Kentucky did. Beth had a polished wood arch over the entrance to her place, and he slowed down again.

"You know what? Yeah, come here. We're almost done."

"I'm turning in now. I'll just wait in front of the house."

"Thanks, Blaine."

Blaine scanned both sides of the road as he eased down it, and he saw signs of overwhelm everywhere. Bluegrass Ranch had every blade of grass at exactly the same height, and nothing was allowed to fall into disrepair. Conrad oversaw a team of fifteen men and women who kept the six-hundred acre ranch and it's dozens of buildings in pristine condition.

They worked six days a week, and it was clear that Beth needed help here. The fences were still standing, and her horses grazing out in the front pasture seemed healthy. It was just the little things that fell to the side when someone didn't have the help they needed to keep up with all the details.

Blaine had no idea what it took to raise a child alone and run a farm, even a small one. Beth's was probably a hundred acres, and that was plenty to overwhelm anyone.

He came to a stop in front of the farmhouse, which had a wide porch spanning the whole front of it. Tam would love that, and Blaine pulled out his phone to look at the designs he'd started on Sunday evening.

He wasn't sure she'd let him expand her grandmother's porch, but he wanted to put together a plan and present it to her. She'd said she'd always wanted a house with a wrap-around porch, with plenty of shade so she could sit outside with her dogs and order leather without getting a sunburn.

He'd scanned in a sketch he'd started, and he made a few notes for what he needed to fix. He kept glancing up to the whitewashed farmhouse in front of him, and he suspected Tam would love the pillars, as well as that amazing swing in the corner.

Acting quickly, he jumped from the truck and headed toward the house. Trey could come out at any moment, and Blaine didn't want to be caught outside of his vehicle. He climbed the steps, noticing the porch was painted a light blue. Beth wasn't falling behind on keeping up the house or the porch.

He turned toward the corner and lifted his phone to take a picture of that swing. It was gorgeous, with the back of it made out of a wagon wheel. The rest of the frame looked like it was made from old, about to disintegrate wood, but Blaine suspected it had been distressed to look like that way on purpose.

Someone had put a burnt orange cushion on the bottom and decorated with mustard yellow and turquoise pillows.

He snapped another picture and sent it to Tam. *For your new porch?* The words went through easily, but the picture took forever to upload.

My new porch? Tam asked, but Blaine headed back to his truck without answering. Back in the air conditioned truck, he hesitated with his thumbs hovering above the screen. How did he answer her?

"Dumbo," he muttered to himself. "The new porch

was a surprise you weren't going to bring up until you had something ready to show her."

The passenger door opened, and Trey climbed in the truck, interrupting Blaine before he could answer Tam. A heavy sigh came with his brother, and Blaine looked at him. "Rough talk with Beth?"

Trey kept his eyes on the farmhouse. "No, she just apologizes over and over."

Blaine watched Trey for a moment. "You can talk on the way to the clothing store. Cayden called and said Spur was pacing."

"Great," Trey said. "Us being late isn't helping, I'm sure."

"Spur gets how things go on the ranch," Blaine said. "How many times have you heard him say animals can be unpredictable?"

"At least a thousand," Trey said, laughing. "I just hate being the animal."

"You weren't," Blaine said. "It was TJ."

"Yeah," Trey said, his voice indicating that his mind was far away. Blaine glanced at him, but Trey didn't say anything else, so he let it drop. Trey had never asked him about Tam, and Blaine appreciated the space his older brother gave him.

The phone rang, and Blaine yelped at the volume of it. He and Trey reached to turn it down at the same time, and he wasn't sure which one of them managed it. Thankfully, the volume reduced, and he tapped the green button to connect Tam's call.

"Hey, you're on speaker," he said, glancing at Trey. He had his keen eyes on Blaine now.

"You never answered my question," she said.

"Yeah, I was at the Dixon farm, and Trey came out. We're on our way to the tuxedo shop."

"Does Beth Dixon have that swing on her porch?"

"Yes, ma'am," Blaine said, noting the interest in Tam's voice. "I thought you'd like it."

"What did you mean by my *new* porch?"

He glanced at Trey, who hadn't looked away from him once. He rolled his eyes and waved at him, but that only made Trey smile. "I'm working on something," he said to Tam. "I don't want to tell you about it yet."

"Intriguing," Tam said, and Trey muttered the same thing.

"Okay," Blaine said, annoyed with his brother. "I'll see you tonight?"

"What will you be wearing?"

Trey coughed, and heat filled Blaine's face, despite the innocence of the question. "It's a community drive-in clean-up project. I'm going to wear the same stuff I've been wearing all day on the ranch." He looked at Trey. "We're going to be picking up trash and moving debris."

"What are you talking about?" Tam asked.

"What are *you* talking about?" Blaine repeated.

"The drive-in clean-up is tomorrow," Tam said, giggling. "We're going to that line dancing class tonight."

Trey burst out laughing, and Blaine picked up his phone and disconnected the Bluetooth. He held the device to his ear to find Tam laughing too. "My brother is being ridiculous," he said.

"I think the line dancing class is going to be a riot too," she said.

"I'm not going," he said.

"What?" Tam sobered quickly. "Why not?"

"Because I don't need to embarrass myself any further." He glared at Trey, who mimed zipping his lips.

"Blaine," Tam said. "You said you'd go with me."

"I'm regretting a lot of things I said I'd do," he said.

"What? What else are you regretting?"

"The wedding is on Saturday, right?"

"Oh, right," Tam said. "Be sure to get your suit at the tailor's too."

"I picked it up yesterday," he said. "But thanks for the reminder."

"So... What are you wearing tonight?" she asked again, a playful note in her voice.

Blaine could admit that he'd had a great couple of weeks with Tam. They hadn't been arguing as much, though they went back and forth about some topics from time to time. She claimed to be working on an amazing new saddle, but she wouldn't let him into her shop to see it.

"Blaine?"

"The same stuff I wear when we go out to dinner," he said. "We're doing that, too, right?"

"Do you want to go to dinner?"

"I don't want to make dinner," he said.

"I'll make dinner," she said. "I'm already home from the shop."

"You are?" Blaine glanced at the clock on the dashboard. "It's three-ten."

"I finished the saddle." Her pride and satisfaction with herself echoed in her voice.

"Can I see it?"

"I brought it home," she said. "So come by when you're done with your brothers."

Blaine suddenly wanted to be done with his brothers, but he kept driving toward the tuxedo shop. "All right. See you in a bit."

He ended the call and looked at Trey. "I hate you, by the way."

"Come on," Trey said, chuckling again. "You and line dancing." His laughter grew. "That's funny."

"Tam wanted to do it," he said.

"Yeah." Trey grinned at him. "Are we gonna talk about you and Tam?"

"No," Blaine said. "No, we are not."

"Come on," Trey said. "I just want to know how it happened."

"I asked her out," Blaine said. "That's usually how it works, Trey."

Trey looked thoughtful. "Just ask her out."

Blaine heard something in his brother's voice. "Who do you want to ask out?"

Trey drew in a deep breath through his nose. "I...think I'll think about it a little bit more first."

"I won't tell anyone."

"No, I know," Trey said. "I just need to figure a few things out first."

Blaine nodded, because he knew what that meant. He debated about saying something the rest of the way to the shop. He pulled up to the tuxedo store and parked the truck. "I know what you need to figure out, Trey, and trust me when I say it's not going to happen until you ask her out."

Trey looked at him, nodded, and said, "You're probably right. I'm just not sure how to do it yet."

"If I knew who it was, I could help you."

Trey reached for the door handle when Cayden came out onto the sidewalk. "Let's talk later, okay? Cayden looks like Spur's been yelling."

Blaine took in the frantic expression on Cayden's face, and he killed the engine and got out of the truck quickly too. "Sorry," he said.

"He's saying he doesn't need to wear a tuxedo to his wedding," Cayden said. "Can you imagine what Mom will do if he doesn't?"

"We're on it," Trey said, striding into the shop while Blaine apologized one more time to Cayden.

Get through this fitting, he told himself, thinking about dinner with Tam at her house that evening. Maybe it would be a good opportunity to kiss her...

---

8

*J*am stood in front of the full-length mirror on the back of her bedroom door. This dress was amazing, and she was glad she'd taken the afternoon out of her saddle shop to get to the mall. She normally detested such shopping trips, but in the middle of the day, with school still in session, it hadn't been too bad.

The dress she wore fell to her calves in soft waves of denim. A white panel across the chest made her look bustier than she really was, and she felt like a proper American cowgirl, especially once she put on her red boots.

She'd never gone wrong with the red boots, and she reached down and brushed something from the front of the right one.

Someone knocked on the front door, and June howled

like an intruder was about to enter. She leapt from the bed, with Jasper in hot pursuit. They barked as they ran toward the door. Jasper retraced his steps to get Tam, as if she hadn't heard the pounding or the two corgis losing their minds.

"Come on," she said. "Hush up." She opened the gate that would keep them in the living room while she answered the door, but both June and Jasper rushed into the foyer. "Come back," she said. "It's just Blaine. Calm down."

Jasper—always more obedient than June—returned to the living room. June took another command, and Tam closed the gate behind her. She opened the door and struck a pose before she met Blaine's smiling eyes.

"Another new dress," he said, taking her in. He entered the foyer and took her into his arms. "I like this one too. It's soft." He ran his hands down her back and looked at her. He hadn't kissed her in weeks—since the hospital. They hadn't talked about why, but Tam knew Blaine well enough to have a pretty close idea.

He wanted this relationship to feel real. He wouldn't be kissing the women he went out with the first time he went to their houses. Tam had told herself a dozen times that the first time he'd kissed her had not been the first time he'd been to her house.

"Are you ready for this?" she asked.

"No," he said, his features darkening. He wasn't as

nearly dark as the rest of his brothers, as he'd inherited some of his mother's lighter characteristics. "But you're making me go, so let's go."

"Line dancing is fun," she said.

"Not when you're fifth," he grumbled, turning to open the door.

Tam grinned, but she kept the real reason she'd wanted to attend this line dancing class beneath her tongue. Blaine would never go if he knew Hayes would be there. Tam's stomach vibrated, but she followed Blaine without a hitch in her step.

She wasn't sure why she wanted Hayes to see her having the time of her life with Blaine, only that she did. It seethed with importance, and when she'd learned he'd be calling the line dancing, she'd signed up immediately.

Blaine was a perfect gentleman, helping her into his truck and letting her pick the radio station. She put it on the country station she knew he liked, because she saw no point in antagonizing him on the way to an activity he didn't want to do.

An electric buzz ran through Tam's blood. She loved line dancing, and she'd seen Blaine smile during the activity too. *High school was a long time ago*, she told herself. Once she'd become an adult, she didn't do things she didn't like doing, and Blaine was obviously the same.

He pulled up to the upscale, restored barn where the dancing was happening, and Tam couldn't help bouncing in her seat a little. "How can you not be excited about this?" she asked. "Look at this place."

The barn was a dark, deep wood that had been decorated with soft white bulbs on long strings that went all the way to the two-story roof. Pillars stretched in front of the huge doors on the barn, with more lights and plenty of shade.

Old barrels served as tables for drinks and small plates of the appetizers that came with the class. Men and women dressed in their best already milled about, and Tam could feel the bass beat of the music rumbling in her seat.

The whole scene was something from a magazine, and Tam turned to Blaine, her eyebrows raised.

He broke, and he shook his head as he chuckled. "I'm happy you're happy," he said. "If you wait, I'll come around." With that, he slipped from the truck and came around to her side to open her door. He offered her his arm, and Tam happily laced her hand through his elbow.

She felt like a queen as they approached the mingling area. Everyone was watching as she arrived on the arm of the most handsome man in Kentucky, and she smiled around at the other people who'd gathered there.

No one was really watching her, but magic still flowed through her system because of the warmth of Blaine's body next to hers. She didn't think she'd see him, but she looked for Hayes anyway. She wanted him to see her glowing in the arms of another man. She wanted him to know he had not broken her. She wanted him to know she was ten times happier with someone else.

The barn hadn't opened yet, but there was food and fans, and Tam's hair blew lightly as she reached for one of the Southwestern rolls she'd had here before.

Blaine sang along with the song he knew and took a cup of soda from one of the waiters walking around. He relaxed more and more with every passing second, and when he put his cup down, Tam led him out onto the dance floor, where a few other couples had started to sway to the western ballad that had come on.

"You can do this," she said. "It's just swaying back and forth."

He could do it, all right. She fit right inside the circle of his arms, and Tam marveled that neither of them had realized it before. Her crushes had always remained a secret, and she hadn't really known how she'd feel with his hands on her waist, and his head right next to hers. He had to bend his neck to do it, but he did as if it was natural for him to want to be as close to her as he could.

Tam breathed in and closed her eyes, letting herself get caught up in the fantasy of a future with Blaine Chappell. The next few decades flowed through her mind in only seconds, and she was so blissfully happy.

A few minutes later, someone came over a speaker system and said, "Welcome to The Old Red Barn. The doors are now open, and our line dancing lessons will begin in five minutes."

Tam opened her eyes and together, she and Blaine moved with the crowd toward the large doors that had been slid to either side of the entrance.

More lights and more magic waited inside, where a real, hardwood dance floor had been lain. Couples could get married at The Old Red Barn, and Tam could admit she had the venue on her list of possibilities for her own wedding.

Blaine hesitated to get near the front, and Tam allowed him to stay in the middle of the crowd. She sent up a prayer that there wouldn't be so many people there that Hayes wouldn't see her. She would pretend not to see him watching her, and she drew in another breath, ready to put on the performance of her life.

He came out onto the stage, and Tam tensed. "Welcome," he said in his smooth voice. "I'm Hayes Powell, and I'm going to be your caller tonight."

Blaine put his hand on Tam's hip, his arm draped along her lower back comforting and perfect for the show Tam wanted to give Hayes. She leaned into Blaine's chest, but he was rock solid and tight, his eyes trained on Hayes.

He demonstrated the dance they'd be doing with a brunette who Tam had seen at the barn before, and then the music started.

Tam grinned at Blaine as they moved a few feet apart.

This line dance required a partner for a few counts, and she hoped Blaine could get the steps right. She honestly didn't care if he did or not. She just wanted him to take her into his arms as she tipped her head back and pealed laughter toward the rafters. She'd hold onto his shoulders with such joy as they laughed together, and Hayes would see how happy she was without him in her life.

She performed the steps easily, especially when she watched the woman on the stage. They went through the steps four or five times at half the speed, one by one. Blaine got the moves right, and he was already exactly where he was supposed to be when she turned around to take her into his arms and dip her.

She giggled and looked up to the stage as Hayes said, "Okay, Brit. Let's get the real thing going." He grinned at her, and Tam knew the power in that smile. Hers faltered as she watched him trail his fingers along the woman's waist, and the two of them smiled at each other.

She moved away from Blaine, and the music began for real. She kept up easily, but when she spun this time, Blaine wasn't there. He arrived a beat too late, and Tam laughed as she grabbed onto him, the scene in her mind exactly what she wanted Hayes to see.

Blaine wasn't overjoyed though, and he said, "Sorry," as he finally dipped her.

"It's fine," she said. "Loosen up, Blaine. It's just for fun." She turned away from him and took a deep breath, looking up to the stage to see if Hayes was watching her. He didn't seem to be; he hadn't even seen her.

They went through the dance again, and this time, Blaine was on time. He did smile then, and Tam pealed out that laughter again.

"You're in a good mood tonight," Blaine said, eyeing her.

She didn't know what to say, so she said nothing. They progressed through the dance, learning it in sections. Hayes didn't look in her direction once, and after about forty-five minutes, Tam was feeling more tired and sweaty than like the picture-perfect woman in love with her new boyfriend.

Blaine looked like he might commit murder if he had to do this much longer, and Tam knew whose it would be: hers.

"One more time," Hayes said. "From the top, all the way through."

Tam could do it, but she seriously doubted Blaine could. He hadn't yet, at least. The music started, and Tam tapped her heel, and put her hands on her hips. She spun, and she got dipped. She held Blaine's hand and did the grapevine, kicking and laughing like this was absolutely the best thing in her life.

If it was, no wonder she wasn't impressing Hayes.

At the end of the dance, Blaine was supposed to spin her, and then they'd separate and do the last step before everyone clapped.

Tam missed a step and turned toward Blaine in a stumble. He caught her, but he got knocked sideways too from her momentum. He grunted as he tried to stop them, but Tam's foot caught on the back of his leg as she tried to tame her movement into a spin.

She knew they were going down before it happened, and then the floor seemed to take forever to come up to meet her. She hit her knee, then her elbow, and finally her face.

Beside her, Blaine cursed as he collided with the floor.

Worse, two more couples fell when they got tripped up by Blaine and Tam being somewhere they shouldn't.

"Everyone stay where you are," Hayes said, and the music cut off. The only thing Tam could hear was the slapping of cowboy boots as someone ran toward her.

Hayes appeared in her line of sight, and a groan pulled through Tam's whole body.

"Are you guys okay?" he asked, and he still had that stupid microphone in his hand. The other people around Tam were getting up and saying they were okay. She was the last of them to get to her feet, aided by Blaine, who wore a dark cloud over his whole face.

Hayes met his gaze and then looked at Tam. "Okay?"

"Yes," Blaine practically barked, bringing her to his side in a possessive gesture that Tam hated. This wasn't how she wanted Hayes to see them—Blaine being all overbearing and overprotective while Tam cowered at his side, her nose about to drip blood.

The first drop fell, and she hurried to put her hands up to her face. "I have to go to the bathroom." She practically ran from the dance floor, pure humiliation filling her. She took care of her nose in the bathroom, and thankfully, it stopped bleeding after only a few seconds.

When she was cleaned up, she left the bathroom to find Blaine leaning against the wall outside the women's restroom. He looked up from his phone, those gorgeous eyes dark and glittering.

He straightened and looked at her. "Tell me the truth, Tamara. Did you want to come to this specifically because Hayes was here?"

Tam opened her mouth to deny him. Such a thing was preposterous. "No," she said, and Blaine cocked his head, his disbelief obvious.

"Okay, yes," she said. "But not for the reason you think."

"I'm starving," Blaine said. "I'm going to get a burger. You want me to come back and get you when you're done here?"

"What?" Tam stared at him. "Of course not. I'll go with you."

He took one step toward her, and he was nowhere near enough to even touch her, but Tam felt his anger way down in her toes. "If you want to be with him again, just say so."

Tam searched his face, shocked he would even think that. So shocked, she couldn't speak. Blaine huffed, growled, and stalked away from her. Tam blinked, her mind racing as she tried to catch up to the situation.

"Wait," she said as he reached the dance floor. He didn't hear her, and he kept going. Tam reached down, grabbed onto her skirt and hitched it a little higher, and ran after him.

9

*B*laine watched as Tam came tearing toward him, her skirt all fisted so she could move faster. She certainly was moving fast. He sat behind the wheel while she yanked open the door and leaned into the cab of the truck. "Wait," she said, panting.

"I'm not going to leave you here, Tam," he said. His mother would never forgive him if he did that. Blaine had all those Southern gentleman manners he abided by, and that meant he'd sit in the truck while she dazzled Hayes if that was what she wanted.

Lord knew he'd done it before.

She climbed into the truck and closed the door. Only the soft blowing of the air conditioner and her labored breathing filled the silence.

Blaine let his displeasure morph into misery, where he wallowed until she caught her breath. His stomach grumbled at him again, but he didn't want to take Tam to dinner. He finally put the truck in drive and pulled out of the parking space.

"I did not come tonight to get Hayes back," Tam said.

Blaine deliberately draped one hand over the steering wheel as if this were a casual drive through the country.

"I came, and I wanted you to come with me, so he would see how amazingly happy I am with you."

Blaine cut a look at her and focused back on the road. His blasted pulse started to bounce in his neck, and he made a turn without thinking about it. "I feel used," he said. "I feel like you brought me here as your fake boyfriend, just to prove a point." He took a breath and kept on going, despite Tam starting to say something too. "I know that's what you originally wanted our relationship to be—me helping you prove to Hayes that you were over him. That's fine. It honestly is. If that's what you want." His stomach clenched, and he concentrated on where he needed to go to deliver Tam back to her house.

Then he could drive to Lexington and get his favorite fried chicken and waffles—alone. He'd drowned plenty of sorrows in fried food and maple syrup before. He could do it again.

"That is *not* what I want at all," Tam said.

"That's what it sounded like," Blaine said. "It felt like that, too, Tam. I don't know who that woman was that I was dancing with in there, but it wasn't you." She'd been so flirtatious, which sure, Tam could be. She'd laughed so loud, and she'd clung to him in an obnoxious way that made no sense to him.

Until now.

"I know," she moaned. "I'm sorry, Blaine. I just thought if he could see us, he'd know he hadn't beaten me."

"Why is it so important that he know that?" Blaine asked. "Why isn't you just living a good life enough?" He didn't understand why she had to prove anything to him.

"I don't know," Tam said quietly, and this time when Blaine looked at her, she was watching the night go by out her window.

He didn't want to push her away, and he sighed and looked out his window too. "I accept your apology," he said, drawing his shoulders up and back. "However, in the future, should you feel like you have to prove something to Hayes, I would appreciate it if you left me out of it."

"I'm sorry," Tam said again, sniffling this time.

Surprise shot through Blaine, and he pulled off the highway quickly, pressing the brake hard.

"Hey," she said, bracing herself against the dashboard.

"Are you crying?" he asked.

"No," she said, looking at him. He opened his door so the cabin light would come on, and he searched her face.

"I was just making sure my nose wasn't bleeding again," she said. A half-smile, half-grimace crossed her face. "I hit the floor pretty hard."

Blaine softened toward her, the misery in her eyes too

much for him to bear. "I'm sorry, Tam. You knew I wasn't a great dancer."

"It wasn't your fault." She giggled, the sound growing as she laughed fully. "I'm the one who tripped over my own feet, then yours, and caused a pile-up on the dance floor."

Blaine laughed with her, reaching over to take her hand. She looked at their joined fingers, and then lifted her gaze to his. "I really am sorry I made you feel used. That was not my intention."

He nodded, his emotion stuffed into a ball in his throat. He looked out the windshield, his night shifting again. "I already accepted the apology," he said. "I don't need another one. I do, however, need some fried chicken. Care to go with me to Bird Stories?"

A few seconds of silence passed, and Tam said, "If I must."

Blaine grinned and swung the truck into a U-turn. "There's the Tam I know."

ON SATURDAY, BLAINE WENT INTO THE KITCHEN AT THE homestead, already annoyed at his collar and he hadn't even left the ranch yet.

"Where are you goin'?" Trey asked. He scrubbed his hands and arms to the elbow, peering at Blaine over his shoulder.

"That stupid wedding," Blaine said, yanking on the fridge door. He'd get lobster and steak in a couple of hours, but his stomach wasn't playing very nice right now. He took out a container of leftover stew Cayden had brought home from Mom's and stuck it in the microwave.

"With Tam?" Trey asked, drying his hands now. "Can I have some of that too?"

"Sure, there's plenty." Blaine opened the drawer and got out two spoons. "Not with Tam. With her friend, Denise."

Trey frowned, and Blaine felt that deeply in his heart. "I don't get it."

"It's so simple, really," Blaine said, plenty of sarcasm in his voice. "I'm going with Denise, because she used to date the groom, so she has to go. Why skip the wedding for your ex, right? But she can't go alone, and she doesn't have a boyfriend. I owe Tam about a million favors, and she's cashing in." Blaine glared at his brother.

Trey just grinned. "What are they serving for dinner?"

"That is not important," Blaine said. "Tam's going to be there too. So I'm going to a wedding for someone I don't know and don't care about, with a woman I've met once—via video chat, mind you—and my girlfriend is going to be there by herself. Tell me how any of this makes sense."

Trey laughed and rounded the peninsula in the kitchen to sit at the bar. Blaine put a spoon in front of him and turned back to stir the stew with the other one.

"Human beings are so complex," Trey said. "None of that makes sense, brother. Not a single thing you said."

"Thank you," Blaine said. "I tried telling Tam, but she just re-explained it all to me as if *I'm* the one who doesn't get it."

The stew wasn't anywhere near hot enough, and Blaine nearly threw it back in the microwave. "We need a new microwave."

"Then get one," Trey said.

Blaine picked up his phone and started tapping to do just that. As he did, Trey added, "Men and women are so different. I don't know how anyone makes a relationship work."

"You and me both, brother," Blaine said without looking up.

Trey cleared his throat. "You and Tam...aren't getting along?"

Blaine glanced up then. "No, we get along as well as we ever have."

"Which means she argues with you about everything." Trey smiled, but he wasn't making fun of Blaine. "You used to get so mad at her in high school."

"I've grown to appreciate that quirk of hers," Blaine said. "Sometimes she makes me think about something in a new way."

Trey looked thoughtful, and Blaine wondered what was running through his mind. He finished ordering a new microwave, put his phone down, and said, "That should be here in three days."

He turned back to the stew and opened the door to stir it again. "So, have you asked out who you were thinking of?"

"No," Trey said. "I don't know. She's..." He let the sentence hang there.

The stew was warm enough to eat, so he slammed the microwave and went to sit beside his brother. "She's what?" he asked, deciding to push Trey a little.

"I don't know if she'd say yes. I don't think she's looking to date anyone right now."

"You'll only ask if you're sure she'll say yes?"

"Wouldn't you?" Trey looked at Blaine, clearly wanting to know.

He had a point. "I don't know," Blaine said. "You didn't seem to ever—I don't know. I know you retreated from the dating scene when you broke up with Lindsey. You've been out since, though. You seem to be willing to ask."

"I ask when I know they'll say yes," Trey said. "I can't get a read on this woman."

"Who is it?" Blaine asked, his curiosity driving toward the roof. "I promise I won't make fun of you or tell any of the brothers."

Trey put a spoonful of stew in his mouth, and before he could chew and swallow, Spur came in the door down the hall, talking loudly with someone on his phone. "...

check with him, Rudy, because that's not what I have in my book."

"That doesn't sound good," Blaine said. "I think that's my cue to leave."

"No," Trey said, tossing his spoon toward the sink. "I was just headed out." His spoon clanged against the sink and bounced out. Their eyes met, and Blaine burst out laughing. Trey joined in, and when Spur entered the kitchen, the storm on his face blew out a little bit.

"What's so funny?"

"Nothing," Trey said, getting up. He retrieved his spoon and faced their oldest brother. "Who was on the phone?"

"Rudy Costas," Spur said, frowning. "Can I have some of that?"

"Sure," Blaine said. "It's not all the way hot or anything."

"I don't care." Spur got out a spoon and leaned over the counter to scoop up some beef and potatoes. "He says the stud fee for Goin' Back Home is sixty, not forty."

"Better get Duke in here," Trey said. "That's a third more."

"It's half more," Spur said. "Half of forty is twenty. He wants fifty percent more." He pointed the spoon at Trey and then Blaine. "Goin' Back Home is barely worth forty." He shook his head. "It's fine. I'm going to talk to Duke and find out what's going on."

"Sounds good," Blaine said, taking his last bite of stew.

His stomach had settled somewhat, and he stood up. "I'm off to get my date."

"Why are you all dressed up?" Spur asked. His face paled. "Is it something for my wedding? What did I forget?"

Blaine laughed with Trey at Spur's panic. "Nothing," Blaine said between chuckles. "It's another wedding you don't need to worry about."

"I can't wait to be done with the wedding," Spur said, his mood blackening again. "It's so much work for no reason."

"I think there's a reason," Trey said as Blaine went down the hall to the door that led outside.

An hour later, he'd collected a very nervous Denise, waited for a flock of geese to cross a street, and arrived at the wedding of Dr. David Frank and Abby Carbon. He immediately looked for Tam and found her wearing a pale green dress that hugged her body in all the right places.

Blaine watched her chitchat with a couple of other women in a rainbow assortment of dresses, and only a few seconds after he and Denise had walked in, Tam turned toward him. He grinned and tipped his hat at her as Denise said, "I need a drink."

She walked away from him, and Blaine went after her. Tam had given him explicit instructions to make sure Denise didn't get drunk today, and Blaine had a suspicion the next three hours were going to be trying. So trying, *he'd* want to drink to forget them.

He arrived at the bar with Denise and waved away the bartender's question as to what he wanted. He leaned against the counter and faced his date. "Tam told me you get three drinks today."

Denise turned toward him, and while she wasn't his type, she was pretty. She had long, dark hair she'd clipped back on the sides, and big brown eyes that could probably devour a man with a single look. "What?"

Blaine smiled at her and leaned closer, having spied the groom as he came out onto the patio. Having a wedding outside in July was ridiculous, but Blaine could ignore the sweat running down his back. "The good doctor is right behind you."

She tensed, but she didn't move. Blaine put his hand on her hip and smiled as if she'd just told him something he was thrilled about. "Three drinks, Denise. For the whole party. You can have them all now and then hang on my arm until you can walk on your own. Or space them out." He chuckled and leaned even closer, his mouth right against her ear. "It's up to you, but I'm not arguing with you about it. Now, put your hand on my shoulder or my arm."

Denise placed her hand on his bicep, and that got her to relax and lean toward him too. "Thank you for doing this, Blaine," she said.

"Sure," he said, though he hadn't been as agreeable

until that moment. "Just so you know, Denise, you don't have anything to prove to him."

"I know it's stupid," she said, but the anxiety still lived in her expression.

"Denise?"

Blaine looked up at the groom, and he slid his arm around her as she turned toward him too. "Oh, hey, David," Denise said, her voice falsely bright. She stepped into him and hugged him, and Blaine just watched.

She returned to his side and indicated him. "This is Blaine..." Her eyes widened, and pure panic filled them. "My boyfriend," she finished.

"Nice to meet you," Blaine said, extending his hand for David to shake. "What are you a doctor of?"

"I have a PhD in Health Sciences," he said.

"I have no idea what that means," Blaine said with a chuckle.

"No one does," Denise said, laughing afterward too.

Dr. David Frank did not laugh, and he looked around like he'd rather be anywhere else. "Excuse me," he said. "Lovely to see you again, Denise." He strode away, and Denise turned to watch him go.

She sagged into Blaine afterward, giggling again. "I have a PhD in Health Sciences," she said in a deep voice, and they laughed together.

"You sure you've only had that one drink?" he asked.

"He's such a tool." Denise sipped her drink and stared after David. "I don't know what I saw in him."

"Sure you do," Blaine said. "He's tall and good-looking, for one. He's probably employed, and he's educated. He has money, and you know, those two first names." Blaine shrugged, watching the man smile falsely at a pair of people a generation older than him. Probably his bride-to-be's parents.

Denise laughed again, though Blaine felt a bit bad for poking fun at the man's name. He couldn't help that.

Tam approached, and Blaine cleared his throat and straightened. "What are you two giggling about?" she asked, her eyes glued to him.

"First," Blaine said. "I don't giggle. Second, you owe me a year's worth of work on the ranch for this."

"Come on," Denise said. "You're having fun."

"Not because of you," he said. "I actually am having fun. I just mean because of this heat. Who gets married outside in July?"

"Abby's been praying for a cold spell," Tam said.

"She didn't pray hard enough," Blaine said dryly.

"Maybe the Lord won't listen to her, because she steals people's boyfriends," Denise said. Tam gasped, and Blaine turned to stare at her too.

He reached out and took her still half-full glass of wine from her. "I think you're done, Denise."

She let him take the glass, and she covered her mouth with her hand. "Did I say that out loud?"

"Yes," Tam said with a small squeak. Her blue eyes

danced, and she grinned like a wolf who'd just found his next meal. "Yes, you did."

Blaine put the half-drunk wine on a tray and took Denise by the elbow. "Let's go find a seat in the shade, okay? If I'm sitting in the sun for this, Tam owes me *two* years of free labor on the ranch."

"I've already done that," she said as he turned. He looked back over his shoulder at her, a smile passing between them that definitely conveyed he'd rather be at this wedding with her than Denise.

She reached up and touched her fingers to her lips, and warmth spread through Blaine from head to toe—as if he wasn't already hot enough.

He found a spot in the shade, and he saved a seat for Tam on his left. She walked down the aisle with the other bridesmaids, and then she came to sit beside him. She pressed her thigh right next to his, and Blaine couldn't help moving his hand to touch hers.

She leaned toward him, and he inclined his head toward her. "You're hot in that tuxedo, cowboy."

He grinned as the preacher started the ceremony. "You don't look so bad yourself," he whispered, and then she laced her fingers through his and held on tight.

10

*S*pur reached to take down the last of the red, white, and blue banners that had been put on the homestead for the Fourth of July holiday. That had marked the one-month mark until his wedding.

Two more weeks had passed, and tonight Spur had called a family dinner. He'd met with Mom and Daddy to talk to them about the meal. He'd called another brothers meeting to tell them what he expected. Olli said she'd prepped her mom and dad, as well as her brother and sister.

"That's the last of them," Cayden said, handing him the banner.

Spur tossed it in the bin and put the lid on. "Thanks for helping with this," he said. "You'll put the ladder away and come help me get all the food, right?"

"Planning on it," Cayden said. "Spur, you need to chill about this."

"Chill?" Spur repeated. "I don't even know how that's possible. I'm getting married again in two weeks." That was insane, and Spur turned around like someone would be standing there to tell him the whole thing was a joke.

Cayden got down from the ladder and put both hands on Spur's shoulders. "Do you love Olli?"

"Yes," Spur said, searching his brother's eyes. "But, Cay. I loved Katie too." He hated this doubt in his soul, and it didn't belong to Olli. It belonged to him. He doubted he could keep a woman like Olli happy for long; he hadn't been able to do so for his first wife.

"You are not the same man," Cayden said. "She is not Katie."

Spur nodded. "You're right. I know." The rising panic subsided, and Spur took a deep breath. "What about you, Cayden? Who are you seeing?"

Cayden sighed and turned to fold up the ladder. "Not many people, I'm afraid. I've been out here and there. I asked Libby out, and we went to dinner. Had a right fine time, but there was no spark." He faced Spur and hefted the ladder onto his shoulder. "I need a spark."

"I know the feeling," Spur said. Every time he even thought about Olli, a whole network of sparks raced through his bloodstream. He loved her. This was just dinner, and if it didn't work out, so what? He'd told Olli once that he didn't care about anything but the two of them. He still didn't, but he'd like Olli's parents to think she'd gotten a good husband and family, not a crazy-loud bunch of men who didn't know how to mind their manners.

Spur took the bins into the front shed and put them away, noting Blaine's neat desk and barbells by the door. He seemed like he was happy with Tam, and Spur hoped that was true. Sometimes Blaine could be his own worst enemy, and as Spur thought it, he realized he could be too.

"No more of that," he told himself as he left the shed.

He met Cayden at the truck, and the two of them headed to Dreamsville to pick up the food. Enough to feed twenty-five people, even if some of them were children, took several trips to carry to his truck. By the time he and Cayden had it loaded, he was ready for the event to be done.

"Maybe you'll meet someone at the wedding," Spur said. "Olli has a lot of female friends she's invited."

"Maybe," Cayden said, smiling in a way that told Spur to stop talking about his dating life. He did, and they moved on to the issue in row house seven, where some weak boards had been found. Half of it needed to be rebuilt, and Ian had started putting together a proposal and a budget.

The ranch had ninety-six pregnant mares now, and Spur had decided that was plenty. Their stud fees were through the roof this year, and he needed to stop spending money. The trays and trays of food in the back of the truck weren't helping that cause, that was for sure.

He pulled up to the banquet hall he and Olli had rented for this dinner, and he and Cayden took all the food inside. Someone had already been there to set up the tables and chairs, and white cloths covered them, with beautiful white china and glinting silver utensils.

"Olli is going to love this," he said.

"I'm surprised there's no centerpieces," Cayden said. "This place is so nice that it seems so plain."

"Olli is bringing them," Spur said. "She's supplying all of the flowers for the wedding from her gardens. That way, she says it'll smell the way she wants it to." Spur wanted Olli to have everything she wanted, and he'd offered to pay for whatever she couldn't.

She'd refused to even take a penny from him, and Spur had considered talking to her mother about it.

"He is here."

He turned toward the sound of Olli's voice, sunshine filling his soul. "Hey, there, baby," he said, taking the enormous black bucket from her. Cut flowers filled it, and how she'd carried it, he didn't know. Water sloshed in the bottom of it, and Spur took it to a side table while she turned to direct Ginny, who carried a second bucket.

"Cayden," Spur said, and his brother turned from where he'd been looking at his phone. He strode toward Ginny, took the bucket from her, and joined Spur at the side table as Olli and Ginny sized up the banquet hall.

"Who is that?" Cayden asked.

"You know her," Spur said, surprised as he looked at Cayden, who had his eyes stuck to Ginny. "It's Ginny Winters. Her family owns Sweet Rose Whiskey." Olli had told him that everyone in Kentucky knew the Winters. That obviously wasn't true, as Cayden had just stuck his thumb in his mouth and was chewing on his nail.

Spur turned around fully, realizing what was happening here. "Go ask her out."

"What? No." Cayden looked at him for such a short time, it could barely be considered a glance. "I don't even know her."

"You like her." Spur stepped in front of his brother and swatted Cayden's hand away from his mouth. "I'm not blind. I can see it."

"She's beautiful," Cayden said, his voice a touch haunted. "And Spur, there was a spark just from me taking that bucket from her."

A grin split Spur's face. "That's great, Cay. Okay." He breathed in deeply and moved back to his brother's side so they faced the two women. "You start to get to know her. She hangs around Olli all the time. She dresses her, and they've been friends for ages."

"I don't want to be set up," Cayden said. "I'll get to know her myself. Do you know if she's seeing anyone?"

"I want to say no," Spur said. "Seems like Olli said she doesn't date much, because of her family situation."

"What situation is that?"

"My guess?" Spur folded his arms and leaned against the table. "It's a lot like ours. Complicated."

"Sounds like a recipe for disaster," Cayden said. He sucked in a breath and spun around as Ginny looked their way.

"Get over here," Olli said. "I need your brilliant mind."

Spur grinned at his fiancée, pushed to a standing position, and said, "Come on, Cay. They need our help and you can see if that spark is as hot as you thought."

HOURS LATER, SPUR HAD SHOWERED FOR THE SECOND TIME that day, dressed in a nice pair of slacks, buttoned up his white shirt, and put on his cowboy casual tie. He sprayed his signature cologne on his shirt, not his skin, as per Olli's instructions, and he stepped into a pair of cowboy boots he'd only worn twice. They still pinched a little, but another couple of outings, and they'd be fine.

He and Olli had decided against formalwear for this dinner, as Olli said they'd be having a rehearsal dinner for the wedding too. That was when she'd inspect everyone's clothes and pass them off. Spur's tuxedo had already been approved, and if the men's wear shop could get it tailored in time, he'd be set.

"Gotta be there in thirty," he yelled to the three men sitting on the couch when he entered the kitchen. Various forms of assent met his ears as he went down the hall and collected his keys.

A few minutes later, he stood on Olli's front porch the way he had many times before. He rang the doorbell, somehow just as nervous to pick her up tonight as he had been for their first date.

For some reason, he thought she'd wake up at any moment and realize what a colossal mistake she'd made by agreeing to marry him.

She opened the door, a smile coming instantly to her face. She scanned him from the cowboy hat to the boots, one hand moving to her hip. "You are perfection," she said, plenty of flirtatiousness in her voice. "I fall more in love with you every time I lay eyes on you."

Spur wondered how she knew exactly what to say to him to get him to calm down. Or get him revved up. Or make him happy. He marveled that the Lord had softened his heart enough to let her in, and such gratitude came over him that he said nothing.

"How do I look?" She turned for him, and Spur's blood ran a little hotter. She wore a cream-colored dress with lots of little ruffly things rolling down it. A denim jacket wrapped around her shoulders, and her sun-kissed hair made her into an angel.

By the time she faced him again, Spur had found his voice. "Gorgeous," he said. "I'm the luckiest man in the world." He swept her into his arms, thrilled when she gave a little squeal and giggled.

They both sobered quickly, and Olli stepped back. "You know it's going to be okay, Spur."

"Is it?" he asked. "Because I'm pretty sure Duke got kicked by a horse today, and Ian smashed his thumb with a hammer. On top of that, I'm freaking out about the wedding, and Blaine is dating his best friend. Oh, and Cayden said when he met Ginny this afternoon, he felt a spark."

Olli blinked at him, absorbing what he'd said as quickly as she could. "Okay, let's start with—Ginny is going to be thrilled." She squealed and reached for her phone. "I have to call her."

"No," Spur practically yelled. "No, you can't tell her."

Olli looked at him in surprise. "Why not? When we first started dating, she asked if we became serious if I'd introduce her to one of your brothers. Or all of them." She grinned like matchmaking was going to be her new favorite hobby.

"He doesn't want to be set up," Spur explained. "He wants to get her number himself, and he wants to do things his way." Spur took her phone from her. "Promise me you won't tell her."

Olli frowned and looked around, obviously hoping another solution would present itself. She finally said, "Fine, I won't tell her. But let's get going so we can put her and Cayden next to each other tonight."

"I thought we weren't assigning seats," he said, reaching back inside to get the door as she rushed by him.

"We're not," she said. "But baby, if you think I can't make sure they end up next to each other, you've got a lot to learn about me still." She grinned at him and went down the steps. Spur could only chuckle, because he knew Olli could do anything she put her mind to.

They arrived at the banquet hall, and he wasn't surprised to find her parents there. They showed up to everything at least fifteen minutes early, and Spur always felt like he was running late when he wasn't.

"Hello, Paula," he said, dropping Olli's hand so he could embrace her mother. He kissed both of her cheeks and shook her father's hand. "Alan."

"Hullo, Spur," he said, smiling up at him.

Olli greeted her parents and looked toward the doors. "Did y'all try to go in?"

"No," her daddy said. "We're just waitin'."

"I hope you're ready for this," Spur said, glancing toward the parking lot as the rumble of an engine got closer. Thankfully, it was just his parents, and they'd be on their best behavior. When Spur and Katie had gotten married, he'd introduced her mother to his parents, and it had gone well. Katie's dad lived in California, and they didn't speak, so Spur had never met the man. Her mom hadn't caused any ripples in the Chappell family, and everything had been easy with regards to trying to bring together two families.

Spur watched with a sinking heart as Ian and Duke spilled out of the back of the truck, both of them with their heads down. Mom followed, and she was lecturing them about proper safety around the ranch, her voice loud enough to carry across the distance between her and the Hudsons.

Spur sighed. "My mother is a special breed," he said.

"She's lovely," Olli said, linking her arm through Spur's. "You just have to know how to get on her good side." She moved forward, taking Spur with her. "Julie," she trilled out. "How are you?" She hugged Spur's mother, who had stopped talking the moment Olli had spoken.

Spur got replaced by his mother, and Olli chatted her up as she took her toward her mom and dad. Spur stayed behind to help Daddy, and the four of them watched Olli and Mom.

"She's incredible," Ian said. "How does she do that?"

"Mom hasn't stopped lecturing since we left the hospital," Duke said, his voice awed too. "Twenty minutes, Daddy. She doesn't even breathe when she's lecturing like that."

"She's just worried about you boys," Daddy said.

"Daddy," Spur said. "Remember how we're not boys anymore?" He stepped slowly with him, though his father was doing much better now.

"I know," he said. "Mom forgets from time to time. She's a good woman."

"Of course she is," Duke said. "The lecturing is somethin' else, though."

"Let's just let Olli handle her tonight," Ian said. "She's doing a great job."

Olli looked over her shoulder, a triumphant smile on her face. Spur smiled and shook his head. He'd just helped Daddy to a seat when the doors to the hall opened again, and more cowboys poured inside. Olli's siblings and their families arrived. The girlfriends and finally, Blaine and Tam.

The only person who wasn't there was Ginny, and Spur looked around for Cayden. He was obviously watching the door too, as was Olli from where she stood with her sister, Lena.

Ginny rushed through into the hall a few minutes later, apologies flying from her mouth. Olli hugged her and said something, and then she turned to find Spur. He knew his role here, and it was at her side, welcoming everyone to their family dinner party.

They reached for one another simultaneously, and Spur pressed a kiss to Olli's forehead. "All right," he said in a loud voice. "Quiet down now." He gave everyone a moment to wrap up their conversations, and he realized how full of love this room felt.

Cayden and Blaine had both been by Mom and Daddy's house to make peace. Those were the only two that Spur knew of, but he hadn't expected miracles. Baby steps were fine too.

"We're so glad everyone could make it tonight," he said. "Families are such a special blessing from the Lord."

Where the words had come from, he didn't know. Olli looked up at him, her smile genuine and perfect.

"There's no assigned seats," he said, getting to the heart of his speech. "Pick a place, get a plate, and get some food. We have the hall until nine, and we're glad to be here to get to know everyone better."

He glanced around, his eyes landing on Trey. "Trey, would you say grace?"

"Sure thing." Trey took off his cowboy hat and gave the rest of the men in the room a moment to do so as well. He offered a prayer for health and safety, and he thanked the Lord for sending Olli and her family into their lives. Spur couldn't help smiling at that, because he felt that same thankfulness down in his very being.

When the prayer ended, he stood back out of the way while everyone else started through the line. Olli held Ginny back with her, and then the three of them finally went down the table holding all the trays of food and loaded their plates.

By the time they got to the tables, there weren't three spaces together. Olli looked at Spur and nodded toward the table where Cayden sat. He had two places there. Spur nodded, and Olli shook her hair over her shoulders.

Watching her made Spur so happy, and he followed in her wake as she approached the table. "Gus," she said to her nephew. "Would you mind going to sit by Papa? I want to sit by Ginny and Spur, and there's no room."

"All right, Auntie Olli."

"That's a good boy," she said, and she picked up his plate and handed it to Spur. He took the boy over to his grandfather and returned to the table to find Cayden right next to Ginny, with Olli on her other side. The empty seat remaining next to Olli was for him, and he chuckled as he sat down.

"Well done," he murmured, glancing at Cayden, who had started talking to Ginny.

"It was like taking candy from a baby," Olli whispered. "Look at them. Aren't they so cute together?"

"Don't get ahead of yourself," Spur said, refusing to look at Cayden or move his mouth too much. He faced Olli instead, and added, "My brothers are in love with you for how you handle our mother. I think we're going to need lessons."

Olli trilled out a laugh that made Spur's pulse fire more rapidly, and she said, "Just set it up, Spur." She leaned closer to him and took a deep breath. Her eyes glittered as she met his gaze. "You smell *fantastic* tonight."

"Thanks," he said. "I kinda have this fiancée who's a genius with scents." He leaned toward her and kissed her, finally settled and ready to get married again, because he was going to marry Olli, and she was perfect for him.

---

11

*T*am tugged at the hem of her dress, hating where it fell. She wasn't in Olivia Hudson's wedding party, and she could wear any dress she wanted. The one she'd purchased had seemed great in the store, but now, it looked all wrong.

The dress was too long to be a party dress but too short to be considered anything else. She'd worn more dresses in the last couple of months than she had in the six months before that. She liked looking good when she and Blaine went out, and she liked seeing that glinting, desirable look in his eyes when she opened her door.

Today, his brother was getting married, and Tam pressed her lips together to refresh her lipstick. "You're kissing him today. To-day."

Frustration streamed through her, and she recognized it in her own eyes. She'd never dated Blaine before, but she felt like he was moving like molasses with her when he'd never done that with anyone else in the past.

They weren't the kind of best friends that kissed and told, but she'd always known when he'd kissed his girl-friends. Her memory had grown fuzzy, but she seemed to remember that he'd kissed Alex within two weeks.

It had taken him that long to even decide if he should date Tam.

She pushed the poisonous thoughts out of her mind, because they didn't do anyone any good. They just made her feel worse about herself, doubt that Blaine really liked her and wanted to be with her, and send her into a tail-spin that she had to work for days to correct.

She'd made some amazing saddlebags in her last tail-spin, and she'd earned great money from the sale. Didn't mean she wanted to distract herself in her shop every time she fell into the dark recesses of her mind.

She turned away from the mirror and went into her closet. Perhaps she had something else she could wear to the wedding. In truth, no one would even care what she was wearing. She'd been over to Blaine's several times in the past couple of weeks, and his brothers treated her the same way they always did—like she was one of them.

Tam pushed hangers left and right, finally concluding that she didn't have anything better than the sunshine yellow dress she currently had on. She bent down to find the shoes she'd thought she'd wear with the dress, finally pulling out the pair of black heels from the back of the closet.

She never wore heels, because she hated them, but she'd worn a pair to Abby's wedding last month. She'd wanted to dance with Blaine so badly, but Denise had claimed him as her date, and she'd needed him.

He'd played his part so perfectly that Tam had actually experienced some pretty severe jealousy. She knew what it was like to stand in the circle of his arms, and she felt so good about herself when he held her close.

"Tam?"

She lifted her head, her heart suddenly tapping far too fast in her chest. Blaine's voice came again, and she hurried out of her closet to find him poking his head into the bathroom.

"There you are," he said. "I knocked and rang the doorbell."

"You did?" She looked down at Jane and Jasper, who had stood up but hadn't made a peep. "That doorbell is on the fritz." She held up her shoes. "I can wear these?"

"With that dress?" He looked down to her toes and back to her eyes. "Sure," he said. "You look beautiful, by the way."

"Beautiful?" Tam took a step toward him, but she did not want their first real kiss to be in her bathroom. He'd kissed her on the front porch and then a hospital bed, and neither of those were her first choice for kissing a handsome cowboy.

The wedding was at the ranch, and Tam had decided that an amazing kiss next to the white fences at Bluegrass Ranch would be perfect.

"Yes," Blaine said, swallowing.

"You've never said I'm beautiful."

"You are."

Tam ran her fingers along his collar, which lay perfectly flat, and trailed her fingertips down his silk tie the color of ripe peaches. "No tuxedoes for the brothers?"

"Thank the Lord," Blaine said, his voice barely above a whisper. "If I had to wear a tuxedo for someone else's wedding, I definitely wouldn't go."

"Even for one of your brothers?"

Blaine looked torn, and Tam knew he'd go. His devotion to his family was ironclad, and he'd told her about how he'd started to rebuild the bridge that had been splintered between him and his mother. Tam was mildly terrified of Julie Chappell, though Blaine said she was starting to mellow out a little.

She hadn't been terribly mellow at the family dinner Spur and Olli had hosted a couple of weeks ago, but there'd been enough people there for Tam to avoid her. She supposed that Duke and Ian had gotten injured on the same day, and that had probably been stressful for her.

"Are you listening to me?" Blaine asked.

"No," Tam said. "Am I late?"

"Yeah." He checked his watch. "We need to go so we're not late."

"I told you I could drive over," she said.

"And I said you weren't meeting me at my brother's wedding." He put a smile on his face and his arm around her shoulders. "I think you're really going to like a wedding on the ranch."

"You do?"

"Oh," he said. "I saw something you need to make." He pulled out his phone and started tapping. Tam went out into the living room, everyone following her. Her dogs liked Blaine, and that was probably why they hadn't barked when he'd come inside.

He showed her the phone. "Look at that."

She took his phone as she sat down on the couch so she could slip on her heels. It was a saddle that had been made into a tree swing. "This is incredible." She abandoned her shoes, studying the picture. "Where is this?"

"A ranch in Texas," he said. "You could make those, right?"

"Definitely." Tam's mind whirred, because she could see so many possibilities with this. "It's like a tire swing, but a saddle."

"A complete saddle," Blaine said. "The chains are laced with reins."

"Can you send me a picture of that? Or that website?"

"Yep," Blaine said, taking his phone back. "Trey just

texted that if I'm not back in five minutes, something bad is going to happen."

Tam slipped into her shoes and stood. "Let's go."

They hustled out to his truck, and he drove quite fast on the way back to the ranch. He pulled up in front of the house and somehow made it through the parked cars that were already there to a spot closer to the garage.

"I think we made it in six minutes," he said, reaching for the door handle.

"Blaine," Tam blurted out. "Can you wait another minute?"

"If my mother or Spur loses their mind because we're not back there, I'm going to throw you under the bus."

Tam smiled and waited until he'd turned fully back to her. "I, um. I'm just wondering when you think you might uh..." She couldn't say it now, and she felt like an idiot. "Let's just go."

She got out of his truck and met him at the front of it. She reached for his hand, ignoring his curious look. He led her through the garage to the back yard, and Tam paused on the threshold of the cement on the patio.

"This is incredible," she said, drinking it all in. She'd been in this yard before, but it hadn't looked like this. Now, it seemed like a place where dreams came true and where fairies lived.

White tea lights lit the space, where hundreds and hundreds of chairs had been set up. Everywhere Tam looked, she saw money. It dripped from the white seat covers with the bright coral ribbons tied around the backs. Every bow was identical, and Tam marveled at how that could even be accomplished by a human hand.

Poles had been erected around the perimeter, with one tall, log-like one right in the middle that held up the highest part of the tent. Fans had been mounted to the pole along the whole height of it, and Tam couldn't believe how cool it was back here.

Pavers had been laid down the middle of the chairs, and the path led her eye to a glorious altar. Sprays of purple, white, and coral flowers decorated the top and front of it, with polished wood peeking through.

Tall vases held flowers too, and Tam took a deep breath. "It smells amazing back here."

"Doesn't it?" another woman asked, and Tam turned toward the pretty woman with the dark blue eyes. "I'm Virginia Winters, Olli's best friend."

"Yes," Tam said, automatically making her voice more refined. "We met at the family dinner. I'm Tam, Blaine's girlfriend."

Virginia glanced at Blaine. "That's right. You make those beautiful saddles, right?"

Tam smiled and said, "Yes."

"Blaine," Virginia said. "You better get inside, because I think Spur is about to pop a vein in his head."

"Right." He squeezed Tam's hand and pressed a kiss to her temple. "See you after, sugar." With that, he left, and Tam faced a woman who was far superior to her.

"He's great," Virginia said, smiling. That gesture softened her, and Tam was able to return it.

"I think so," Tam said. She noticed Virginia turning back to the house, and she seemed quite distracted. "Do you have a place to sit?" she asked. "Because I'm sort of freaking out about having to sit out there by myself."

She turned back to the chairs, glad when Virginia joined her. "My mother is here," she said. "You're welcome to sit by her. I have to be in the bridal party."

"Can I?"

"Of course."

"Thank you, Virginia."

"You can call me Ginny," she said, linking her arm through Tam's. "All my friends do." She smiled as they stepped off the patio and onto the pavers. "That dress is great on you."

Tam laughed, keeping it light and airy. "Oh, now you're lying."

"I never lie," Ginny said. "I know fashion. Olli has me dress her for every important event." She glanced down at Tam's shoes. "I didn't peg you for a heels girl. You should be wearing boots."

"I didn't think I was allowed."

"Honey," Ginny said as she turned down the second aisle from the front. "You watch every one of those Chappells come down the aisle. Every single one of them will be wearing boots." She grinned and introduced Tam to her mother before flitting off to join the bridal party.

The Winters clearly had money too, as did most of the guests Tam saw before the ceremony began. She stood with everyone else, her breath catching in her throat. This whole affair was simply beautiful, and Tam's emotions clogged in her throat as she watched Spur walk down the aisle at the head of a long line of men.

He wore a tuxedo, his tie exactly right and his cowboy hat the most delicious thing Tam had ever seen. She hoped Blaine would wear a hat like that when they got married.

She sucked in a breath, realizing what she'd just thought. Now that the marriage idea had gotten in, though, she couldn't get it out.

Behind Spur came his father, and then Cayden, then Trey, then Blaine. Tam didn't see who came after him, though she knew they were going in age-order. Her eyes locked onto him, and he glided with all the grace of a ballerina, his cowboy hat pretty darn perfect, his suit the color of the midnight sky on a moonless night, and the smile he kicked in her direction made of pure flirtation.

Tam grinned back and waited with bated breath for the bride to arrive. Her family came next, and they filled the front rows. The bridal party came next, each woman wearing a dress in a gauzy, peachy color that didn't seem gaudy or forced. Ginny had probably picked those, and they managed to complement each woman's shape and size.

Finally, Olli appeared on her father's arm, and Tam

couldn't help the gasp and then the sigh that came from her mouth.

She half-turned to Ginny's mother. "That's an Eden Phillips dress."

"It's fantastic for her, isn't it?" she asked. "She's so beautiful."

"She really is," Tam said, and she watched Olivia Hudson step carefully from paver to paver, pure joy radiating from her. She joined Spur at the altar, and Tam sat down. She kept her back straight, because she didn't want to miss anything.

She wanted to take notes and get a live video of every single detail of this wedding. She wanted to pick it all apart and pull out the pieces she liked for her own wedding. She'd never considered Bluegrass Ranch as a possible wedding venue, but now that she'd seen how a back yard could be transformed into a wonderland, she'd definitely be adding it to her list the moment she got home.

A COUPLE OF HOURS LATER, SPUR AND OLLI HAD SAID I-DO, a beautiful and delicious dinner had been served by real waitstaff, and she currently stood in Blaine's arms, dancing.

Pure happiness flowed through her, and while she and Blaine weren't talking, they were still saying plenty. His fingers moved up and down her upper arm, and she had her arms wrapped around him inside his suit coat jacket, her pinky fingers caught through the belt loop on his waist.

"Tam?" he whispered.

"Hmm?" She didn't lift her head from his chest, because this moment was perfect, and she wanted to hold onto it for a while.

"I'm ready to go." He stopped swaying, forcing her to look up at him. "Can I take you home now?"

"All right," she said, though she didn't want to go home yet. "I just need my shoes." She looked around for them, but the heels had disappeared.

"I gave them to...someone." He turned too, searching.

"It's fine," she said. "I don't really like them anyway."

"We have to walk back up to the house," he said.

"Maybe you can carry me," she teased, giggling when he looked at her with surprise. "It's fine, Blaine. It's practically paved."

The dinner and dancing had been in front of the house, near the road that ran around the ranch, under three of the largest tents Tam had ever seen.

"I'm sure someone will find them," Blaine said.

"It's okay if they don't," Tam said, taking her first step onto the dirt road.

They moved away from the party, the music muting the farther they went. The soft light from the tents got left behind, and Tam took a deep breath of the clean air.

"I love Kentucky," she said.

"Me too," Blaine said. He drew her closer to him by taking her hand and tugging her into his side. He paused and Tam slowed her steps too. "Tam, I'm falling in love with you."

Everything stopped as Tam processed what he'd said.

He reached for her, cradling her face in both of his hands. "I'm dying to kiss you."

"I've been dying for you to kiss me," she whispered, her eyes drifting closed.

Blaine didn't waste any time, and when his mouth met Tam's, her joy was complete. She pulled in a breath through her nose and grabbed onto Blaine. She pushed her hands into his hair, dislodging his cowboy hat.

He didn't complain, and while he'd kissed her before, neither of them were like this. This was a first kiss worth having and holding, and Tam never wanted to kiss anyone but him.

She pulled away, feeling slightly crazed and completely like she was falling. "I'm falling in love with you too." He smiled, and Tam wanted to kiss him again, so she did.

12

*B*laine kissed Tam in the darkness on the road leading to the homestead, the soft glow from the wedding casting their shadows up the lane. Her hair felt like silk, and she tasted like the chocolate cake Spur and Olli had served at their wedding.

He couldn't get enough of her, and he couldn't have timed a more perfect first kiss. He was definitely counting this as their first kiss, because they'd been dating for a couple of months now. He'd never waited this long to kiss a woman, and the wait was definitely worth it.

He'd told the truth when he'd said he was falling in love with her, and he believed her when she said it too.

"There is nothing fake about this," he whispered, moving his lips to her neck.

"No," she gasped. "Nothing."

"Blaine, is that you?"

He pulled away from Tam quickly, the sound of Duke's voice a real buzzkill. His pulse still pounded, though, and he was no longer even close to tired.

"Yeah," he called back down the road to the shadowy figure coming toward him. "Just taking Tam home." He stooped to pick up his cowboy hat so Duke wouldn't wonder why it was lying on the ground.

"Cool," he said, getting closer. "Will you be back for the sparkler send-off?"

Blaine did not want to come back to the wedding. He was ready to be out of his suit, and if he knew Spur, so was he. He and Olli were staying in Louisville that night, and they were flying to Texas for their honeymoon cruise in the morning.

"Mom will lose it if everyone's not there."

"Mom's been on the verge of losing it for weeks," Blaine said.

"You're tellin' me," Duke said, arriving. "Hey, Tam."

"Hi, Duke." Tam's fingers slid down Blaine's arm and into his fingers. She pressed in close behind him, and Blaine tilted his head down toward her as his brother sighed.

"Allison broke up with me," Duke said.

"What?" Blaine asked. "When?"

"An hour ago?" Duke sighed again. "If you're not going back to the wedding, maybe I won't have to." He looked over his shoulder toward the festivities, clearly not wanting to go back.

Blaine wanted to help his brother, because he'd been dating Allison for six months. That was too long for her to break-up with him at his brother's wedding. Why hadn't she just waited until tomorrow?

"I'm sorry," Blaine said. "You don't have to go back. Come on. Come with us." He glanced at Tam, who looked like she'd just lost something important. He knew how she felt, because he wasn't finished kissing her yet.

Thankfully, at the homestead, Duke said, "I'm going to go find some of those peanut butter cups Cayden hides in the cupboards. Text me when you get back."

Blaine said he would, and he helped Tam into his truck. "That's a rotten thing to do," he said once he sat behind the wheel. "Breaking up with him at a wedding?"

"I agree," she said. The rest of the drive happened in near-silence, the radio on at a low volume. Blaine found he didn't have much to say but a lot to think about, which was fairly typical for him after something huge had happened.

Telling Tam he was falling for her and then kissing her was fairly huge. *Really huge*, he amended inside his head.

At her house, he opened her door for her, and she slid to the ground. He didn't give her an inch as he took her into his arms and kissed her again. She giggled against his lips, but the kiss quickly turned as passionate as the one on the road in front of the homestead.

Blaine could honestly kiss her all night, but his

Southern manners kicked in, and he pulled away. "It's Saturday tomorrow," he murmured. "I have a little bit of work to do around the ranch, and then maybe you and I can just watch movies on your couch."

"I have to finish that purse order," she said, her fingers curling over his ears. "I should be back by noon, though."

"I'll bring lunch," he said, stepping back. "Okay?"

"Yeah, okay," Tam agreed. Blaine took her all the way to the porch, where he'd kissed her before. He suddenly turned shy, ducking his head as she opened the door. "See you tomorrow."

"Bye, sugar." He lifted only his eyes to watch her enter her house, bending down to pat the corgis who always came to greet her. June came out onto the porch, and Blaine chuckled as he crouched down to stroke her. "You go on now," he said to her. "Your momma's tired."

The dog went back inside, and Tam lifted her hand in a wave goodbye before closing the door.

Blaine practically floated back to the ranch, where he found Duke on the couch in the homestead, several peanut butter cup wrappers strewn around him. After changing out of his suit and into a T-shirt and a pair of gym shorts, he collapsed onto the couch with his youngest brother.

"I don't want to talk about it," Duke said. He'd put an old basketball game on the TV, and Blaine stared at the moving people on the screen.

"Fine with me," Blaine said. "You never have to tell me

anything you don't want to." He closed his eyes and just took a deep breath.

"She said she met someone else," Duke said.

"That sucks," Blaine said.

"Yes," Duke said. "It does. I mean, I get she works with a lot of guys, but I don't get what they have that I don't."

"Maybe their abs are more impressive."

Duke scoffed, and Blaine smiled though he didn't open his eyes. "They're just cowboys, like me."

"First," Blaine said. "You're not 'just' a cowboy. You're far more than that."

"Yeah? What am I?"

"You're a Chappell," Blaine said, sitting up and opening his eyes. "You know every bloodline in the horse racing industry, and you book the top studs that will make sure Bluegrass continues to be the best place in the whole dang South to buy a winning horse."

Duke turned to look at Blaine.

"If she can't see that, it's her loss," Blaine said.

"Thanks, Blaine," Duke said. Time passed, and Blaine wasn't sure if it was seconds or minutes before Duke asked, "You and Tam next?"

Blaine smiled at the thought of waiting for Tam at an altar like the one where Spur had stood. He'd seen her face as he'd walked past her standing in the second row, and everything about this wedding had enthralled her.

Tam was as tough as women came, and she was brilliant with horses and leather. At the same time, she loved frilly things and flowers and the smell of fruity things.

"Maybe," he said.

"What do you mean, maybe?" Duke asked. "Haven't you known her for twenty years?"

"Yeah," Blaine said.

"I remember crushing on her when I was thirteen."

Blaine's eyes widened as he gaped at Duke. "You're kidding."

Duke chuckled and shook his head. "Not even a little bit. She was *hot*, Blaine. You just never saw her that way." He reached for another peanut butter cup. "I'm pretty sure Conrad did, though. He almost asked her to Homecoming."

"He did not."

"He did, but someone else asked her first." Duke's dark eyes shone like liquid oil. "She's fun to be around; in high school, we all thought she was gorgeous. She still is, if you like blondes."

"I like blondes," Blaine said, wondering if he'd really just never seen her the way Duke was talking about.

"I know you do," Duke said. "You haven't dated a non-blonde ever."

"But not Tam," he said quietly, frowning.

"Yeah, why not Tam?" Duke asked. "She's been right there forever."

Blaine already felt stupid for not seeing Tam all this time. For the car mats on her thirtieth birthday. For not even realizing his feelings had changed at some point. How did he answer *why not Tam?*

"She's my best friend," he said, shrugging. "I guess I never really thought to look at her as anything but that."

"You're lucky someone else didn't snatch her up." Duke's phone rang, and Allison's name sat on the screen. He swiped the phone up, sucking in a breath, as he jumped to his feet. He walked away from Blaine saying, "Allison, hey," in a near-breathless voice.

Blaine's frown deepened, because he wasn't sure Duke should be so happy to have his now ex-girlfriend call him, only an hour after breaking up with him. He couldn't control Duke, though, and he certainly knew better than to try to control how someone's heart reacted to someone else.

His pulsed steadily in his chest, and he stayed on the couch until the door opened and Trey and Cayden came inside, both of them talking at the same time.

"There you are," Trey said. "We were wondering where you disappeared to."

"Just wedding-ed out," Blaine said, looking up at them as they took off their ties. "How was the sparkler send-off?"

"Bright," Cayden said. "Fun. Spur looked about ready to claw off his tie." He grinned like that was the funniest thing ever.

"He probably was," Blaine said. "I know I was. Getting married is entirely too much work."

"He's done it twice now," Trey said, looking around at everyone. "I'd like to get there at least once. Hopefully *only* once."

"I think we all would," Cayden said, and Blaine nodded.

He stood up and turned off the TV. "Well, I'm beat. I was just waitin' for you two, so I knew you were home."

"Thanks, *Mom*," Trey said, grinning at him. Cayden laughed, and even Blaine cracked a smile. The three of them went down the hall that led to the bedrooms, and Cayden veered up the steps to his room.

Blaine and Spur lived on the main floor, though Spur had been moving his stuff out steadily over the past few days. Olli lived right next door, so he wouldn't be far from the ranch, and she had a big house with lots of room for Spur's cowboy boots and hats.

They'd sat at the kitchen table one night a couple of weeks ago, sketching out a place for a corral and barn where Spur could keep All Out, the horse he loved to bits and pieces. Then he could saddle up and ride to work every day. As far as Blaine knew, that was still the plan, and he glanced at the door at the end of the hall, which was Spur's bedroom.

"He's not far," Trey said.

"I know," Blaine said.

"I think I'm going to ask that woman," Trey said. "Next time I see her, I'm going to ask her if she'll go to dinner with me."

Blaine grinned at his brother and clapped him on the bicep. "That's great, Trey. I'm sure she'll say yes." He watched his brother unbutton his dress shirt. "What's not to like?"

Trey shrugged. "There's got to be something women don't like about us. I mean, none of us have managed to make a relationship stick for very long."

Blaine's throat closed, and he nodded. "Maybe there is. Or maybe you just haven't found the right person." *Or seen them*, he thought, Tam's pretty face floating through his mind.

She was hot. Duke's words assaulted him, and Blaine supposed his teenage self had thought Tam was hot. He'd just never considered her girlfriend material.

He sure did now, and the kiss they'd shared down the lane accelerated his heartbeat even now.

"Let me know how it goes," Blaine said, and he continued down the hall to his room while Trey followed Cayden upstairs. Once behind the safety of his closed and locked door, Blaine brushed his teeth, examining his eyes as he did. He thought about kissing Tam, and holding Tam, and possibly being married to Tam.

They were great friends already, and he didn't anticipate that changing. They had great chemistry together too, as Blaine's blood seemed to turn into popping candy every time she touched him. He knew Tam wanted to get married, and if he asked, she'd say yes.

"For the right reason?" he asked himself. He wasn't

sure, and he needed more time to get his feelings and thoughts to align.

He knelt to pray, taking several seconds to breathe in and out first. "Lord," he whispered. "Help me to have clarity when it comes to Tamara Lennox." His mind started to quiet already. "I'm so grateful Spur and Olli got married today. They seem so happy and bless them that they will be happy."

He wanted to be happy too, and he prayed for that next. "Help me make good decisions that don't take months, okay? Help me be less indecisive and more proactive." With nothing else in his mind, he added, "Amen," and crawled into bed.

Sleep took a while to come, because the fantasy of him and Tam married and living in her grandmother's house played through his mind, and it was a very, very good fantasy.

13

*T*rey Chappell took off his gloves and clapped them together to get the dust off. That never truly worked, as everything he owned was perpetually covered in dirt, no matter how much clapping or washing he did.

About the only time he didn't feel the grit of dirt on his hands was when he went to church. He hadn't done that for a while, though, and a frown pulled his eyebrows down as he headed for the hay barn.

Part of his job of working with the trainers and various owners who rented stable space was to make sure they had the supplies needed for the hundreds of horses that lived and trained at Bluegrass Ranch. That required a lot of good-quality hay, and they grew that right here on the ranch.

With it this late in August, Trey needed to start

checking their supply. They'd just finished their third cutting a couple of weeks ago, and the heat wave the South had been experiencing had slowed the growth of the hay. He'd still get another cutting from it before autumn started and he needed to get the ground ready for next spring's planting.

He entered the hay barn, which was really one of the biggest buildings on the ranch. Trey managed the rotation of the hay to make sure they were using the oldest hay first and storing the newer bales. That way, the susceptibility to mold was reduced.

The building ran for a hundred yards, with a tightly maintained walls and roof, because water and hay did *not* go together.

The scent of hay and dirt met Trey's nose, and he took a long breath of it. He loved the smell of earth and grass, sky and water, and the hay building epitomized all of those things. He took the clipboard from the nail next to the door and checked the date he'd been here last.

Just three days ago, because hay maintenance and the agriculture on the ranch was a full-time job. They employed a full-time ag manager to take care of the field scheduling and rotating, the baling, the cutting, the storage. He oversaw the maintenance of the equipment required to plant, grow, and harvest the hay, wheat, and barley they grew on the ranch.

Tucker Marshall also checked the hay barn every week for signs of mold, rot, and water, and he'd marked the clipboard yesterday as clear. The building was half-full of hay, and that would last them through the end of the year.

Still, a thread of worry snaked through Trey. With only one more cutting, Bluegrass might have to buy hay for their boarders over the winter. If that was the case, Trey would rather buy it right now. The price would be cheaper, and he'd be able to sleep easier from now until April.

He left a question for Tucker about purchasing more hay after their next cutting and quickly read the note about the placement of the flag. He frowned as he realized Tucker was saying it had been in the wrong place yesterday.

I left it, because I wasn't sure what you were doing. Shouldn't it be on the left, though?

Trey's heartbeat skipped as he looked up. Though the light in the hay building wasn't nearly as bright as outside, he could clearly see the bright orange flag they used to mark where the next bales should be taken from.

It was on the right side, and stuck quite a bit lower than where Trey had last left it.

"TJ," he muttered to himself, trying to decide if he was excited or upset. TJ Dixon loved the hay building almost as much as Trey. The problem was, the five-year-old shouldn't be in the building, especially alone. "Especially if he's going to touch things."

Trey frowned, definitely a little bit annoyed. At the

same time, if TJ had been here, that would warrant a visit to his mother. An image of Bethany Dixon's dark hair, dark eyes, and slim figure moved through his mind.

This was his chance. He'd told Blaine he'd ask Bethany to dinner the next time he saw her. That had been a few weeks ago now, but he hadn't had a reason to go down the road to her place, so he hadn't seen her.

He could now.

"TJ?" he called, though he didn't expect the child to be there. He liked coming into the hay building, but his favorite place to hang out was in the hay loft in the barn closest to his mother's farm.

Trey walked down the middle of the building, the bright orange flag they used to mark where the next bales should be taken from beckoning to him. He reached it and sure enough, it was far too low for a man to have placed it there.

It was on the wrong side too, and Trey plucked it out of the hay where TJ had put it and moved it back where it belonged. That way, whoever came to get hay would know which side to take from. They started down on the end next to the wall, taking what they needed from top to bottom, left to right, the way one might read a book.

The flag stayed on the far right, only getting moved back a row when the last bale was taken from the one in front of it.

Trey looked back into the recesses of the hay building, the space getting darker and darker with every step he took. "TJ Dixon," he called. "If you're in here, you better answer me."

No one did, but Trey went all the way to the very back of the building. There were no little boys.

Tucker had left the note yesterday, so TJ had probably been here yesterday morning, or the day before that.

Something pricked at his mind, and Trey left the hay barn, got behind the wheel of his truck, and rumbled over to the barn where he'd found TJ several times. He didn't blame the kid for coming to Bluegrass Ranch. The southeast barn was a tall, beautiful, dark red structure that had a loft with a slide back to the ground out the window. As a five-year-old, Trey had loved coming out to this barn with his father—or anyone else who'd take him—just to go down that slide.

He pulled up to the barn, noting that the front doors had been thrown wide open. That usually only happened if Duke needed the small tractor they parked inside to do something with the chickens, goats, or sheep they kept on the ranch.

Sure enough, the tractor was gone, and the back doors on the barn stood open too, letting sunshine in from both ends.

Trey cocked his head as he heard a high, child-like voice talking. Singing, really, and Trey smiled as he went toward the ladder that led up to the loft. He made his boots land heavily on the thick rungs, and by the time he poked his head up into the loft, TJ had quieted.

He'd disappeared too, though he'd left one of his army men behind. "I know you're here, TJ," Trey said, finishing the climb into the loft. "I heard you singing, and I see one of your commanders." He stooped to pick up the toy, looking at the man's plastic face. He wore a frozen frown, his dark eyes displeased as he forever gave his troops a command he didn't like.

"Come on out, now," Trey said. "I'm not mad."

"You're not?" TJ asked, though he still didn't appear.

Trey sat down on the bale of hay someone had dragged into the middle of the loft. "Nope. Come on. Tell me who this guy is." He held up the action figure, and a moment later TJ peeked around the edge of a stack of hay in the corner. Trey smiled at him, hoping to put the child at ease.

He'd definitely have to take him home, but he wasn't going to lecture Beth about TJ being on the ranch. The likelihood of him getting hurt while he played with his toys in the hay loft was slim to none, and while that had been Trey's initial concern when the boy had started crossing fences almost a year ago, he didn't worry about that now.

What he worried about now was his own heart getting broken by the beautiful Beth. He'd liked her from the very first moment he'd taken TJ home. She wore sadness in her countenance, though, and that came radiating out of her eyes even when she smiled.

She was completely overwhelmed with the task of

running her farm alone, raising TJ alone, and taking care of everything absolutely alone. Her husband had died about two and a half years ago, and she'd been doing the best she could.

She was always kind when Trey brought TJ back, offering him sweet tea and cookies and plenty of apologies. Trey had always waved away everything but the food, and even when he didn't find TJ on the ranch, he was the one who took him back home.

"So," he said, holding up the action figure. "Who is it?"

"That's Commander Barry Barnes." TJ came to a stop right in front of Trey and took the doll. "He got left behind by his troops, and he didn't make it."

"Hmm." Trey took in the boy's dirty clothes and mussed hair. "When's the last time you showered?"

"I don't take showers," TJ said.

"A bath then," Trey said with a smile. "Because, boy, you stink." He grinned at TJ, though he did smell like cow manure, dirt, and old wood.

"Last night," he said. "No school today, so Momma won't make me bathe 'till church tomorrow."

"Hmm, church tomorrow," Trey said. He wasn't planning to go to the chapel tomorrow, but TJ didn't need to know his personal reasons for taking a step back from his religion. "Get your shoes, bud. I'll walk you home."

"Don't have shoes," TJ said, looking at Trey with wide, innocent eyes. "Could I maybe just stay here with you?"

"Why's that?" Trey asked, standing up. "This is a

working ranch, son. Ain't no place for a little boy." He'd started wandering the ranch from the time he could walk, but TJ was different. He wasn't a Chappell, and no one wanted to be responsible for any injuries the boy might incur on their property. It was a liability issue Trey especially worried about.

"There's nothin' to do at my house," he said.

"Is your momma working?"

TJ nodded, and Trey's heart divided. He wanted to see Beth. He wanted to make TJ happy. They'd both suffered so much already. Would it hurt to let TJ tag along with him for an hour or so? He'd still get to see Beth...

"All right," he said. "How about this?" He sat back down on the hay bale. "You can come around with me and check on stalls for an hour. One hour." He held up one finger and looked right into the boy's hopeful eyes. "But you can't do it without shoes." He glanced down at TJ's feet. "And you have to check with your momma first. She worries about you, bud." He put his big hands on TJ's slight shoulders, but the child bore the weight of them. "You should never come to Bluegrass without shoes on, okay?"

"Okay," TJ said.

"Okay." Trey smiled at him and ruffled his hair. "I'll walk you home where you'll get shoes and I'll ask your momma if you can tag along with me for an hour."

"One hour," TJ said.

"One hour," Trey repeated. He stood again and

headed for the steps. He'd taken TJ home plenty of times, and they both knew the path well. Trey's heart pounded when he stepped from Bluegrass to Dixon Dreams, because he had two questions he wanted to ask Beth.

TJ ran ahead of him up the steps to the deck and through the back door, calling for his mother. Trey couldn't hear him after a moment, and he muttered to himself as he went up the steps.

The back door had been left open, and Trey touched it with two fingers. "Beth?"

Everything inside the house was deathly silent and still. Trey smelled something off, and his heart crashed against his ribs. "Beth," he called. "It's Trey Chappell from next door."

He hurried past the kitchen table and around the island, thinking she'd be on the other side, perhaps passed out on the floor. She wasn't there, but Trey could definitely smell blood.

"TJ?" he called next, and he heard the little boy's footsteps running toward him. "Where's your mom?"

"I don't know," he said. "I got shoes."

"We need to find your mom." Trey hadn't been anywhere else in the house but the kitchen, and Beth wasn't there. "Where's her room?" He scanned the front of the farmhouse, where Beth had couches and chairs, a TV and a beanbag for TJ. She wasn't there either.

"This way." TJ skipped back the way he'd come,

detouring down a hall that curved around to the side of the kitchen.

Trey followed right behind him, reaching out and grabbing TJ's shoulders before he could go inside his mother's bedroom. "You wait out here, okay?"

"Okay," TJ said, not picking up on the anxiety flowing from Trey like water through a sieve.

He took a deep breath and stepped into the bedroom. "Beth?" he called again. "It's Trey from next door." If she didn't know who he was by now, Trey would be equally surprised and devastated.

He heard sniffling from the bathroom, and light spilled onto the wood floor in the bedroom from that direction too. "Are you okay? I'm coming in. It's just me. I left TJ in the hall."

Trey's heart pounded as he approached, his desperation for Beth to say something making his vision blur for a moment. Every time he'd offered to help her, she'd refused him. Once, he'd said he'd bring a crew and come help put up her wheat, and she'd argued with him for ten minutes.

Beth really didn't like accepting help, though it was Trey's opinion that she desperately needed it. He'd tried to tell her that getting help wasn't a sign of weakness, but she'd just kept shaking her head until he'd stopped talking.

Trey had the distinct impression she was going to have

to accept his help this afternoon whether she liked it or not.

He arrived in the bathroom doorway and took in the scene in front of him as quickly as he could.

Beth stood at the bathroom sink, blood dripping from her hand. Tears ran down her face, and when she looked at Trey, it was if all of the strength she'd been using to keep herself together fled.

"Okay," he said, stepping over to her as her face crumpled and she swayed on her feet. "I got you. It's okay."

She sobbed, a horrible, gut-wrenching sound that chilled Trey's blood and made his whole heart hurt. "I cut myself," she said, her voice stuttering and tinny. "It was an accident, and I can't get the bleeding to stop."

Trey didn't dare move too far from her, and he kept one leg behind her completely in case she passed out. "Can I see?"

She nodded, gaining some semblance of control over her emotions. "It's across my palm. I was out in the stupid barn trying to get down another length of sprinkler pipe that Danny had lashed to the wall." She held out her hand slightly and lifted the one pressing a blue cloth over her palm.

"I was on the ladder, and I just kept swiping at it, and —" She cut off, her breathing labored as she struggled to talk and inhale at the same time.

"How long ago did this happen?" he asked, taking over the job of removing the cloth from the wound. The blue was soaked with blood, and he wasn't sure why he hadn't whisked her off to the hospital yet.

"I don't know." Her body shook, and Trey edged forward to shore her up with his leg as he got the cloth to release.

He peered at her palm, and there was no way that gash was going to heal by itself. The muscle was plainly visible on both sides of the wound, which went from thumb to pinky, and Trey caught a flash of white before he quickly pressed the cloth back over the wound.

"I'm taking you to the emergency room," he said, looking at her. "Don't argue with me."

She nodded, no argument in sight.

"Great," he said. "Let's go."

14

*B*ethany Dixon couldn't stop sniffling, and she battled the pain in her hand, the worry in her heart, and the embarrassment that Trey drove her truck while she cried in the passenger seat, a thick towel wrapped around her hand.

TJ rode in between them, each hand clutching one of the army men he loved so much. No one said anything.

Bethany's hiccups sounded above the radio in her truck, but Trey didn't seem bothered by it. His hands didn't clench the wheel. He didn't drive particularly fast or crazy. He was the ultimate picture of calm, collected, and oh-so-sexy cowboy.

She kept her gaze out the window, desperately trying to fight against the urge to scream. She really didn't have time for a five-inch gash across her palm. She had hay to put up, and fields to tend to. She had pregnant mares who needed constant attention, and a garden that needed to be cleared, the fruit trees picked, and all of those fruits and vegetables canned, pureed, sauced, or frozen.

TJ needed a ride to school every morning, and someone to go pick him up in the afternoon. He needed a haircut, and new shoes, and probably ten thousand other things Beth didn't even know about.

The weight of her life threatened to crush her, and another sob worked its way up her throat. She couldn't quite contain it, and the resulting sound was somewhere between a scoff and a yell.

"We're almost there, sweetheart," Trey said, and Beth turned her head to look at him. He probably called every woman *sweetheart*, but somehow, her heart thought he'd reserved the word just for her.

He glanced at her, and their eyes met for a moment. He shifted in his seat and made the last turn to get on the road where the hospital sat. Only thirty seconds later, he pulled up to the emergency bay and said, "Get out on my side, TJ. Stay close to me now, y'hear?"

"Yes, sir," TJ said, following Trey out of the truck.

"Close the door, bud," Trey called to him as he rounded the hood. He opened Beth's door for her, his dark eyes sparking with concern...and something else Beth couldn't identify, because she couldn't hold his gaze for very long.

"Come on," he said. "You lean on me all you need to, Beth, okay?"

"I'm okay," she said, sliding out of the truck, both hands still clasped together. Something pulled on her palm, and she sincerely hoped the fabric of the cloth hadn't started to fuse to her wound.

His eyes flashed with black fire now. "No, you're not." He leaned closer. "It's okay that you're not. Admitting you need help is not a weakness." He didn't give her a chance to respond before he backed up, tugging her with him. He closed the door behind her and said, "TJ, you're right here at my side. All the time. Come on now."

TJ did exactly what he said, and Beth's chest caved in on her. She had to beg TJ to find his shoes and brush his teeth, but there he was, obeying Trey's every demand.

Inside, Trey took charge of checking her in, and he told the nurse behind the desk—who he seemed to know —that it was a high priority. Only five minutes later, another nurse called Beth's name.

Her legs shook as she stood, and her vision swirled. She moaned, though she didn't remember telling her voice to make that sound.

"We need a wheelchair," Trey called as he took her into his arms. He held her right against that rock-solid chest, and Beth didn't have enough mental power to even speak to him. Her whole body felt limp and cold, and she knew enough to feel him set her in the wheelchair. "Stay with me, Beth," he said, his hand on her shoulder. "TJ and I are right here. TJ, tell your mom that story about the barn cats."

She focused on the sound of her son's voice, and that alone kept her awake until they arrived in a curtained-off room. Someone helped her onto the bed, and someone hooked her up to an IV. People touched her forehead and her chest, her neck, and then her hand.

She cried out when the cloth was torn away from the wound, and she distinctly heard someone say, "Push one thousand milligrams of ibuprofen. This is going to need a lot of stitches."

"I'll get Dr. Watts," someone else said, and then the activity seemed to slow.

Trey filled the empty spot at her side, his warm fingers brushing her hair off her forehead. His other hand filled her uninjured one, and he said, "Squeeze my hand if you can hear me, okay, Beth?"

She put all of her energy into squeezing his hand. He chuckled and said, "Good, sugar. That's good." His lips landed on her forehead too, and he started talking about a couple of horses at Bluegrass that were giving Spur and Blaine trouble.

His voice was like the rolling Kentucky hills. Beautiful, and deep, and full of amazing things. Beth could get lost on the tide of it, and he seemed to know it, because he called TJ over and had him start to tell her about the moon rock project he was doing at school.

Eventually—she didn't know how long—she opened her eyes, and everything stayed stationary. Her hand didn't hurt as bad, and her head wasn't throbbing anymore.

"Hey," Trey said with a smile. "There you are."

"I didn't pass out."

"I know." He laced his fingers though hers again, and when he gazed down at her now, there was an edge of adoration in those eyes. Her heartbeat sprinted now, and she had the urge to fly from his presence.

Her mind moaned with a single word. *Danny.*

He'd been gone for thirty-one months now. Over two and a half years. Beth had managed to keep the farm, and it was actually making a little bit of money now. A very little bit. Her father had been helping her for a long time, and Beth really wanted to get out from underneath the bills, the debts, and her guilt that she needed her dad's money to clothe herself and her son.

The doctor entered, and Trey stepped back. Beth talked to him, and he confirmed that she needed stitches in her hand. "Two layers," The doctor said, poking at the fleshy part of her hand and the gaping ravine between the two halves of it the knife had made. "It's a good, clean cut, though, so it should heal nicely."

"How long?" she asked.

"At least twelve weeks," the doctor said. "I might put you in a brace to keep it stationary for the first six. You use your hands so much, and you don't want that to split." He looked at her. "You'll have to hire some help, Miss Dixon. You can't use this hand for *at least* twelve weeks." He was the very stern, not-great-bedside-manner type of doctor, but Beth found herself nodding.

"If you try to use it, you'll just be back here at square one," he said. "Zero, actually, because it'll be torn up. You might have permanent damage and lose mobility for a lot longer than twelve weeks if you don't just let it heal."

"She'll let it heal," Trey said. "I'll help her."

"You don't need to do that," she said quickly, looking from the doctor to Trey and back. "He's just my neighbor."

"Neighbors are the perfect people to ask for help," Dr. Watts said, and Beth laid her head back. "Let's get this numb, and I'll get you fixed up."

He did just that, with Beth turning her head away from her left hand and clenching her teeth while he did. He finally stood and stretched his back. "I'm going to wrap it tightly for now," he said. "I want you to follow-up with your primary care physician in seven to ten days and have him check these."

Dr. Watts continued to give her care instructions for the stitches, including that she couldn't get them wet when she showered, but she needed to keep them moist with Vaseline so the skin didn't dry out and pull.

In all honesty, she tuned out after the first couple of sentences. Her brain couldn't handle any more than that anyway. Trey seemed to know exactly when she couldn't absorb any more, and he listened to the doctor, tapped notes on his phone, and took the paperwork for how to keep the wound clean, when to change the dressing, and how to manage the pain.

Her stomach growled, but she didn't think she had the physical strength to stand up. She watched Trey crouch down and say something to TJ, who nodded. He cared about her son; she could see it right there on his face. Then he stepped over to her and said, "I'm going to go get you both something to eat. I'll be back in fifteen minutes."

"You don't need—"

"If you say I don't need to do that one more time, I'm going to go nuclear," he said, his mouth pressing together into a thin line afterward. He glared at her, and Beth finally nodded. "Thank you," Trey said, his voice terse.

He turned away from the bed and left the room, his shoulders strong and his step sure. She wondered what it would be like to always know exactly what she was doing, with exactly who, and exactly how.

The last two and a half years had been nothing but failure after failure, and the familiar desperation clogged her throat. Even more familiar were the tears that came to her eyes. "Come here, baby," she said to TJ, who climbed up into the bed with her and snuggled into her right side. "Were you over at Bluegrass again today?"

"Just for a minute, Momma," he said, his voice somber and quiet. "Trey said I could work with him for an hour. We was comin' to ask you permission."

"It's were," she said, letting her eyes drift closed. "It's we *were* coming to ask you permission."

"We *were* comin' to ask you permission," TJ repeated. He was the sweetest child, and Beth loved him dearly.

"You can't go over to Bluegrass, baby," she whispered.

"Trey said if you said I could, then I could."

"I'm tellin' you right now, you can't."

"Why not?"

"Those cowboys have a lot to do over there," she said. "You can't get in their way." She didn't believe for a single second that Trey wanted her five-year-old as a shadow for even an hour. He was just being nice, because Trey Chappell was the kindest man she'd ever known.

"But Momma—"

"Don't talk back to me, baby," she said. "That's that."

TJ huffed, but he didn't argue again. Relief filled Beth, and she enjoyed the steady beeping of the machines. They meant she was alive, and she thanked the Lord that He hadn't taken her and left TJ an orphan.

He'd already taken Danny, and both God and Danny had left Beth with a mess of snakes disguised as a ranch. She sighed as she pressed against the anger and bitterness that had accompanied her around Dixon Dreams since the day she'd found out the ranch was in debt up to the rafters, and Danny had known and not told her.

"All right," Trey said, and Beth opened her eyes. "I've got a cheeseburger and fries for you, little man. Come over here and eat now."

Beth smiled at Trey as he smiled at her son. She liked how he put "now" on the end of a lot of sentences. He sounded very Southern when he did, and he sure did have the gentlemanly manners down too.

He looked at her. "I got you the chicken parm sandwich. Salt and vinegar chips, because I've seen those on your counter before and know you like them." He put a bag on the wheeled tray and pushed it over to her. "They wouldn't let me bring in the soda, so I took it back out to the car. You'll need the caffeine once you get home." He grinned at her, and Beth wanted to pull him into a hug and tell him how grateful she was for him.

She said, "Thank you," instead and ate her dinner.

He ate a double bacon cheeseburger and all of his fries, cleaned up, and said, "I'll go check on where we're at." Trey left to do that, and Beth closed her eyes and prayed.

"Thank you for sending Trey Chappell."

He came back a few minutes later, all of the paperwork in his hand. "You've got to sign, and I can take you home. They're filling your prescription now; we can get it on the way out."

She signed with her right hand while he held the clipboard, and then he took it all back out to the nurses.

He helped her to the truck; he drove through the pharmacy pick-up window and got her pain medication; he put TJ in the bathtub when they all got back to the farmhouse.

Beth sat on her couch in her cooled house, not much else to do. She had a list of chores a mile long she hadn't completed that day, and she'd be behind for weeks because of it.

Trey came back down the hall and sat beside her, a sigh leaking from his mouth. "He's gettin' himself scrubbed." He took off his cowboy hat and did a bit of scrubbing through his hair too.

"Thank you, Trey," she said again. "For everything. I'd probably be passed out on the bathroom floor without you." She dared to meet his eye, and he gazed at her.

"Of course." He settled his hat back on his head, and everything about him was just one shade past mysterious. "Now, what are you going to do about your farm?"

She sighed. "I'll have to do what Dr. Watts said, and hire people in." She couldn't afford to do that, but she saw no other choice.

Trey nodded. "Let me know if you want me to send you a list of guys we've used at Bluegrass. We're always lookin' for more help at certain times of the year."

"Sure," she said. "I want that list."

"Great. I'll get it and send it to you tonight." He rested his elbows on his knees and focused on the ground. "I better get going. I just wanted to..." He paused, and Beth sensed a shift in his demeanor.

"You just what?"

He looked at her, pure vulnerability in those beautiful eyes now. He was so handsome, and yet so approachable. "Would you like to go to dinner with me sometime?"

Beth's eyes widened, and her mouth fell open. "What?"

"Dinner," he repeated as if she really hadn't heard him. "It could just be something simple here at the farmhouse. I'll bring it, so you don't have to cook, and we can... talk. Get to know each other better." He kept his steady gaze on her, and she couldn't look away from him because something electric moved through her body at the speed of light.

"Or we can go out," he said, dropping his head again. His cowboy hat hid most of his face now. "I can help find a babysitter for TJ, and we can go to your favorite restaurant."

"No," she said.

Trey flinched, and he got to his feet in one fluid motion. "Okay. I'll leave you alone." He walked away a few steps. He kept his back to her as he kept talking. "Your pain meds are right here on the counter for tonight. You should take those before you go to bed. I wrote down my number for TJ, so he can call me if he needs any help. I'll get you the list of cowboys, and you can do that tomorrow."

No? she thought. Why had she said no?

She just didn't want him to get a babysitter for TJ. She could call her dad, and he'd take his grandson. She blinked, trying to catch up to what was happening. Things were moving too fast. So fast.

"I'll send someone over tomorrow to make sure your

animals get fed," he said. "Everything else can be put on hold."

She still didn't know what to say, and he was moving again. Moving fast, toward the back door. He opened it and turned back to her. "Okay, Beth?"

"No," she said again.

He sighed and rolled his eyes. "You can't run this place by yourself with your hand in that condition."

She'd just meant *no, it was not okay*. He couldn't leave. She needed him to back all the way up to his first question. The one about going to dinner with him.

"Blaine will come over tomorrow. *Please* be nice to him." With that, Trey walked out the door, closing it gently behind him. She watched him cross her back porch without a single stutter or glance over his shoulder toward her, and then he disappeared as he went down the steps.

Tears came to her eyes again. "No?" she repeated aloud, immediately sucking in a breath. "Dear Lord, why did I tell him no when I meant to say yes?"

15

Tam used her hydraulic press to cut the saddle skirt and a couple of other pieces, using her measurements to get each thing exactly the right size. She loved watching the pieces of a saddle come together into a whole unit, and she picked up her head knife and laid the template she'd made for this particular western saddle over a large piece of rawhide.

She cut this by hand, as she was getting paid for a custom saddle that would only be used by one cowboy on one horse. As such, Tam could charge a premium price, and the cowboys at Cattle Ridge Ranch would pay it.

It wasn't the first custom saddle she'd made for the men up there, and she was hoping it wouldn't be the last. She worked steadily, first cutting out the saddle by hand and then shaving down the edges of each piece she'd cut or pressed so it would lay precisely flat on the saddle tree.

She glued, crimped, and nailed the saddle horn pieces into place, using a strong needle to punch through the layers so she could then sew it too. Her hands had started to ache in the past few weeks, and she reached for her compression gloves before continuing.

As she turned back to the saddle horn with two needles now, the door to her shop opened. She expected Blaine to walk inside, but instead it was Cara.

A smile burst onto Tam's face, and she left her needles on the workbench. "Hey," she said, laughing as her sister ran toward her. They embraced, and Tam closed her eyes as she held Cara. "It's so good to see you." She stepped back and held Cara by her shoulders. "What are you doing here?"

Tam wasn't a tall or thick woman, but compared to Cara, she felt like both. Another person entered the shop. Cara turned toward her boyfriend and extended her hand toward him. "We wanted to see what you were doing, and you weren't home."

"If I'm not home, I'm here."

"Or at Bluegrass, and we drove by there. Your truck wasn't there."

"You can't miss that new truck," Tam said with a smile. She'd told Blaine last week that she was glad she'd let him talk her into getting that electric blue Velociraptor, and he'd laughed and laughed.

Tam smiled just thinking about him, but she played it off like she was thrilled her sister and her boyfriend had come to see her. She hugged Chris hello and watched as he and Cara exchanged a private glance between them.

"You don't have to stop," Cara said. "I want to see how you do this. Talk as you go."

"It's boring," Tam warned. "You can tell me to stop anytime." To her, it wasn't boring. She loved what she did, especially when she got to create custom designs. "This saddle is for Jamie McGrath out at Cattle Ridge," she said. "I've cut all the pieces, and I've started to put them all on the saddle tree."

She indicated the semi-saddle shaped apparatus on the workbench. "I've just finished the saddle horn. Sort of. I have to sew it and cut off the excess leather around it there." She picked up her double needles again and looked at Cara. "How was the first week of school, Chris?"

"Good," he said. "Busy."

"Third year of law school," Tam said. "I can imagine." She couldn't really, because Tam had never formally gone to college. She'd taken several community classes on accounting and how to run a business. She'd gone to farrier school, but she very rarely shoed horses these days. Sometimes Blaine would ask her to come look at one of their horses in a pinch, but that was all. She'd taken her leather-working courses for certification, and she'd apprenticed for the best saddle-maker in Kentucky.

Now *she* was the best saddle-maker in Kentucky, and she listened as Chris talked about his classes, and Cara told them about what was new at the bank where she worked full-time as an assistant manager.

She'd gotten her degree in finance, but Tam knew her goals and desires were a lot like Tam's. Marriage. Family. Stability. Cara was a bit of an adrenaline junkie, and she and Chris liked to spend their weekend on dirt bikes and four-wheelers, ham sandwiches in insulated bags and cans of cola that got shook up too much.

"Why aren't you guys out in the Cumberland Plateau this weekend?"

Cara put both hands on Chris's chest, her smile wide and playful. "*Someone* didn't get up on time."

"I'm adjusting to my new schedule," Chris said with a smile. "Besides, Cara wanted to look at diamond rings."

Tam dropped her head knife, her surprise instant. She gaped at Cara and Chris. "Did you get one?"

"Close your fishy mouth," Cara said with a laugh. "No, we haven't even gone yet. He slept so late, and we came straight to see you."

"I see why you're down this way now," Tam said, bending to get her knife. "The diamond shop."

"You're an added bonus." Cara grinned at her sister. "Chris really did want to see what you do. I've told him it's pretty amazing."

Tam focused on her sewing, her fingers moving quickly as she'd done this countless times in the past. "Once it's sewn, I trim the leather with that forked knife there." She had a whole table of tools she used, and

Blaine had once said she could easily operate a torture chamber from her shop.

"We also want to hear about your hot cowboy boyfriend." Cara giggled. "Is he any closer to proposing?"

"I'd like to hear about him too," Blaine said, and Tam dang near bobbled her needles. He grinned at Cara, who squealed and ran to greet him too. He laughed as he swept her into a hug, and his smile stretched across his face as he shook Chris's hand. "You've got a whole audience this morning," he said to Tam, placing a kiss on the back of her neck as she bent over and kept sewing.

"Mm," she said. "I can't leave until I have the saddle seat strapped to the tree, so if you want me out of here anytime soon, you won't distract me." That was already happening, as he kept his hand on the hip opposite of Cara and Chris.

Tam had mentioned to Cara once—*one* time—a couple of weeks ago that she wasn't sure what Blaine was waiting for. They'd known each other for a very long time. He obviously liked her. He'd even said he was falling in love with her at Spur's wedding, and that was three weeks ago now.

He kissed her like a man in love, and Tam knew she was kissing him like that. She fell for him a little bit more every time she saw him, and she'd started to see him living with her in her grandmother's house.

He'd helped her paint the kitchen and living room last weekend, and this weekend, she was helping him at Bethany

Dixon's farm. Beth had cut her hand yesterday, and Blaine and Trey had organized a large group of men and women to go help her get caught up on the work around the ranch.

Blaine had said they wanted to help her get ahead, and that he planned to go over every few days to make sure Beth was doing okay. Tam loved his giving and generous heart, and she was more than willing to sacrifice her weekend for someone like Beth.

She was good people around Dreamsville, and Tam didn't think she'd have any shortage of people to help her.

"What are you doing now?" Cara asked.

"She's skiving each piece to fit perfectly against the tree," Blaine answered for her. "Then she's gonna get that sander and make it all real smooth. She's meticulous with it, using this knife, and shaving and skimming until she sees something the rest of us don't."

Tam smiled to herself as she continued to shave off bit by bit, making the leather form to her will. She did shave it down until she felt it form where it was supposed to. She put the tin on to give it more rigidity, nailed it down, and covered that with leather too. "This is the part that gets shaved and sanded," she said, smiling at Blaine.

"I was a step too early."

"About five steps," she said, enjoying it when she could tease him with something she knew that he didn't. That happened so rarely that Tam needed to take advantage of it when she could.

Once that was done, she picked up the piece of leather she'd punched from her hydraulic press. "This is the swells," she said, gluing the piece to the front swell that went up to the saddle horn. "And this is the cantle."

She put leather along the back seat of the saddle, gluing and shaping and pressing with her hands. They continued to ache, and she shook them out.

"You okay, baby?" Blaine asked.

"Can you get me some painkiller?" she asked. "It's in my office."

"Sure thing." He went that way, and Cara raised her eyebrows at Tam.

"What?"

"What's wrong with your hands?"

"Nothing's wrong with them," Tam said, though they did hurt. Her very bones ached. She'd be fine once she took some pills. "I've been working a lot this week is all. I work with my hands, and I just wear these gloves as a precaution."

"Okay," Cara said. "So I don't need to tell Mom."

"You do, and I'll never talk to you again." Tam meant it too, and she glared at Cara. "It's nothing."

Blaine returned with the painkiller and a bottle of Coke from the fridge in her office. He held out the pills, and Tam took them. She swallowed it all with the cola she loved, and she grinned at Blaine. "Thanks."

He smiled back and took the Coke bottle from her.

"How long are we lookin' at?" He surveyed the saddle tree, and so did Tam.

"We're gonna run," Cara said. "The jeweler is open now."

"Okay." Tam left her tools and walked Cara and Chris outside. The sun shone down merrily, and she hugged them both and thanked them for coming.

Cara grabbed her a second time and said, "I see the way Blaine looks at you. He's definitely going to ask you soon."

"You think so?" Tam pulled away and looked into her sister's eyes.

"He's probably just making a plan for how to do it."

Tam nodded, but she knew Blaine wasn't making a plan for an elaborate proposal. He hated stuff like that, and truth be told, so did she. Blaine was probably so far inside his head, he was trying to figure out if he should ask her or if he shouldn't. That would take a while, and Tam told herself to be patient.

"Have fun at the jeweler," she said. "Text me pictures, okay?"

"I will," Cara said with a squeal as she ran to the passenger door of Chris's truck. Tam wondered what it would be like to be a decade younger and still so hopeful. Tam felt like she was viewing the world through jade-colored glasses. She watched Cara and Chris leave, and she went back inside.

"I'm almost done," she said. "I need thirty more minutes."

"Okay," Blaine said, looking up from his phone. "Trey's got a crew going over there now, so we'll just go with the second wave, after lunch."

"Oh, are you going to buy me lunch?" Tam grinned at him, and Blaine grinned right on back.

"Tell me what you want," he said. "I'll make it happen."

"I know you will." Tam stepped right into his arms, tipped her head back, and kissed him. This was the hello she'd wanted to give him when he'd first arrived, and he took her face into his hands and kissed her back.

"Blaine," she whispered.

"Mm?" He swayed with her, his forehead resting against hers. "What are you thinking about us?"

"A lot of things," he said, a completely maddening and vague answer. "You?"

"I'm thinking my little sister went to the jewelry store with her boyfriend so they could look at diamonds, and I'm thinking I'd like you to take me to do that." Tam expected Blaine to pull away and search her face, but he didn't. He ran his hands down her back to her waist, where he tucked one hand in her back pocket and the other through the loops on her apron.

"I can do that," he said.

Tam stepped back and looked up at him. "Really?"

"If that's what you want."

"No," Tam said. "It's not about what *I* want. It's about what *we* want."

Blaine smiled down at her. "Do I propose at the jewelry store?"

"No," Tam said, something stinging in her chest.

"Let me make sure I get it right," he said. "We go shopping together, so you can pick out the ring you want. Then I keep it until an undisclosed time, at which point, I ask you to marry me. You'll squeal and say yes, and then you'll start pulling out your folders that detail the wedding of your dreams."

Tam smiled at him, the sting completely gone now. "Yeah, that's about right," she said. She sobered. "How long have you been thinking about this?"

"About what?"

"Marriage. Proposing."

"I don't know," he said. "You?"

"Since you kissed me at Spur's wedding," she said, wrapping her fingers around the back of his neck. "That was a *great* kiss."

Blaine chuckled and dropped his head. She wished he would say more, but he didn't.

She stepped out of his arms, the familiar taste of disappointment on the back of her tongue. "You did get one part a bit wrong," she said, picking up her tool to shave down the leather again. "I have folders with wedding plans, but I won't be making them myself. I plan to lay them out and have a discussion with my fiancé. Then *we'll* plan the wedding we both want."

She didn't look at him, her focus staying on the saddle as she trimmed the outside of it so it wouldn't chafe the horse. She took the cut and shaved leather to the warm water tub and soaked the leather.

With it nice and pliable, she folded it over the saddle tree, making sure every inch was smooth and exactly where it needed to be. She strapped it in place and said, "I'm ready."

"I'll call for pizza," he said. "Trey said they need food at Beth's place. Are you okay if we eat there with everyone?"

"Of course." Tam moved over to the sink and washed up.

Blaine drove them to Beth's, and Tam enjoyed the silence between them. They'd been getting along really well since the incident at The Old Red Barn. They hadn't spoken of Hayes either, and she hadn't heard from him or seen him any of the times she'd been to town.

At Beth's farm, a dozen trucks had crammed into the driveway, and Tam's heart warmed at the way the community had come together to help her. She and Blaine got out of the truck, and she saw cowboys working in the front fields, cowboys mowing the lawn, and cowboys up on the roof. There were people working the fences out front, and people sweeping the porch, and even people way out in the pasture trimming the trees.

"This is amazing," she said.

"Come see the swing," he said, and Blaine reached for her hand. She put hers solidly in his and let him lead her up the steps. The swing with the amazing wagon-wheel back appeared, and Tam's whole soul lit up.

"I love this." She practically skipped over to it and sat down, letting it swing back. Blaine joined her, taking off a couple of the pillows so he had room. She snuggled into his side, though they should go find Trey and have him direct them to what else needed to be done around the ranch.

Blaine didn't seem to be in a hurry though, so Tam stayed right where she was. He used the toe of one foot to keep them gently swaying, and Tam said, "You're right, Blaine. I want a swing like this at my house."

"It's nice, right?"

"So nice."

His arm around her tightened, and she let her eyes drift closed. They snapped back open when she heard a man say, "It's okay, Beth."

She found Trey and Beth Dixon standing just outside the front door. Beth reached up with her good hand and ran it through her hair. Tam could see Trey's face, but not Beth's.

"This is not charity," he said. "Can you please not argue with me about everything?"

Beside her, Blaine tensed, which caused Tam to do so

as well. He stopped toeing them back and forth too, and the farmhouse seemed to hold its breath.

"I'm trying," Beth said. "This is very hard for me."

"I know." Trey's eyes stormed as he looked at Beth. "It was hard for me to come here too, Beth." He looked past her and saw Blaine. His eyes widened, but Blaine put one finger to his lips.

"I meant to say yes yesterday," Beth said, and that took Trey's attention straight back to her. "I was so surprised when you asked me out, and I was saying no, I didn't need you to help with a babysitter for TJ. My dad can take him anytime." She reached up, her hand hovering between her and Trey.

"You said no twice," he said, his back straight but his head down. It was clear Beth wanted him to take her hand, but he didn't.

"The second one was that it wasn't okay for you to leave."

Trey looked so hopeful, and Tam wanted to yell at him to take the woman's hand. He finally did, and he lifted it to his lips, where he pressed a kiss to her wrist. He said something else to her that wasn't loud enough for Tam to hear, and he gathered Beth into his arms.

A soft smile touched his lips as his eyes drifted closed, and Blaine leaned his head down. "He's been telling me about this woman he's liked for months. Guess I know who it is now."

"He likes her so much," Tam said, finding the scene in front of her so sweet. "They're so cute. Look at them."

"I'm lookin' at 'em," Blaine said, pushing against the deck with his foot again. "Tam, I think we should go look at rings."

She looked up at him, shock traveling through her body. "Really?"

"Really." He smiled at her. "What are we waiting for?"

Tam didn't know what he was waiting for; she was waiting for him to ask her. She kissed him, but it only lasted a few seconds, because Trey said, "Stop kissing, you two. You're not here for a romantic interlude in the swing. There's work to do."

She grinned at Trey and stood up. "Yes, sir," she said. "Where do you want us?"

16

*B*laine pulled into the next jewelry store, peering up through the windshield at the sign. It seemed to have been knocked askew, and the fact that it was located in a strip mall next to a chicken restaurant didn't ease his mind.

He couldn't believe he'd told Tam they should go ring shopping. His heart hopped around in his chest, almost like it was trying to flee.

She'd been extraordinarily busy the past couple of weeks, because fall seemed to be the time that cowboys wanted new gear. Harvests were getting pulled in; pregnant mares were well into their gestation periods; fields were prepared or almost prepared for winter.

Late autumn was when the cowboys around Bluegrass Ranch made sure all the fences were ready for possible snow too. All the roofs on all the buildings serviced. Tack got inspected and thrown away if it was worn out, new items purchased, and everything cleaned.

If a cowboy or a cowgirl wanted a new custom saddle, they ordered from Tam. If they wanted new saddlebags, they ordered from Tam. If they had a significant other who would like anything made out of leather for the upcoming holidays, they ordered from Tam.

She was always slammed from September to February, her workload actually easing after Valentine's Day and through the summer.

She hadn't brought up ring shopping again, as she'd been working seven days a week. Blaine often went to her shop and sat with her while she sculpted and sanded, threaded and sewed, carved and created.

He was plenty busy around the ranch, as their annual yearling sale approached. Stands were getting rebuilt and refinished, buyers were being invited, and the horses were getting prepped.

Spur, Blaine, and Cayden had plans to start going through their stock and deciding what to sell and what to keep. They made a lot in sales every year, but they also kept horses, trained them, and entered them in the big races too. Plenty of money there as well.

He'd finished her porch project, but he hadn't shown it to her yet. Neither of them had spoken about diamond rings or engagements or a wedding.

Today, he'd told her he needed to pick up some lumber for one of the barns on the ranch, which was one hundred percent true. He'd also collected a load of lumber for her front porch, and he'd decided to scope out the top three jewelers in Dreamsville. They could go to Lexington if she didn't see anything in town she liked, and while Blaine didn't know what kind of ring Tam would like, he hadn't been able to determine which store was best besides his overall impressions from the outside.

This one was definitely at the bottom of his list.

His stomach growled though, so he got out of the truck and approached the store. He'd see what the customer service was like, and then he'd get a chicken sandwich. Perhaps this place did have all the details right.

A chime rang on the door when he opened it, and that set Blaine's nerves on fire. A fairly typical jewelry store spread before him, with glass cases, watch stands, and glinting gems everywhere he looked.

No one came out from the back, and no one waited in the front. Blaine looked around, thinking he could've brought in a decently-sized rock, smashed the first case, and grabbed whatever he could get his hands on by now.

Ten more seconds, and he could be back in his truck.

Those ten seconds passed, and still no one appeared. "Definitely not this place," he said, turning around to walk right back out.

He was probably being a little bit of a diva, but he wanted to be taken care of from the moment he stepped inside a jewelry store to the moment he left. He knew what wedding rings cost, and for that amount of money, there could be someone standing next to the door simply to greet him.

His stomach shook as he walked back to his truck. He couldn't believe he was even thinking of doing this again. He suddenly understood Spur's anxiety and bad temper the month before he'd gotten married.

Blaine had never made it that far, and he didn't want a long engagement. He should probably talk to Tam about that soon. That was one of the main reasons he hadn't asked her to marry him yet.

Well, that, and he wasn't entirely sure he'd decided how he felt about her. He had been falling in love with her a little bit more every single day. When would he know when he was all the way in love?

He'd just gotten behind the wheel when he remembered his hunger. Instead of going into the chicken restaurant alone, he pulled out his phone and called Tam.

"Blaine," she said, pleasantly, her voice far away, a clear sign that she'd put him on speaker. Sure enough, he could hear the tell-tale scraping of her knife against a piece of leather. "What's up?"

"Can you take a break for lunch?" he asked. "I'm in town, and I thought maybe we could just sit down for an hour or something."

The knife stopped moving, and silence came through the line. "Tam?" He pulled his phone away from his ear and looked at it. The call was still connected.

"Lunch?" she asked.

"Yeah," he said. "There's this chicken place next to a jewelry store, and I thought—"

"Wait. Why are you at a jewelry store?" Her voice came into clear focus as she took him off speaker.

Blaine shifted in his seat, though he had no reason to be embarrassed. He hadn't done anything wrong. "I was just checking out the selection of retailers in Dreamsville," he said.

"I'm on my way," Tam said. "Where are you?"

He rattled off the name of the jeweler and the chicken restaurant, and she said, "I'll be there in ten minutes," before the call ended.

Blaine leaned back and closed his eyes; the radio played softly in the background. If his stomach wasn't so angry with him, he might have been able to fall asleep. When he was sure ten minutes had passed, he opened his eyes and started looking for Tam.

He didn't see her, but he did catch sight of a woman through the glass of the jeweler, and he decided to give them a second chance. The chime brought her head up this time, and Blaine smiled before he realized who he was looking at.

Alexandra Alloy.

She wore a black skirt suit that rounded at the bust and hips but went inward at her waist. Her blonde hair had more gold in it, like honey, and he remembered her blue-green eyes so well. She'd often looked at him with laughter in them, and sometimes desire. At the end there, she seemed more annoyed with him than anything, and he'd seen those eyes when they were nothing but ice.

After a few seconds of the two of them staring at one another, she said, "Blaine Chappell."

That got him to move, and he actually took a step into the store rather than out of it. "What are you doing here?"

"I own this store," she said, her smile instant and wide. "Isn't it great?"

It's next door to a fast food chicken restaurant, he wanted to say. He frowned with the effort it took to be nice by nodding. He looked into the first case, seeing that it was practically empty. "I didn't know your family was into jewelry," he said, meeting her eye again.

"They're not," she said, the smile slipping away. "I am."

"So are you not doing those fundraisers anymore? All that stuff with the Breeders Association?"

"I still do a few things," she said coolly, lifting her chin.

Blaine nodded again. He'd been around Alex and the upper echelon of the horse racing society enough to know what her body language meant. She wasn't still doing a few things in the Breeders Association. She wasn't going to her fancy parties and luncheons, wearing her ridiculous hats with feathers and sequins, or raising money for jockeys and horses who sustained injuries during their racing careers.

She was running a nearly-empty jewelry store next to a chicken restaurant in a strip mall. For some reason,

Blaine expected to feel some sort of satisfaction. Vindication, perhaps. Something.

He only felt sadness.

"Are you ring shopping?" she asked, coming a case closer to him.

He kept his focus down in the case, wanting her to know she hadn't been the reason he'd cooped himself up at Bluegrass Ranch and never dated. "Yes," he said simply.

"Oh, who are you dating?" Alex asked, curiosity in her voice.

He looked up at her at the same time the door chimed. Alex looked past him, and he turned to find Tam entering the shop.

He put a wide smile on his face and walked toward her. "Hey, baby." He drew her into his arms and kissed her, the way he'd done many times before when he saw her for the first time that day.

He kissed her until she giggled and ducked her head, saying, "Blaine, we're in public."

He knew right where he was, and he laced his fingers through hers as he turned back to Alex. "I think you remember Tam, don't you, Alex?"

Beside him, Tam sucked in a breath. "Alex," she said.

Alex narrowed her eyes and moved to stand behind the first case. The glass and little bit of metal was all that separated them, and it definitely felt like a face-off to Blaine.

"Oh, the best friend," Alex said, her eyes sliding down

Tam's body. Tam wore dirty jeans and a faded T-shirt that had seen some leather glue it its lifetime. "Nice to see you again."

"We're actually dating," Blaine said. "We're here to look at engagement rings, actually." He wanted to tape his mouth shut so he wouldn't say *actually* again. He'd almost sounded like he was bragging.

To his surprise, Alex burst out laughing. When neither Tam nor Blaine did, she quieted. "Oh, you weren't kidding."

"No," Blaine said, frowning. "I'm not kidding." Why would she think he was? Was the idea of him and Tam so laughable? Had she not seen him making out with her a moment ago?

Alex looked back and forth between Tam and Blaine. "I just don't see it, I guess." She bent her head to look in the case. "I'm not sure we have anything for you."

"You mean *you* don't have anything for us," Blaine said, his fingers tightening on both hands. "Unless you have a mouse in your pocket."

Alex rolled her eyes. "There are other jewelry stores in town, Blaine."

"You don't want my money?" he asked, shocked. The Alex he knew had cared about money a great deal.

Alex's eyes widened for a moment, as if she'd just realized what she'd said. Her jaw clenched, and the stubbornness he knew so well manifested itself in her eyes next. "No," she said. "I'd appreciate it if you left."

Blaine really wished he'd had that rock when he'd entered the first time. He shook his head and smiled. "Good luck, Alex."

"Good luck to you too, Blaine." She glanced at Tam and looked like she'd smelled something bad. "Tam."

Blaine didn't take a breath until he was outside. His thoughts raced, and he paced away from the store, practically dragging Tam with him. "I don't believe her."

"What is she doing there?" Tam asked.

"She owns that place. Something must've happened with her family." He needed to do a search. He should call his mom and ask her too, as she ran in all the same high society circles Alex did. Or had.

He reached the end of the sidewalk and realized he didn't need to go that way. "I wonder what happened to put her in that lame shop. Did you see that case? It hardly had anything in it." He didn't mention her lackluster customer service from the first time he'd entered the store.

"Blaine," Tam said, but he couldn't hold still. She released his hand as he went back toward his truck. He collected his phone from the cab and called his mother.

"Blaine," Tam said again, and he just lifted his hand to indicate he'd like her to wait a moment, please.

"Mom," Blaine said the moment his mother answered. "What's going on with Alexandra Alloy?"

"What do you mean?" Mom asked.

"She's running a jewelry store on the west side of

Dreamsville," he said. "Next to Pirates of the Cari-chicken."

"I'd heard there'd been some sort of falling out in the Alloy family," Mom mused. "I don't know the details, though."

Some sort of falling out. That sounded like Alex to a T. She poisoned everything she touched. It just took some people longer than others to realize it.

"Why?" Mom asked. "Where are you?"

"At the jewelry store," Blaine said without thinking.

"You're at a jewelry store?"

"Uh."

"Is Tam with you?"

He turned and looked at her. She wore displeasure in her eyes, and Blaine looked past her to Alex's storefront. "Yes," he said, his brain slowing down by the second. "I have to go."

"Are you buying an engagement ring?" his mother shouted, but Blaine arced the phone away from his ear and hung up.

He stuffed his phone in his pocket and returned to Tam. "Chicken sandwich?"

She glared at him, and Blaine had an inkling as to why. He opened the door and waited for her to go inside. She did, but she didn't look happy about it. Blaine cast another look in the direction of Alex's shop and followed Tam.

They didn't speak as they ordered, and Blaine picked

up the tray with the fast food on it. Tam led the way to a booth in the corner, and he put the tray down before sliding in opposite of her.

"I'm an idiot," he said.

Tam picked up her chicken sandwich and started unwrapping it. "Why's that?" She looked at him with those piercing blue eyes, and Blaine saw her annoyance.

"Uh, for, um, calling my mom?"

Tam shook her head. "Try again."

Blaine didn't want to try again. "Just tell me why you think I'm an idiot."

She took a bite of her sandwich instead, her eyes never leaving his. He couldn't even get himself to unwrap his sandwich, so he picked up a French fry instead.

After she swallowed, she said, "I don't think you're an idiot."

"You're mad."

"I'm not mad. I'm *frustrated* that you called me to come have lunch with you, only to find you talking to Alex and automatically becoming so obsessed with her that you had to call your mother."

"I'm not *so obsessed* with her," he said.

"Why do you care why she's at that store and not running some stupid fundraiser somewhere?"

"I don't."

Tam shook her head. "Yes, you do."

Blaine didn't know what to say. He did care, and he didn't know why. "You cared that Hayes would see you'd moved on. Maybe I want her to see that I've moved on. That I'm okay."

Tam rolled her eyes. "She doesn't care, Blaine. She wouldn't even sell you a ring. She asked you to leave."

Blaine's irritation with her sparked. "She asked *us* to leave."

"She doesn't even believe there is an us," Tam said.

A knife went through Blaine's heart. "Yeah, what was that about? Her laughing like that?"

"She's not worth my time," Tam said. "I'm not going to waste a moment worrying about what Alex Alloy thinks about me."

Blaine normally wouldn't either, but something seethed under his skin. What was so unbelievable about him and Tam being together?

He pushed Alex and her reaction to his relationship with Tam out of his mind. Tam was right; Alex wasn't worth his time, and he shouldn't waste a moment worrying about what she thought.

17

"I'm sorry, Tam," Blaine said. He stood next to her truck with her, his head bent down. "I—you have to get back to work." He looked up and their eyes met. "Can I bring dinner by tonight?"

"I'm going to my parents', remember? It's their anniversary."

"Is Chris going with Cara?"

"I don't know," Tam said. She wasn't sure if she wanted Blaine to come or not. He'd met her parents plenty of times over the years, obviously. They knew she was dating him. She'd thought she knew how serious they were getting, but the scene in the jewelry store had rocked her a little bit.

She could still hear Alex's incredulous laughter, and while she'd told Blaine she wasn't going to waste a moment caring what Alex thought about her, she hadn't actually been able to get to that point yet.

She refused to look to the right to see the shop. "Stacy will be there. It could be...ugly."

Blaine nodded. "Okay, so I'll see you tomorrow then."

"That's probably best." She put her hand on his chest and slid it up until her fingers curled around the back of his neck. "Tell me what you're doing the rest of the day."

He sighed, but he put one hand on her waist, and things started to settle in Tam's mind. They were fine; they were okay. It didn't matter if Alex didn't believe they were a couple or that she wouldn't sell Blaine an engagement ring. She wasn't the only jeweler in town. She wasn't a jeweler at all.

"I'm going to go with Trey over to Beth's," he said. "Her hand is healing up real well, but she still needs a lot of help."

"How are things going with them?"

"Uh, he doesn't really say," Blaine said. "From what I can tell, they're either slow or just friends."

"He hasn't taken her to dinner?"

"Not that I'm aware of," Blaine said.

"What are you doing tonight?" She really wanted to hear him say he wasn't going to keep looking into this situation with Alex. She knew Blaine, though, and when his curiosity took over, he could become obsessed about something. Or someone.

She really didn't want him obsessing over his ex-fiancée. Hadn't he been upset with her for doing the same thing?

Tam still thought about Hayes from time to time. She did want him to know he hadn't beaten her or broken her. The best way to do that would be to get engaged, but Blaine wasn't asking.

It's your fault, she thought. *You work so much in the fall.*

"Probably gonna go hang out with Olli and Spur," Blaine said. "They're hosting a movie night in Olli's back yard."

"That sounds fun." Tam leaned into Blaine, glad when he held her close. "I'd rather do that than deal with Stacy and her negativity."

"Come by when you're done," he said, dipping his head to kiss her. Thankfully, this time he kept the kiss chaste. He kissed her the way she'd expect him to in a parking lot.

Embarrassment heated her face as she thought about the way he'd kissed her in that jewelry store. He'd wanted to prove to Alex the exact same thing he'd been upset with her about proving to Hayes.

"Tam?" he asked.

"Yeah?"

"I don't want a long engagement."

She pulled away and looked up at him, searching his face for the answers she needed. "Because of last time?"

"I just don't see the point," he said.

"I'm not going to cheat on you."

"I know that."

"There might be some aspects of the wedding that will take time to plan."

"Like what?"

"The venue," she said. "Some places get booked out for months or years."

Blaine toed the ground, his eyes trained on it again, the cowboy hat he wore a barrier between them. "I was thinking we could get married on the ranch. It's available any day."

"The ranch?"

"You saw it for Spur's wedding. It was beautiful." He looked at her, his expression open and vulnerable. "Right?"

"It was," she conceded. She'd just never thought of getting married outside, on a ranch.

Why not? she asked herself. "Okay," she said. "We won't have a long engagement. You still have to ask first."

"You still need to find time in your schedule to come look at rings with me." He raised his eyebrows as if he was using them to raise the ante on her.

"I know." She sighed. "Let's go one night this week. I can schedule it in to be done by five, and we'll have dinner and look around."

"To be clear," he said. "I'm not going to buy you the ring. I just want to see what you like. Get a feel for your style."

"Yes," she said dryly. "You've explained it to me a

hundred times." He wanted to get her a ring she'd love, but he wanted it to be a surprise. The shopping trip was just to "gather ideas."

"Just being clear."

"You're in the clear, Blaine." She stepped out of his arms and added, "I should go."

"Yeah." He reached past her and opened her door. "Call me when you're on your way home from your mom's so I know you survived."

She smiled and got behind the wheel. "Okay."

"Blaine leaned in after her and kissed her again. "Okay. Be safe, Tam. Love you." He closed the door and turned to go back to his truck.

Tam could only stare at him, noting the way his plaid shirt pulled across his shoulders and the curve of the brim on his cowboy hat.

"Love you?" she repeated. They'd been talking about marriage and wedding planning and looking at rings. Sort of. He'd mentioned it a couple of weeks ago, but they hadn't actually looked at any diamonds, nor talked about it again.

"You literally just talked about getting married on the ranch," she said. "Not having a long engagement." She put the truck in reverse and backed up. She never wanted to come to this strip mall again.

They hadn't said "I love you," to each other. Six weeks ago, he'd said he was falling in love with her. He hadn't said he was all the way there.

Tam stewed on his words all the way back to her shop. She worked steadily throughout the afternoon, Blaine never far from the front of her thoughts. She did have to push him aside from time to time as she focused on carving the design in the leather saddle seat. Otherwise, he ran rampant through her mind, and everything felt so tangled.

When it was time, she made sure the two saddles she'd shaped that day were strapped tight for the drying process, and she went home to shower. She stood too long in the hot water, thinking. She'd forgotten if she'd already washed her hair, so she did it again just to be sure.

"Let's go," she said to Jane and Jasper after rushing through her hair and makeup. "We're late." She hated being late, and she honestly wasn't sure where the time had gone.

She drove to Dreamsville, where her parents still lived in the house they'd moved into all those years ago when they'd relocated from Tennessee to Kentucky. When she pulled up, the driveway already held two extra cars, and she knew she and the corgis were the last to arrive.

"Come on, guys," she said, opening the back door for them to jump down. Jasper barked as he did, always the more vocal of the pair.

Tam followed them to the front door, where they both waited with their paws up on the step. She opened the door, and Jasper barked again, alerting her father of his arrival.

Her daddy laughed and scooped Jasper right into his arms. The dog licked his face and kept squirming to get closer. Tam closed the door behind her and drew in a deep breath. She put a smile on her face, realizing it was a game face she was donning.

When she turned around, she caught Daddy bent over as he put Jasper back on the ground. "Hello, baby," he said, straightening.

"I'm not too late, am I?" she asked, stepping into his arms.

"Heavens, no," he said. "Your mother just took the pecan pie out of the oven. We've got loads of time."

"That's dessert, Daddy," she said, shaking her head. "Oh, I got you a present." She reached into her shoulder bag and took out a small box.

Daddy looked at her, his bright blue eyes glittering like sapphires. "I'll give it to Momma."

"No, you open it," Tam said, glancing over his shoulder toward the kitchen. It sat around the corner, but Tam could hear voices back there.

"She'll want to see it."

Impatience ran through Tam, but she nodded. She didn't know what else she was supposed to do. "Okay," she said. "Happy anniversary."

"Thanks, baby." He turned and went into the kitchen with the gift, and Tam followed. Not only was Chris sitting next to Cara at the bar, but Stacy had brought her boyfriend too. Tam didn't know how to treat Rupert. He and Stacy weren't married. They weren't engaged. They did live together in a town about an hour north of Dreamsville, which Stacy had not made a secret. She said they lived in Huntington, because it was a good "buffer zone" for both of them. What she really meant was her family couldn't pop in on her whenever they wanted.

Since they weren't married and they weren't engaged, Tam wasn't sure how to think about Rupert. He was a know-it-all who talked down to everyone around him, and how Stacy could stand to be with him for more than an hour was a mystery to Tam.

"Tam, baby," her mother said, grinning widely as she hurried toward her. She embraced Tam, who closed her eyes and held on tight.

"Hi, Momma."

"Oh, you smell like that shop," her mom said, pulling away. She still wore the fond smile, though, so Tam knew she was teasing. "Where's Blaine?"

"I didn't know Blaine was invited, Momma," Tam said, shooting a glance at Cara. "No one told me."

"Of course he's invited," Momma said, backing up. "You two are practically engaged from what I hear."

Tam frowned. "Where'd you hear that?" She pinned her youngest sister with a glare. "I'm not wearing a ring, so I wasn't sure."

"Cara's not wearing a ring either," Mom said. "She knew."

Tam looked at Cara, who shrugged. The more likely

scenario was that Cara hadn't known. She just didn't care if her parents wanted Chris there or not. *She* wanted him there, therefore, he was there.

She looked around at the people in the kitchen, hating that she was all alone. "Hey, Stace," she said, keeping her voice light as she stepped over to her sister. The girls were about five years apart, and Stacy would be thirty just after the New Year.

Tam hugged her, but it was like embracing a bag of bones. She said hello to Rupert, who looked like he'd gotten at least half a dozen new tattoos since she'd seen him last. He owned a tattoo parlor in Huntington, and Stacy's reasoning for never coming to things was his busy work schedule.

"How are things at the shop?" she asked him. Rupert loved to talk about himself, and he started into a story that Tam lost interest in after about thirty seconds. She kept humming and nodding though, secretly wondering if she could text Blaine and have him come to dinner.

"We're ready," Momma said, and Tam put the idea out of her mind. He'd show up about the time they finished eating, and she didn't need to call more attention to herself.

"Can you just open the gifts already?" Cara asked, grinning.

"You guys brought gifts?" Stacy asked, looking from Cara to Tam.

"I did," Cara said.

"So did I," Tam murmured, almost afraid to speak too loud. Stacy would not be happy about being the only one there without a gift.

"I've made your mother wait all day for her gift," Daddy said, and Stacy scoffed.

"It would've been nice if someone had told me gifts were required."

"They're *not* required," Cara said, glaring at their middle sister.

"No one told me to bring my boyfriend," Tam said, also shooting a look in Stacy's direction. Everything was about her, all the time. Tam honestly didn't know how she survived on a day-to-day basis. She was always playing the victim. Someone had always done something wrong by her.

How she and Rupert got along, Tam would never understand. It didn't matter if she understood a relationship she wasn't part of, just like it didn't matter if Alex didn't think she and Blaine were a real couple.

At the same time, Tam was starting to have serious doubts about Blaine. Maybe it did matter what other people thought. If they couldn't even put on a convincing performance of their mad love for each other, what was the point?

You've never had to convince anyone, she told herself. *The relationship is real.*

"Come sit down, girls," Momma said as Daddy piled all the gifts at her spot on the table. Tam turned away from Stacy's sharp eyes and went over to the table. She'd always sat to her mother's left, and she went to take that seat.

She'd just settled down and taken a sip of the sweet tea there when Stacy said, "Tam, Rupert's sitting there."

She looked up. "What?"

"I'm sitting here," she said, indicating the chair next to Tam. "That means Rupert is going to sit there."

"I always sit here," Tam said.

"Big deal," Stacy said, her voice cold. "Go sit on the other side."

Why she thought she could just boss Tam around, Tam wasn't sure. She found herself standing and vacating the seat Stacy wanted for Rupert, and she went behind her mother to the other side of the table. Cara and Chris had taken spots on this side, and one lonely spot remained next to her father.

There was no place setting for Blaine, and she wondered if her mother even realized that. She didn't seem to, and Tam faded into the background as her parents opened their gifts. Her mother let out a long sigh when she opened Tam's gift—a pair of wine bottle charms she'd ordered months ago.

"The stones are the birthstones for the month you got married, and then each of our birthdays." She smiled at her mother, who looked up from the delicate charms with tears in her eyes.

"That's wonderful," she said. "Thank you." Tam nodded, glad she'd brought a smile to her mother's face.

Cara had gotten them an espresso machine, and both Momma and Daddy exclaimed over that for a good minute. Daddy wanted to make the coffee right now so they could have it after dinner, but Momma managed to keep them on track.

"We need to eat while it's hot," she said, settling at her place.

"You need to open my gifts," Daddy said.

"They're not going to be anything gross, are they?" Stacy asked.

"Stacy," Tam said. "Come on."

"What? You don't know what married couples do, because you've never been married."

"Neither have you," Tam shot back.

"Girls," Momma said, and Tam felt bad for engaging with her sister.

"Sorry," Tam said. She looked at Stacy. "Sorry, Stacy."

Her sister did not return the apology. She held her head high, her chin slightly elevated too. She watched silently as Momma opened a new cookbook, exclaiming over it, and then a beautiful bottle of red wine.

"Thank you, Kenneth."

"That is for later," he said, his grin very much saying there was something secret between the two of them.

They kissed, and Stacy groaned. "Gross," she said.

"It's not gross," Cara and Tam said at the same time.

"How old are you?" Cara asked. "I swear, Stacy, sometimes you act like a child."

"So do you," Stacy shot back.

"They're our parents," Tam said. "Don't we want them to be in a loving, committed relationship?"

"I do," Cara said.

"People in those kinds of relationships kiss," Tam said. "It's not gross."

"It is to me," Stacy said. "I'm allowed to have my own opinions."

"Maybe you should learn to keep them to yourself, though," Tam said. For some reason, she really wasn't going to take anything from Stacy today. Maybe it was her own ragged nerves. Maybe she simply couldn't add more to her already overstuffed mind.

"Don't tell her what to do," Rupert said.

"Whatever," Tam said, looking back to the head of the table, where her parents stood watching and listening to their children bicker and bite at each other. Tam didn't know how to stop herself from doing it. She'd taken so much from Stacy over the years, and she just couldn't keep doing it.

"Go on, Momma," she said.

Her mother reached for another present, and Stacy said, "I think that's from us."

"No, it's not," Cara said. "Daddy got that for Momma."

"Didn't you bring that one, Rupert?"

He looked at Stacy with such an utter look of confusion and surprise, and Tam didn't understand what she was doing. Literally everyone in the room knew Stacy and Rupert had not brought a present for the anniversary party.

"I think we brought it," Stacy said.

"What's in it, then?" Tam challenged, her sassy side rearing its ugly head.

"It doesn't matter," Momma said, slipping her fingernail under the wrapping to open the gift.

"It matters," Tam said, jumping to her feet. "If they brought this gift, they'll know what's in it." She snatched the box from her mother before she could get any more of it open. She held up the boxy package. "So what is it?"

"Wow, it's no wonder you're not married or engaged yet," Stacy said. "Honestly, who wants to live with the control freak?"

Though she'd heard it before, her sister's assessment of her still stung. Tam ignored her, which was what she should've done in the first place.

She handed the package back to Momma with a murmured apology. She returned to her seat, a very disgruntled wave of emotion flowing through her. Why had Stacy even bothered to come?

Probably for the free food, Tam thought. Rupert ate an entire tray of fresh shrimp by himself, and Tam couldn't help watching him as he sat on the other side of the table from her.

Soft music played in the background, and Daddy said, "Time for dessert."

"Thanks for inviting us," Cara said.

"Of course," Momma said. "This is about our family now, not just the two of us."

"We are the beginning of us," Daddy said, and Tam wasn't sure what that was supposed to mean.

Momma went into the kitchen and retrieved the pies she'd made. "Cherry, apple, or pecan."

"That's all you've got?" Stacy asked.

Cara opened her mouth to say something, thought better of it, and just looked to Mom.

Three pies for seven people was plenty, and Stacy hadn't even responded when their mother had asked for suggestions for the pie flavors for this very party only a week ago.

Momma and Daddy worked together to dish up the pie and add as much ice cream as someone wanted.

Afterward, Momma handed Tam a cup of coffee, and said, "Come sit with me on the porch."

"Are the screens down?" Tam asked. "Because the bugs are a real issue right now."

"Yes, we've got them all zipped." Momma led the way to the screened-in porch, and Tam sighed as she sat down beside her on a comfortable couch. "Tell me about Blaine, dear. Why did he not come? Really."

"I told you why," Tam said. "I didn't know he was invited."

"You're still seeing him?"

Tam frowned, confused by this line of questioning. "Yes, Mom. Of course."

"You can't say of course," Momma argued. "Hayes had broken your engagement for three weeks before you told me."

"That's because it wasn't hard to get everything cancelled," Tam said. That had been partially true. They'd still been more than sixty days from the wedding, so cancelling had been somewhat easy. Dealing with the emotional aftermath of the break-up had not.

Tam hadn't wanted to tell the story again, so she hadn't said anything to her parents to spare herself the pain. That wasn't a crime; she was allowed to protect her own feelings.

"Where is Hayes?" Stacy asked, and Cara threw her a look.

"He's back in Dreamsville," Tam said slowly. She hadn't seen him since the line dancing incident, and he hadn't tried to call her. Or if he had, she wouldn't know, because she'd blocked his number. "His father has cancer, so he came back to help with the dealership and be with his dad."

"Darren's doing really well," Daddy said, smiling around at everyone as if they all got along like peaches and cream. "That's what I heard. The surgery got out a huge tumor in his lower intestine, and he's doing much better."

"That's great," Cara said, and Tam nodded her assent too. Maybe Hayes would leave town once his father was feeling better. Then Tam could move forward too and try to forget everything that had happened since she'd asked Blaine to be her fake boyfriend.

He's not fake, she told herself, and intellectually, she knew he wasn't. In some other ways, though, he was.

The heavens parted, and her thoughts aligned.

What she was really worried about was whether they'd been kidding themselves this whole time. Her reaction to Hayes; his to Alex. People not believing that she and Blaine were together.

Was she really past Hayes?

Was Blaine really over Alex and ready for a real, lasting relationship?

Did she and Blaine even *have* a real, lasting relationship?

She took a bite of her pie, but the normally delicious pecan filling just felt like soggy cardboard in her mouth. She hated these doubts, because she'd thought she'd finally moved past them. She'd thought she and Blaine just needed each other.

She'd been wrong. She needed some sort of outside validation that she and Blaine were a real couple. She needed to know he wanted her. She needed to feel like while their romantic relationship had definitely experienced some bumps up until this point, that he hadn't started to see her in a romantic way simply because she'd confessed to a having a crush on him.

Horror struck her right between the ribs, making eating difficult. She kept doing it, ignoring the conversation flowing around her.

What if Hayes hadn't come back into town?

What if she'd never told Blaine about her crush?

What if all of this—the last few months with Blaine— really *had* been fake, and that was why no one could really see the two of them together?

18

$\mathcal{T}$rey pulled up to the white farmhouse, something not quite right about it. He and Beth were supposed to be going to dinner that night—finally. He'd finally followed-up with her about the invitation, and she finally felt like the ranch was caught up to a point where she could take a night off to go out with him.

Her father was coming to stay at the farmhouse with TJ, but Trey didn't see another truck or car in the driveway. He got out of his truck anyway and went up the steps to the front door. His anxiety skipped through his whole system, but he managed to raise his hand and press the doorbell.

It was then that he smelled the smoke.

He spun around, searching for the tell-tale sign of fire. It wasn't strong enough to be outside, and that only struck terror inside his heart. "Beth?" he called.

"Coming," she yelled. She opened the door a few seconds later, and it was obvious that she was nowhere near ready to go to dinner. She wore a pair of jeans with a white paint smear up the left thigh, a T-shirt with actual holes along the collar, and her hair in a high ponytail.

She looked like she'd just come in off the ranch.

She still had her palm wrapped, though the bandage was much smaller now. The first layer of stitches had been removed, and the doctors were pleased with her healing. She'd thought that meant she could start to do more, but she'd found out the painful way that she couldn't.

"What's goin' on now?" Trey asked, trying to peer around her.

"TJ thought he could try making his own scrambled eggs," she said, her expression frazzled. "He set the egg carton on fire. We're fine. It's all fine." She turned and walked away from him, those narrow hips swaying and her dark hair doing the same.

"So I'll come in," Trey muttered to himself, entering the farmhouse and closing the door behind him. The kitchen sat at the back of the large space, and he followed Beth there. TJ sat on a barstool near the sliding glass door, and smoke rose in thin wisps from the kitchen sink.

"I can get this cleaned up," he said. "If you want to go finish getting ready."

"I'm fine," she said, picking up the frying pan from the sink and dumping the contents of it into the trashcan.

Trey looked at TJ, who watched him with wide,

remorseful eyes. Trey wanted to wrap the little boy in a blanket straight from the dryer, give him a box of candy, and hold him until he ate it all and fell asleep in a sugar coma.

That was exactly what his mother had used to do for him, and Trey needed to get over to his parents' house and make peace with them. Sometimes they could just be so pushy, and he didn't want to go to church.

His mother worried about the salvation of his eternal soul, but he'd told her it was his decision to make.

"Beth," he said. "Let's just reschedule."

He expected her to argue, so when she said, "Okay," and braced herself against the countertop with her one good palm, Trey was equal parts disappointed and surprised.

"Okay," he said.

"My dad's not here anyway," Beth said. "I'll go call him right now."

Trey wondered if a date with her would ever happen. Right now, it wasn't looking good for him. She left him in the kitchen with TJ, who hadn't moved or made a sound.

"Are you in time out or something?" Trey asked.

TJ nodded. "Mom was mad about the eggs."

"You probably shouldn't be using the stove." Trey wasn't even sure how the little boy had gotten the burners lit. He'd have to stand on a chair to twist the knobs at the back of the stove.

"Yeah, probably not," TJ said. "Can I get down now?"

"I have no idea," Trey said. "I'm not in charge here."

TJ balanced on the barstool and brought his knees up to his chest. Trey wasn't sure if he should stick around and wait for Beth to get off the phone, or just go. He hated the awkwardness between them tonight, though there'd been a little these past few weeks as he'd come to help her every two or three days.

He'd come every afternoon and evening if she'd let him, but Beth was a particularly stubborn woman who knew exactly what she wanted. Trey had felt more like a nuisance than a benefit every time he came to help her.

Trey finally wandered over to the couch and sat down. Several minutes later, Beth breezed back into the kitchen. "I changed my mind," she said. "I want to go to dinner." She wore a pair of short shorts and a blue, green, white, and brown striped shirt.

Trey's mouth turned dry, and he stood. "You sure?"

"Yes," she said, barely meeting his eye. "My dad will be here in five minutes." She looked at TJ. "Come on down."

The little boy practically jumped from the barstool and flew into his mother's arms. Trey smiled at the familial gesture, and he listened as Beth told him he couldn't use the stove without permission.

"Tell me what permission is, baby," she said, stroking his hair off his forehead.

"It means you tellin' me yes," TJ said. "If you tell me yes, I can do something, I have your permission."

"Good boy," she said. "You have to *ask* to do things, TJ.

Grandpa is bringing pizza. There was no reason for you to be making eggs."

"I was hungry," the little boy said.

"Not hungry enough to starve to death." She smiled at him and straightened. "Now, go say hi to Trey and then make sure the dogs have water in their bowls on the back patio."

TJ came skipping over to Trey, and he bent down to scoop the wisp of a boy into his arms. "Hi, Trey," he said.

"Hi yourself, TJ." He smiled at the little boy. "I'm glad you're not in trouble anymore."

"Me too."

Trey set him back down. "You better get those dogs watered, though. Animals need fresh water."

"Do you water animals, Trey?"

"All the time." He glanced at Beth, who was looking at her phone, and went with TJ as he walked outside to the patio. He brought up the first bowl and skipped back down to get another.

Trey held them for him, and when they had all four, he turned back to the house. Voices met his ears, and he slowed. "...I might not be ready."

"It's been almost three years, Beth," a man said, and Trey assumed that to be her father.

"I know *exactly* how long it's been since my husband died," Beth said, her voice dripping with acid.

A sigh filled the air. "If you're not ready, don't go out with him," her dad said.

"I can't just blow him off."

"Sure you can. You just say you aren't feeling well. Your hand hurts. Whatever. You can't go."

Trey didn't want to hear another word. He entered the house with the dog bowls, his pulse storming inside his chest. Did she not want to go out with him, because it was him asking? Was she really going to cancel because she wasn't ready and not for some other reason?

Thankfully, Beth and her father had fallen silent the moment Trey had come inside.

"We just wash these out, or...?" He looked at TJ, and he would miss the little boy. He'd likely wander onto Bluegrass Ranch at some point in the future, and Trey might have the opportunity to see Beth from time to time.

"Yep," TJ said. "Fill 'em up and put 'em back out. You don't got dogs at your ranch?"

"Sure," he said. "We've got dogs. But we're not a cattle ranch, buddy. We raise horses, and they don't need to be herded by dogs."

"You have those sheep," TJ said. "Dogs like to herd sheep."

Trey chuckled. "That they do." He finished washing and rinsing the bowls and started to fill them. "It would be easier to take these back outside and then fill them."

He handed one bowl to TJ. "Take this one, bud."

TJ did as instructed, and Trey brought out the rest of the bowls. "Be right back. Don't wander off now."

"Yes, sir," TJ said, gazing at something in the distance.

Trey went back inside and found a large bowl in the drying rack. He filled it with water and made the trip outside. It filled two of the bowls, and Trey returned to refill the bowl.

Tam and her father certainly looked like he'd interrupted them, and Trey wanted to whip out his pocketknife and literally cut the tension and apprehension right out of the air.

"You must be Clyde," Trey said, smiling at the older gentleman. "I'm Trey Chappell." He glanced at Beth, who should've made this introduction. She seemed so out of it tonight. He shook her father's hand, and hoped he passed the test when Clyde looked him up and down.

"Chappell? Is that right?"

"Yes, sir," Trey said. "We're right next door."

"I'm Clyde Turner. You have a beautiful ranch."

"Thank you," Trey said. "I'll tell Spur you said so." He turned to Beth, who just stood there staring at him. "I think I'm going to go," Trey said. "I'm not feeling well tonight."

"It's been hot lately," Beth's father said.

"You don't have to go," Beth said.

"But I'm going to." Trey tried to smile at her, but he couldn't quite pull it off. He put his hand on top of his hat and nodded. "Goodnight, Beth." He faced her father again. "Sorry to make you drive all the way out here."

"It's okay," Clyde said, his keen eyes missing nothing.

Trey nodded and headed for the front door. Clyde said

something behind him, but it wasn't to him, and Trey didn't have the mental energy to find out if Beth would put any action behind what she'd said.

She didn't, and a sting punctured his heart. As he drove back to Bluegrass, he realized she actually *had* put an action behind what she'd said.

She wasn't ready to date, despite the almost three years since Danny's death. So she hadn't come after him. She hadn't texted him, and she wouldn't either. If Trey wanted to go out with her, he'd have to ask again.

"Maybe just let it lie," he told himself as he trundled down the dirt road toward the homestead. "Your life will be so much easier."

He parked, still undecided as to what to do about Beth, and went to see what his brothers were doing. Spur and Olli had hosted a couple of movie nights, but tonight, the homestead was full of soda, candy, and laughter as everyone *except* Spur and Olli had gathered in the living room for a night of video games.

"Trey's back," Conrad yelled, and an uproar filled the house. Trey just wanted to go to his room and figure out what to do about Beth, but he found himself swept into the group of brothers, each of them vying for him to be on their team for the next race.

19

"You just text her," Blaine said to Trey. "Ask her how she is, and if you can come over."

"I don't want to intrude," Trey said. "I feel like I'm pushing myself on her." He turned his back on Blaine to hang up a length of rope he'd just coiled. "No one wants to feel like he's the only one interested in the relationship."

"You don't know she's not."

Trey turned back to Blaine, and he looked so frustrated. Blaine knew the feeling keenly. He and frustration were good friends, especially since last weekend when he'd made a mess of things with Tam.

They'd texted and talked a little bit since, but things weren't the same, and Blaine knew it. Tam had to know it too. Sometimes, in the past, they just ignored the awkward things between them, and they eventually went away.

Blaine didn't think that was going to happen here. Not only that, but he didn't want to act like a seventeen-year-old. He wanted to have a meaningful, open, honest relationship with Tam.

"You think Tam and I are a couple, right?"

Trey looked up, surprise in his eyes. "What?"

Instant embarrassment shot through Blaine. "Nothing," he said.

"It's something."

Blaine turned away and bent to pick up some errant reins. He ran his hands along the length of them, feeling the dust and dirt, and it grounded him. "Tam asked me to be her fake boyfriend for when Hayes came into town," he said, looking out the open barn door. The sun seemed dimmer today, as there had been a big fire a bit up the road, and the smoke was hanging in the air today.

"I didn't really want to, but I started thinking about her in a new way, and we started dating."

"For real?" Trey asked.

"Yes," Blaine said, ducking his head. He started rolling up the reins. "For real. Hayes didn't believe it. We ran into Alex last weekend, and she didn't believe it either. Now, I'm so deep inside my own head, and..." He exhaled heavily. "It's been a hard week. She's just working a lot."

"You still disappear at night," Trey said. "You're not going to see her?"

"I've been spending a couple of hours with Featherweight." He handed the reins to Trey, their eyes meeting. "I'm pathetic, just like Alex always said."

"No, you're not." Trey yanked the reins from Blaine, his eyes flashing with anger. "Don't say that. She doesn't get to have any influence over you anymore."

"Yeah, but she still does sometimes," Blaine said. "I *hate* that she does."

"Then do something about it," Trey said.

"I will, when you do something about Beth."

Trey glared, and Blaine gave his attitude right back to him. "It's different," Trey finally said. "You're already dating Tam, and you guys are extremely good together. I never doubted once that you were having a real relationship with her." He clapped Blaine on his shoulder and went to retrieve another saddle from outside.

When he came back inside the barn, he added, "I knew you two were dating before you even went out. She showed up at the house all perfumed and curled, and she asked for you, and...I knew."

Blaine nodded, reaching for the leather cleaner. "I'll do this one."

"Great," Trey said as he pulled his ringing phone out of his pocket. "Because this is Beth."

"Really?" Blaine asked.

Trey turned the phone toward Blaine, and it was Beth.

"Answer it before it goes to voicemail." Blaine took the soft cloth out of the warm water in the sink and got to work, Trey taking his phone call outside.

When he finished, and the saddle gleamed like it was brand new, Blaine took out his phone and called Tam.

"Hey, stranger," she said, her voice set on super-flirt.

Blaine chuckled, pieces of himself flying back into the right place with the simple sound of her voice. "It's been a long week, hasn't it?"

"Yes," she said with a sigh.

"Where are you in your work?" he asked. "Could I take you to dinner?"

"You know what? Dinner sounds amazing." She let out another long breath, and said, "I need an hour. Will that be too late?"

"Nope." Blaine said he'd come by after he showered, and he was just going in from the barn now.

"See you soon," Tam said, and Blaine hung up. His step had more bounce as he made the walk back to the house, and he took several long minutes to clean up, shave the outer edges of his beard so he looked neat and trim, and get out the bottle of cologne Spur had given him.

He put on his best jeans, a black polo and put his brown leather jacket over that. He opted for his brown cowboy hat and his brown boots to tie himself together from head to toe.

As he looked at himself in the mirror, he sighed. It didn't get any better, and he hoped his efforts to look good for her would be noticed by Tam. He'd seen the spark of attraction in her eyes plenty of times over the past few months, and he really needed to see it again tonight.

Out in the kitchen, Trey sat at the counter with a bowl of cereal in front of him. "You're going out," he said.

"Yeah. Why aren't you?"

"I didn't ask," he said. "Before you say anything, she asked me to help her with the horses tomorrow, which is a *huge* step for her. *Huge.*" He grinned at Blaine, who smiled on back at his brother.

"Good luck tomorrow," Blaine said. "If I don't see you in the morning." He nodded at Trey and left the homestead. Out on the front porch, he caught sight of Conrad and Hilde sitting on the top steps, hand-in-hand as they talked. Neither of them looked upset, but they didn't look happy either.

Blaine was tired of trying to make sure everyone around him was doing okay. His heart was too small for all of his brothers, his parents, Tam and her family, and everyone else. His neighbors, and Olli and Spur, and the cowboys he worked with.

He just wanted everyone to be happy.

He wanted himself to be happy.

Better get to Tam's, then, he thought, wondering why he cared what anyone thought about his relationship with her. They didn't have to live inside it. Only he and Tam did, and a whole speech started in his mind as he backed up and turned around to head down the lane toward the highway.

"Shoot," he said when he looked at the clock on the dashboard. He was late already, and he considered going to Tam's house instead of her shop. She hadn't said where she'd be, but he'd assumed the leather shop, as she'd been working from sunup to sundown for a couple of weeks now.

When he turned the corner to go down the street to her shop, he saw her bright blue truck still parked out front. Relief filled him that he'd chosen the right location, and he pulled in next to the black truck parked next to Tam's.

She had customers come to the shop to pick things up all the time, but Blaine didn't wait in his truck. He'd gone into her shop when other people were there plenty of times. He didn't hesitate as he opened the door and entered.

Tam stood chest-to-chest with another man, up on her tiptoes as she said something in a high voice. The problem was, the man was also shouting something at her, and Blaine froze as he took in the scene.

"Hey," he yelled over them, and both Tam and— Blaine's heartbeat shot through his body like a cannon— Hayes looked at him. "What is going on here?"

Hayes grabbed onto the lapels of his jacket and pulled it forward, as if adjusting his clothes. He wore a frown on his face, and Tam didn't look happy either.

"Nothing," she said, stepping away from Hayes.

"I want an answer," Hayes said.

"I don't have to answer to you," she said. "Now, I'm leaving, and I'd like you to leave my shop."

"No," Hayes said. He took several quick steps toward Blaine too, and it was almost like he and Tam were racing to see who could get to him first. "I want to know the truth."

"The truth about what?" Blaine asked, shooting a glance at Tam. "How long has he been here?"

"Not long."

"Half an hour," Hayes said, shooting her a look.

Blaine's blood turned cold, and it couldn't quite move through his body the right way. "Thirty minutes, huh? You guys probably had such a great talk in that amount of time." He folded his arms, hating that he'd taken so long to get ready. Tam hadn't even looked up to his hat or down to his boots.

"Don't," Tam said.

"Don't what?" Blaine asked. "A half an hour, Tam?" Jealousy snaked through him, striking at all of his organs. He knew exactly what this felt like, and exactly how long it would take the poison to infect his whole body. He knew exactly how long it took to recover from, and exactly how agonizing those years would be.

Even worse, because this was Tamara, his very best friend on the whole Earth, and he felt her slipping away from him with every breath he took. He wouldn't have her to talk to after this ended. He wouldn't have her to text in the middle of the night when he couldn't sleep and his feelings of self-doubt crept in. He wouldn't have her to call on for help around the ranch, and he wouldn't have her to ride with when nothing else in the world made sense.

"I just want to know if your relationship is the real deal," Hayes said.

"No," Blaine said at the same time Tam said, "Of course it is." Her voice echoed in the empty silence, and she looked at Blaine with pure shock on her face.

Blaine took a deep breath and looked at Hayes. Oh, how he disliked this man. Why was he even here? Did he think he could win Tam back if she admitted they'd started this fake relationship to fool him into thinking Tam was over him?

"When she heard you were coming back into town, she asked me to be her boyfriend. I wasn't sure, because I don't think she has a darn thing to prove to you." He cleared his throat, his fists curling tightly at his sides. He couldn't look at Tam, because she'd made a squeaking noise when he'd started talking.

"But she thought she did, and...certain things were said and done, and we started dating."

Hayes kept the frown on his face as he looked from Blaine to Tam and back. "And now? it's real or fake?"

Blaine shrugged, because he was pretty certain Tam was going to pummel him the moment they were alone, and he'd rather not take his heart out of his chest and give it straight to her to shatter. "We're still working on the details," he said.

"I hate you, Blaine Chappell," Tam said, her voice deadly quiet. "And I hate you, Hayes Powell. Both of you get out of my shop."

Blaine looked at her, the perfect rage on her face, her fists clenched at her sides, her eyes bright with unshed tears.

Tears.

His heart tore right in half. "Tam," he started.

"Get out," she said, taking a menacing step forward. "Now. Both of you. Go!" She looked wild and ferocious, and Blaine turned to open the door. His heart pounding in terror, he left the shop, Hayes right behind him.

"Don't call me," she said. "Either of you. Don't stop by ever again. We're done." She punctuated her words with a loud slamming of the door that actually made Blaine cringe. He ignored Hayes as he walked to his truck.

He had no idea what he was doing. He existed outside his own mind, his own existence. He just knew he didn't want to be there anymore. He was so tired of thinking about Tam, and what he should say to Tam, and what should happen next between him and Tam.

He normally wouldn't have left her alone with Hayes, but tonight, he fired up his truck and backed out of the parking lot first.

He normally wouldn't have left town without letting someone know where he was going, but that someone was Tam, and he couldn't tell her.

As he put the town of Dreamsville in his rear-view mirror, Blaine had the distinct realization that he'd just lost everything. His girlfriend, his best friend, and his chance for a happy future.

am lay face-down on her bed and cried. June kept whining, her head very close to Tam's. Jasper paced up and down the length of her body, licking her feet every so often.

She hated crying almost as much as she hated dealing with her sister. She usually didn't cry at all, except for a few instances in her life.

The hole in her soul was simply too wide to fill with doing dishes, cutting leather, or online shopping. She couldn't fill it if she had an unlimited amount of chores, orders, and money, as the agony of it went on and on. It radiated deep down into her heart, and clear up into her mind.

It was endless, and painkillers didn't touch the hurt cascading through her.

The worst part was she had absolutely no one to call.

You could call Cara, she thought, but she didn't move. Besides, her sister was busy with her own life and her own boyfriend, and the one person Tam wanted to talk to she'd told never to call her or come by again.

Her tears started anew, and Tam simply let them flow from her. She had no other choice, because this heart-break was simply the worst she'd ever experienced.

THE NEXT MORNING, SHE WOKE IN HER CLOTHES, HER NECK aching and her face crusty. It took several seconds for her to realize where she was, and she sat up with a start, her heart beating rapidly.

She fumbled for her phone and checked the time. "I'm late." She swung her legs over the side of the bed before she realized she owned her own business, and she could go into the shop whenever she wanted. She had no appointments that day and two saddles to finish.

Everything from yesterday rushed at her, and Tam found she couldn't stand up. She couldn't stomach the thought of showering or going to the shop. Her breath shook in her chest, and she couldn't possibly carve and shave with such trembling in her body.

Before she could give it too much thought, she tapped out a couple of texts and sent them. Daniel Harrison and Cody Benson could wait another day for their saddles. No one would die. The world wouldn't end. They'd still pay, and Tam would still have a great reputation around Lexington.

The texts sent, she sighed and put her phone back on the nightstand. Without a job to keep her time occupied, Tam thought about what she liked doing best.

Blaine came to mind instantly. She liked spending time with Blaine. If she and Blaine had free time, they liked to ride horses together on Bluegrass Ranch. It was surprising to Tam that in all the months they'd been dating, they hadn't saddled up once and enjoyed the evening air together. They used to do that so often.

Her whole body ached, the worst of it right behind her breastbone. Her head felt too heavy to hold up, and she laid back down in bed. She curled her knees to her chest and tried to hold her emotion inside. She failed, and a horrible, wrenching sob filled the bedroom.

She wondered if her grandmother had felt like this after her husband had died. She wondered if she'd cried right here in this very bedroom, in a bed very much like this one.

Down the hall and somewhere in the house, one of her dogs barked, and Tam sat up. They had to go out. They deserved to be fed. A plan formed in her mind, and she got up. Her legs shook slightly as she went into the bathroom and started running cold water over a washcloth.

She pressed it to her face, putting a lot of pressure on

her eyes to try to get them behave. "I don't want to spend the whole day crying," she said, tipping her head back. "Please."

She lowered the washcloth and looked at herself in the mirror. Only a pathetic, weak woman looked back. She shook her head. "No."

She would not take the blame for what had happened last night. That was Blaine Blasted Chappell. He'd told Hayes about their stupid plan, and while yes, it was an asinine plan, it wasn't like they'd even gone through with it.

Never once had their relationship been fake. Never once had they pretended to be dating when they weren't.

Determined now, she strode through her house to the back door, where both Jane and Jasper waited to go out. Neither of them had come to get her, and that surprised her too. "There you go, guys." She slid open the door and the corgis stumbled over each other to get out.

Tam left the door open and went back down the hall to shower. She put her clothes in the laundry basket, scrubbed everything in the shower, and dressed in blue jeans and a pink and white checkered shirt.

She was going to go horseback riding today. Bluegrass Ranch wasn't the only gig in town, and she fed the corgis, grabbed a protein shake, and headed out.

Instead of going straight to the stables where she'd ridden before, she made the drive into Dreamsville to visit her parents. She enjoyed them when it was just her and Cara and them. Or just her and them. As long as Stacy wasn't there, Tam liked seeing her mom and dad.

She stopped by Dough Boy and bought a half-dozen muffins to take. Maybe if she had something to do with her hands and mouth, she'd be able to contain her emotions.

A sigh leaked from her mouth as she pulled into the driveway. Her smile came naturally when she saw her parents sitting on the front porch in the pair of rocking chairs she and Cara had bought them for Christmas last year.

"Look at you two," she called up to them as she got out. They were so cute, and a familiar pinch radiated through her chest. She wanted to grow old with someone who would make better coffee than her, remind her when it was okay to be sassy and when she should pull back and simply smile, and who would love her no matter what.

She'd thought that would be Blaine. She'd even started thinking about their future together, though her folders with all the wedding ideas had stayed solidly in the filing cabinet.

Her smile wavered as she climbed the steps. "I brought muffins."

"What kind?" her mother asked.

"It's an assortment," Tam said, reaching the porch. "Blueberry, peach, and lemon poppyseed."

"I want the blueberry," Daddy said, getting up to hug Tam. She clung to him without meaning to, and when he tried to pull away and realized it, he held on tight. "Oh, okay." He patted her back. "What's wrong, baby?"

Her mom got up and took the muffins she held against her father's back and asked, "Tamara? You're crying, sweetheart."

"Blaine broke up with me," she said, her eyes burning like the devil himself had lit them on fire. "Or I broke up with him. Something."

Don't call me. We're done.

She pulled away from her father, heaving in the largest breath she could. It stuck in her throat, and she choked.

"Come sit down," Momma said. "Kenny, move that box." Her mother took her by the arm and led her to the rocking chair. "Tell us everything."

Tam just shook her head, because she couldn't retell the story. She felt like she'd lived a thousand years in the course of a single night, and she couldn't rub any more sand in her eyes.

"It'll work out," Daddy said as he brought out another chair and sat down. "You and Blaine are like left and right. You work together so well." He looked at Momma. "Tell her, Shirley."

"Look at her, Ken."

Tam looked down at her hands, her embarrassment and shame too much to hold upright. "I'm going to miss him so much."

"Just go talk to him," Momma said.

Tam shook her head. "I can't." This pain would fade. She'd endured a similar situation when Hayes had left, and she knew if she just put in enough time, she'd start to feel like herself again.

"What happened?" Momma asked again.

"What kind of muffin do you want, my Tams?" Daddy asked.

"Lemon poppyseed," she said. "Please." She lifted her gaze to her father's. "I just came because I belong here. Can you just let me be? I don't want to talk about it."

"Of course," Momma said, leaning back in her chair. "You absolutely belong here, Tam. You belong with that man, too."

"Well, he doesn't want me," Tam said miserably. "I'm not saying another word. I'm going to eat my muffin, and I'm going to get some potato chips later, and if you really wanted me to feel better, you'd make those caramel chocolate chip brownies."

Momma chuckled and closed her eyes. "I can do that."

Tam took the top off her lemon poppyseed muffin and took a bite. The large chunks of sugar combined well with the tart lemon, and Tam moaned as the flavors exploded across her taste buds.

"I'll go get some milk," Daddy said. "Or do you want juice, Tam? Coffee?"

"Milk," Tam said, because she wanted to feel young again. She didn't want to think about how old she was, and how she'd been transported all the way back to the starting line. Worse, as she had to figure out how to get back to the race at all.

After Hayes had left, she'd sat on the sidelines for a long time, and if she did that again, she'd be thirty-seven before she even suited up and arrived at the starting line.

Then what? she asked herself. Dating around. Dating apps. Getting to know a man took a long time, and when Tam looked to the future now, all she saw was a blank slate.

Nothing.

There was nothing for her anymore.

The morning wore on, and Momma and Daddy spoke to one another in calm voices about a neighbor, then about a movie they wanted to see, and then about the groceries they needed. Daddy left to do that, and Momma went into the kitchen to start on the brownies Tam wanted.

She dozed in the rocking chair, the relief from her thoughts what she hoped heaven would be like. Free from worry or care. Happiness and light and joy.

She woke when she heard a car door slam, and her first thought lingered on Blaine. A groan came out of her mouth, and she stood up to go find a restroom. After taking care of that, she joined her mother in the kitchen.

"Momma?" she asked as her mom got out a package of bologna.

"Sandwiches for lunch?" she asked. "The brownies will be done in only a few minutes, but they need to cool."

"Sandwiches are fine," Tam said, easing onto a barstool. Her back ached, and her mother looked at her when she groaned.

"How are you feeling?"

"My back hurts," Tam said. "I've been working seven days a week for a few weeks to keep up with the orders."

"I'll get you some pills."

Tam didn't even try to argue. She let her mom get her the painkillers, and she sipped the sweet tea her mother put in front of her to swallow them down. She smiled at her mom, and it pinched her face.

Thankfully, her mom just turned around and pulled bread from the drawer. Tam took a deep breath and steadied herself. "Momma?"

"Yes, baby?"

"Did you and Daddy ever fight?"

"Definitely," Momma said, shaking her head and laughing lightly. "He wanted to name you Ophelia." She burst out laughing, and Tam reveled in the sound of it. "I won that one, thankfully."

Tam would like her arguments with Blaine to be as simple.

Her mother turned and put a plate with a bologna and tomato sandwich in front of Tam. "I know that's not what you meant, Tam." She gave her a soft, kind smile. "I don't know what happened with Blaine, but it's as plain as the nose on your face that you love him."

"Sometimes love isn't enough, Momma," Tam said. "I loved Hayes too, you know."

This hurt worse, though. Tam knew it hurt worse, because she'd lost the man she loved and her best friend with only a few words.

Get out. We're done. Don't call me.

It was amazing to her that some three-word phrases could heal, and some could do so much harm.

"I know you did, baby." Momma turned to the stove when the timer went off. She stuck her hands in a pair of oven mitts. "He wasn't right for you, and I think you knew it. We told you our feelings, and you were so determined to have him." She pulled the brownies out and put them on the stovetop. "Sometimes parents have to let their children do what they want."

"You and Daddy are really good at that. Just look at Stacy."

"Stacy." Momma sighed and shook her head. "She's a special breed of human." She came around the counter and sat next to Tam. "So are you, Tam. You're *smart* and *beautiful.* You're so talented, and you can do anything you put your mind to."

"Thanks, Momma." Tam put her hand over her mother's.

"If you want to get Blaine back in your life, do it."

"It's not that easy, Momma."

"Of course it is," Momma said, her fingers tightening on Tam's forearm. "You're smart and beautiful. You know exactly what that man likes, and you know how to make yourself look amazing. You get over there, and you take his very favorite thing, and if you put your mind to getting him back, you can get him back."

"He doesn't want me," Tam said, her voice choking again. "Just because I want him doesn't mean he wants me."

"He wants you," Momma said. "I've seen that man look at you, Tam, and he doesn't just want you. He loves you."

"As a friend, Momma." Tam looked into her mother's eyes, desperation filling her. "He loves me as a *friend*. I want to be his wife, and I want to build a family with him." She shook her head, the wonderful future she'd fantasized about going up in dust.

"Tell him that."

"We were talking about marriage," Tam said. "He said he'd take me to look at engagement rings." She shook her head, the memories so painful. There was simply too much to explain to Momma right now.

"See? He loves you as more than a friend if you were talking like that."

"Maybe," Tam said, refusing to hope her mother was right. She picked up her sandwich and took a bite, instantly getting transported back to when she was eight years old. Her mom used to make her come in from riding her bike or swimming in the watering holes around Tennessee for lunch, and she'd served sandwiches five days a week.

Sometimes bologna, sometimes peanut butter and peach jam, sometimes cheese and mayo. She smiled at the pure memory, the happiness she'd experienced as a child at the forefront of her mind. "Thank you, Momma."

"You bet, Tam." She hugged her arm. "I love having you here, but Tam, you're too strong and too capable to hang around the porch with two old people." She smiled, and Tam giggled before taking another bite of her sandwich.

"I'll just say this, and then I'll be done badgering you about Blaine." She paused, though, and Tam finally gestured for her to go on. "You'll always belong here. We love seeing you. You know what you want, and you just have to be brave enough to go get it. If that's Blaine, that's Blaine. If it's to come spend a morning in a rocking chair with your parents, that's fine too."

Tam didn't want to do that, and both of them knew it.

"You started your own business with a loan of five thousand dollars to buy rawhide," Momma said as she got to her feet. "You worked in a garage without air conditioning until you could afford shop space. You traveled if you needed to. You learned to carve. You bought the tools with credit and paid them off."

She pulled a carton of cream out of the fridge. "If you want that man, you can have him." She set the cream next to the brownies, which were still far too hot to eat. Momma dished them up anyway and poured cold cream over them.

"You just have to ask yourself one question: What do you really want?"

21

"Yes, a week," Blaine said, aware of his acidic tone. He honestly did not care about going back to Bluegrass Ranch. He had plenty of money, and someone else could step up and get the fields finished, monitor the horses for a few days, and worry about everyone in the family.

Blaine was done with all of it.

"Blaine," Cayden said, and he also wished he wasn't on speaker with the three brothers older than him. Spur had called, but they'd staged an intervention of sorts, and Blaine was glad he hadn't told any of them where he'd gone.

He felt stuck in the middle of two extremely hard places, the same as he'd been his whole life. As the fourth son, he was constantly between the older brothers and the younger ones.

Right now, he was stuck between Kentucky and Georgia, in a tiny Tennessee town he'd forgotten the name of. He'd driven all night, found somewhere to sleep, done that, and then answered Spur's texts with one about how he wasn't coming back to the ranch for a while.

Spur's first words out of his mouth when Blaine had answered the phone were, "Define a while, Blaine."

"What?" Blaine asked.

"What's goin' on now?" Trey asked. "You left for a date last night, and you didn't come home."

"Didn't have a date," Blaine said, the sight of Tam's angry face right there in his memory. *I hate you, Blaine Chappell.*

Get out.

Don't call me.

We're done.

I hate you, Blaine Chappell.

She'd said that to him before, but in a teasing, flirtatious voice. The one she'd used last night hadn't held any of that. Not a single touch.

He deserved what she'd said to him. He shouldn't have reacted to Hayes being in her shop the way he had. He shouldn't have said he and Tam weren't dating.

"I don't like you out there alone," Spur said.

"I'm fine," Blaine said.

"What if your week becomes more?" Cayden asked.

"It won't," Blaine said, but he wouldn't promise any such thing if they pressured him to.

"Go on," Spur said. "I want to talk to him alone." Scuffling came through the line, and then Spur's voice didn't echo quite so much when he asked, "Blaine, do you remember what you told me to do when I was having trouble with Olli?"

"Spur," Blaine said. "This is a hundred percent different."

"How so?"

"You're you, and I'm me."

"I don't get what that has to do with anything," Spur said.

"I know you don't," Blaine said. "You're the oldest, Spur. You've always had ten times the confidence I have. You've been married twice. No one has ever cheated on you." He stopped talking, because Blaine didn't need to go on.

"You asked me if I wanted to do the right thing," Spur said. "I know you do too. You told me I didn't want to hurt her. I know you don't want to hurt Tam either."

"Already did that," Blaine said, his throat sticky. "She hates me."

"She does not."

"She said so," Blaine said, collapsing onto the bed and running his hand down his face.

"She did?"

"I was cruel to her," Blaine said. "I reacted instead of thinking. I—I don't deserve her anyway."

Spur took the longest time to respond, and when he did, all he said was, "Follow your heart."

Blaine nodded and let his phone fall to his lap. He looked around the hotel room, trying to find the right thing to do. He didn't want to get hurt either, and he was definitely hurting.

"I miss her already," he said out loud.

He and his brothers had not always gotten along. When problems happened, Blaine had learned how to apologize and ask for forgiveness. He thought of his mother, who had been working hard to be better than she'd been before.

Blaine had spoken to her and cleared the air. Could it really be that simple for him and Tam?

He didn't see how. Ever since he'd shown up on her doorstep and kissed her, everything had been so complicated. Blaine took forever to work complicated things through his mind, and he really disliked that about himself.

Right now, he disliked almost everything about himself, and he didn't even know how to live and breathe through the next minute. Somehow, that happened, and he focused on the next breath in, and then out.

If he could do that for long enough, he might be able to figure out how to do something besides breathe.

～

THAT EVENING, HE ATE ALONE IN A BOOTH IN THE CORNER OF a sports bar. The restaurant was loud, with TVs mounted on every available surface. He ignored the baseball on the screen, because the only sport Blaine cared about was horse racing.

He wasn't even really sure he cared about that. He thought he should, because he was a Chappell, and Chappells had been working in the racehorse industry for generations. He did have the love of horses in his blood, and he'd miss the Kentucky sky if he didn't go back. The white fences and emerald green grass. Featherweight and his whole family.

He'd go back to Bluegrass Ranch; there was nothing out here for him.

The real problem was, there was nothing back there for him either.

22

*B*eth paced in front of the barn, throwing a look toward TJ every now and then. The boy was right where she'd told him to stay. Having the kittens living out of the woodpile helped, and her son reminded her so much of her husband.

As usual, whenever Beth thought about Danny, her pulse quickened and then stopped. She pulled in a shallow breath and held it, the world spinning for just a moment. As quickly as the vertigo had come, it dissipated, and Beth could breathe again.

The whole episode had lasted three or four seconds, but Beth hated them. If she had enough of them throughout the day, they left her drained and exhausted. Trying to maintain the hundred-acre ranch did that by itself; she didn't need episodic grief to take her down too.

She'd asked her therapist on Friday afternoon how

much longer she'd have to deal with the panic, depression, and random tightening of her chest. Sam hadn't given her a timeframe.

"You know, Beth, everyone deals with things on their own timetable."

She hadn't liked that answer. She wanted someone to tell her she'd feel better by Halloween. Then, once the calendar flipped to November first, she'd be better.

"Where are you, Trey?" she muttered to herself, her boots crunching over the loose gravel in front of the barn. She wrapped her hand in a thick brace whenever she left the house, because she didn't want to take any chances. She still had a long road ahead of her before she'd have full use of her hand, and she thanked the Lord every day that it was her left hand and not her right that had been cut.

She could still make scrambled eggs and macaroni and cheese. She could still type decently fast and write checks. She could tie her shoes and brush her teeth. Everything would've been harder had her dominant hand been the one with forty-seven stitches in it.

Those had actually come out a few days ago, and Beth's hand pulsed with pain as a reminder. Afterward, she'd taken the highest dosage of painkillers she was allowed and laid down in her bedroom, all the black-out curtains drawn.

Her daddy had come to take TJ for an afternoon of miniature golf and wading in the river, and Beth tried not to think about the dozens of tasks around the ranch that needed doing.

Trey Chappell had been coming every few days to help her. He usually brought a crew of at least six men, and they made sure the horses were thriving, all her equipment was still working, and any major issues were taken care of.

She could feed chickens and goats, and she did. She did the daily feeding of the horses too, and while she couldn't clean a stall, she could open a gate and move an animal from one pasture to the next.

The hand she used to mouse around on the computer worked fine, and Beth was able to check her accounts and keep up with her bills as best she could.

Like lightning, a hot flash of fury hit her. It sizzled through her whole body and left quickly. She really wanted that to stop too, but she suspected those particular feelings came from such a deep place that they'd be with her for a while.

She turned toward TJ when she heard someone talking. Trey approached him, and he clearly hadn't seen her yet. She ogled him, because she could.

Trey Chappell was a glorious specimen of a man, and she waited for the guilt to hit her. It did, but only as a tiny splash, not the tsunami that had threatened to engulf her just last week. He was tall, with plenty of dark hair curling out from underneath his cowboy hat. When he looked at her, his eyes shone like her hardwood floor after she'd polished it, the dark, deep color of them like rich soil.

He always wore a shirt in some sort of plaid, usually in blue or green. Today's had blue *and* green, with yellow in there too. Jeans. Big belt buckle. Cowboy boots.

He was perfection.

He crouched down with TJ, who pointed underneath the logs stacked against the shed there. The back lawn met the front of the shed, and the farmhouse sat beyond that.

Trey laughed, and Beth couldn't help smiling. She didn't think either of them would be once she talked to him about the Sweetheart Classic.

Her fingers twined around one another, and she pulled in a breath when he straightened and looked in her direction. A smile popped onto her face, but her feet shifted, betraying her nerves. Even if she wasn't about to ask him to do something crazy, she'd be anxious about him being on her farm.

He'd asked her out, and she'd floundered it. She'd told him later that she meant to say yes, and he'd seemed so hopeful. Then he'd come, and she was sure he'd over-heard her and her father talking about how she wasn't sure she was ready to date.

He'd made up an excuse and left. Beth had been wondering what she was so afraid of ever since.

She hated change with the fierceness of a cornered alley cat. If someone had asked her five years ago what her future held, she wouldn't have put *widow* in the fantasy. So much had changed with Danny's death that Beth didn't even recognize her life or herself inside it. The woman she'd once been had definitely died with her husband, on that lonely stretch of road where he never should've been.

"Hey, Beth."

She pushed her dangerous thoughts away and focused on the man in front of her. "Thanks for coming, Trey."

"Sure," he said easily.

"I hope I'm not keeping you from your own chores."

"Nah." He reached up and pushed his hat back. "We've got people to cover 'em today." He smiled at her and reached for her hand. He paused, his skin only an inch from hers. Plenty of energy flowed from him to her, and Beth sure did like it.

"You can hold my hand," she said.

Trey's eyebrows went up. "Can I?"

"Yes." She took his hand as it hovered there in front of his body, and an internal sigh moved through her. "I need help with the horses today, because they need to be inspected, and I can't use both hands to look at their shoes."

"All right," Trey drawled. "Let's do it." He went with her into the barn, which had a row of stables down the left side.

Bluegrass had dedicated stables, with long row houses where the horses lived. Beth had five horses in this barn, and three stables which could house two dozen each. She didn't have quite that many horses right now, but sometimes the farm operated at full capacity.

She boarded horses. She bred them. She sold them. She offered horseback riding lessons. She raised cattle. She did anything she had to do to pay the mortgage and keep the farm. That first summer after Danny's death, she'd sold produce from a table at the Farmer's Market in town.

She could still remember standing there, pure humiliation filling her as people walked by. She'd never felt so invisible. She'd never felt so desperate. She'd never gone back.

She plucked a binder from the shelf inside the barn. "How about you inspect, and I'll make the notes?"

"Sure," Trey said. Sometimes they argued, but usually only when Beth didn't want him to do something. He'd claimed he'd love to have TJ follow him around Bluegrass, but Beth didn't buy that for a second. She hadn't let her son go next door and bother the cowboys there.

TJ seemed to do whatever he wanted though, and she'd first met Trey when he'd brought TJ home after finding him in the hay loft.

"All right, Buttercup," Trey said as he unlatched the door. "I'm comin' in." He entered the stall, and Buttercup just stood there and looked at him with doleful eyes. He inspected her legs and feet, saying, "She needs new shoes."

Beth made a note, and she had a feeling a lot of the

horses would need new shoes. She quieted the rising panic by reminding herself she had a budget for this.

After the fourth horse, Beth swallowed, breathed, and asked, "Have you heard of the Sweetheart Classic?" she asked.

Trey looked up at her as he exited the stall. "Sure," he said.

"You guys ever enter that?" She couldn't quite hold his gaze, and she looked to the fifth stall in the barn.

Trey went toward it. "No," he said over his shoulder. "Number one, it's not a qualifying race. Number two, it's...odd."

"Odd?" Beth's heart skipped a beat and then picked it up again.

Trey entered the stall with Midnight Moonlight and did the inspection. "Shoes," he said. "He's got something with his teeth too. There's spots on this side." He had his hands in the horse's mouth, and Beth wanted to tell him to be careful.

She made the notes while he joined her. "The Sweetheart Classic isn't horse racing. It's an amateur community event."

"Right," she said. "There's still money to be won, and a horse."

Trey smiled at her like she was a small child with big dreams that would never come true. "I suppose."

"We can't all be billionaires," she said, her idea of asking him to enter the Classic with her disappearing. She turned and left him standing in the barn, her goal the stables past the walking circle and the huge garden she planted every year.

The sight of it made her tired, because it was time to harvest, and she had only done about a quarter of the work. There was much to do following the harvest too. She knew how and had made applesauce in the past. Creamed corn she froze in bags. Pumpkin pie filling. Squash soup.

She didn't want the food to go to waste, but she couldn't possibly harvest it all and preserve it too.

"Hey now," Trey said, catching up to her. "What are you talking about?"

"I want to enter the Classic," she said, keeping her gaze straight ahead. Talking to him about this while she was slightly irritated with him was actually a good idea. She could deliver the facts and send him home to think about her proposal.

"You've got a horse you think can win?"

"Yes," Beth said. "Somebody's Lady."

"Then enter her."

"She needs some training up," Beth said. "But I could get her ready. I just can't enter her."

"Why not?"

She sighed and paused in the shade of a tall willow oak. In just a few more weeks, all the leaves would turn a beautiful shade of red and fall to the ground. Beth wouldn't be able to rake them by herself, and she pressed against the hysteria threatening to overtake her.

She just had to keep swimming. She wouldn't drown.

"It's the *Sweetheart* Classic," she said. "Run on or near Valentine's Day. You can only enter a horse as a..." She cleared her throat. "Only..."

"Married couples who own the horse together can enter." Trey looked up from his phone, shock plain on his face. "You have to be married to enter the Sweetheart Classic."

"That's right," she said, walking again. Looking at him was too hard.

"The prize money is half a million dollars," he called from behind her.

Beth knew, and she couldn't even imagine what that kind of money could do for her and TJ. She shook her head at her idiocy. She'd allowed herself to dream, and she shouldn't have done that.

Trey caught up to her again, and Beth cut a glance at him. He seemed thoughtful, and she didn't want to interrupt him.

At the same time, she needed to get these words out before they poisoned her. "I was thinking you and I could enter."

"We're not married," he said.

"We could get married," she said, her whole face heating with just those words.

"The deadline to enter is November first."

"Yes."

"That's what? Seven weeks from now?"

"How long do you think it takes to get married?"

Trey put his hand on her arm and said, "Can you stop? I need to get something straight."

She stopped, her heartbeat pounding furiously fast in her chest. She looked everywhere but at him, and he simply waited for her to meet his gaze. When she finally did, she saw his carefully masked face and had no idea what he was thinking.

"Start at the beginning," he said.

She looked away, and he reached up and gently guided her face back toward his. "Look me in the eye and tell me what's going through your head."

She appreciated the soft quality of his voice, because he'd just made a pretty hefty demand. She cleared her throat again. "I need the money, Trey. Plain and simple." She'd only ever told her father about the financial situation on the ranch. "My horses won't win derbies or stakes. Somebody's Lady can win this, and I want to enter. One of the requirements to be able to enter is to be married and own the horse together."

She shrugged. "I know a few cowboys, but I know you the best. I figured...we could get married real quick. You give me a dollar for Somebody's Lady, and I put your name on her certificate. We enter her. We win." She looked away again, despite his demand. "I could give you some of the money, if you want."

"I don't want or need the money," he said.

She knew he didn't. The Chappells had more zeroes in their bank accounts than royalty.

"Then what?" he asked.

"Then what?" she repeated, looking at him again.

"Yes, Beth. Then what? We enter her. We win. Then what?"

"Then...you can file for divorce. It's five months, Trey. Only five months. For five hundred thousand dollars."

Trey exhaled and looked up over her shoulder, toward the northern sky. "You want us to *pretend* to be married."

"Yes."

"Do I have to live here?"

"I don't see why you'd need to," she said. "It's really just a piece of paper. In and out at City Hall. No one would have to know."

Trey chuckled, the sound dark. It grew into a full-blown laugh, and Beth didn't like it.

"Sweetheart, they'll know," he said, focusing on her again. "You enter that horse with my name on it, and your name on it, and people will know."

She lifted her chin, disliking how he made her feel small. "Then we pretend it's real. So what if people know? We'll be like, yeah, we got married. We're making it work."

"Then I *would* move in here." He wasn't asking this time.

"There are a lot of details to work out," Beth said, her

courage fading fast. "I thought I'd bring it up today and you can take some time to think about it."

"Hmm." He nodded, looked at the ground, and started walking again. "Let's get these horses inspected. My mother wants me to come to lunch at her place today, and I said I would."

"Okay," Beth said, scampering after him. They worked through the rest of the horses, and Trey didn't say another word about the Sweetheart Classic.

He laughed with TJ at the farmhouse while they washed up, and he sent her son back outside to get his shoes, which he'd left by the woodpile and the kittens.

"I don't know what it is with that kid and his shoes," Trey said with a smile in his tone. He turned away from the back windows and faced her, the grin slipping from his face. "I'll bring the guys sometime this week to get the garden cleared," he said. "I'll think about what you said, and I'll have an answer for you then, okay?"

"Okay," she said, glad the word was only two syllables. "Take your time."

He nodded, touched the brim of his hat, and came toward her. He stopped in front of her, his dark eyes blazing with desire, hope, and danger. So much danger.

He leaned down, and Beth tipped her chin up. Every fiber in her body beat with her pulse, and Trey slid his hand along her waist. His lips brushed her cheek and continued toward her ear. He held her in place, his mouth at her ear, and whispered, "I like you, Beth Dixon."

Trey stepped back, and Beth reached for the counter behind her so she wouldn't fall. The nearness of him made her muscles weak, and the whispering buzz of his voice in her eardrums rendered her breathless.

"See you soon," he said, and he left the farmhouse. Beth stared toward the back windows, only moving a few minutes later when her son came skipping into the house while he sang one of his favorite songs from the shows she let him watch on TV.

"Did Trey leave?" he asked.

"Yeah," Beth said, clearing the emotion from her voice. "Yes, he had to leave." She flashed a smile at her son, noting his disappointment. *Join the club*, she thought.

If he'd agree to marry her, though, then he might not have to leave...

23

Tam sat on the front steps of the homestead at Bluegrass Ranch, sheer will holding her in place. A box of cheesy garlic knots from Mindie's rested beside her, and she scanned the dirt lane leading up to the house constantly.

Spur had said Blaine would be back in time for work on Monday morning. Cayden had confirmed it. When Tam had showed up at the house, Trey had said they expected to see Blaine any time now.

That had been an hour ago.

The garlic knots were cold, and Tam's patience and willpower were wearing thin. "Where are you?" she asked, clenching her fingers into fists inside the front pocket of the hoodie she wore.

It was almost October, and a cool wind had arrived in Kentucky. The sun went down, and the door behind her opened. "Still out here?" Cayden asked. He came to sit beside her on the steps, and he sighed as he let his hands hang between his knees.

"Maybe I should just go," Tam said. If he confirmed it for her, she'd take it as permission and get the heck out of there. She had nothing prepared to say to Blaine, though she'd had plenty of time.

She'd finished four more saddles this week, a piece of her heart etched into each one. Part of Blaine was too, and she wanted to tell him. She needed to apologize for saying she hated him. She needed him to know *she* wanted him, and then he could decide if he didn't want her.

"Maybe give him a few more minutes," Cayden said.

Tam nodded, her jaw clenching.

"Can I ask you a question?" he asked.

Tam took her eyes from the empty road and looked at Cayden. He seemed unsure and pretty nervous. "Sure."

"If you sent a text to a man that said you were just so busy right now, but you'd like to get to know him in the future, what does that mean?"

Tam wanted to know who the woman was, because context was important. She'd seen Cayden circling Virginia Winters at Spur's wedding, but that was months ago. Blaine hadn't said anything about him dating, but they didn't spend their time together gossiping about his brothers.

"I don't know," Tam said, her brain misfiring. "Probably that I was really busy right now, and when things at my job or in my family slow down and life feels easier for me, I'll go out with you. But right now, it just makes me more stressed, and I don't want to be stressed when I meet up with you." She sucked in a breath and met his eyes, which had widened during her monologue.

"I'd want to feel relaxed and ready to have a good time. I'd want to feel sexy and flirty, and make sure you knew that all of my attention was on you, not whatever project or assignment I'd left at work, unfinished." She shrugged and looked back out to the road, though she'd have heard Blaine's truck if he'd arrived. "That would be what I would mean."

"Okay," Cayden said.

"Why?" Tam asked, glancing at him out of the corner of her eye. "Who said that to you?"

"Ginny Winters," he said, sighing afterward. "We met at the wedding, and I've seen her over at Olli's and Spur's a couple of times. I asked her to dinner, but she sent me that text instead."

Tam smiled at Cayden and laid her head against his shoulder. "Ginny Winters doesn't play games, Cayden. Whatever she says, she means." She straightened, the sound of a truck's engine getting closer. "Also, you shouldn't ask her out via text. She is far more sophisticated than that."

She stood as Blaine's truck crested the hill. "Dear Lord, here we go."

"Sophisticated?" Cayden stood too, but Tam didn't

have enough mental energy to focus on him and the man driving toward her. "We'll talk later." Cayden turned and left her standing on the top stair.

"Mm," she said, not even sure what he'd said to her. Her feet took her down to the sidewalk, where she remembered the garlic knots. She hurried back up the steps to retrieve the box of Blaine's favorite food.

She felt like a dunce carrying it toward him. A blast of loud music filled the air for only a moment, and then a truck door slammed.

Keep going, Tam coached herself. *A few more steps. Don't stop.*

She made it around the trucks parked in front of the house, and Blaine and his truck came into view. She stopped, her fingers tightening on the box of food.

"What are you doing here?" he asked, his voice low and his cowboy hat pushed all the way down over the tips of his ears.

"I came to apologize," she said. "I brought cheesy garlic knots from Mindie's in a potentially disastrous attempt to get you to forgive me with cheese, bread, and butter." She twittered, the sound so nervous.

"You don't need to apologize to me," he said, taking a few slow steps toward her. The darkness hid his whole face, and she really wanted to see him.

Frustration grew inside Tam. "Yes, I do," she said. "I don't hate you, and I shouldn't have said I did."

"I overreacted."

True, and he was admitting it, which only endeared him to her more. "I want you to call me. I want you to come by. I don't want this to be the end of us." She took a shuddering breath. "I want to be your wife, and I want to build a family with you." She looked down at the white box that held cold breadsticks, her eyes burning. "I'm sorry that I hurt you, and that I said things I didn't mean, and I know it's idiotic to think I can buy forgiveness with bread."

She looked up at him. "I'm willing to wait if you need time. I know everything about you, Blaine Chappell, and I'm in love with you." She took the few quick steps to erase the distance between them. "Please, take the knots and say something."

She certainly needed to stop speaking. She thought of her mother, and how strong she'd said Tam was. A sense of accomplishment filled Tam for having the strength to come here and say all she had. She'd held back with Blaine for so long, and she really didn't want to do that anymore.

"I don't want the garlic knots," he said.

Tam recoiled from him as if he'd thrown ice water in her face. Sputtering, she had no idea what to say. She couldn't look at him, because what kind of sadist watched another person rip their heart out and squeeze it into a tiny ball?

"I just want you," he said.

Tam's gaze flew back to Blaine's. "You want me?"

"Yes," he said. "*I* was the idiot at your shop that night. I shouldn't have let Hayes bother me, but I did. I said terrible things that weren't true—we never pretended. Nothing we did was *ever* fake."

Tam's life started to brighten, but she pulled hard on the reins so the hope inside her wouldn't get too far ahead of reality.

Blaine took the box from her. "I don't want these." He dropped the box on the ground. "I love you. I want you."

The air in Tam's lungs whooshed out, and she reached for him. "I'm sorry," she murmured at the same time he said it to her. He gathered her close, and Tam stood in his arms as the things that had been bent and misplaced between them got righted.

He felt solid and warm, and Tam clung to him, still in shock that he'd said he wanted her.

"I didn't think anyone could ever want me," she said.

"You don't see yourself clearly, Tamara," he whispered, pulling back. He leaned down and kissed her, and the future Tam had started to envision for the two of them came roaring back into her mind in full color.

She kissed him back, feeling every stroke of his mouth against hers, every touch of his hand along her back and in her hair. Every sense had heightened, and she enjoyed all the sensations of kissing Blaine Chappell after he'd said he loved her and wanted her.

When he finally pulled away, Tam's pulse hammered through her veins. "Where have you been?" she asked.

"Tennessee," he said. "Did you think I wasn't coming back?" He stroked her hair tenderly, and Tam fell in love with him a little more.

"No," she said. "I knew you'd come back."

"I'm that predictable, huh?" He smiled at her, and Tam returned the gesture.

"It's not about predictability," she said. "I went to see my parents the day after we broke up. My momma told me I knew how to get what I wanted, and she asked me what I wanted. I thought about it for a day or two, and everything always came back to you. That's how I knew you'd come back." She ran her fingertips down the side of his face. "Plus, I called Spur, and he said you'd be back in time for work on Monday."

Blaine burst out laughing, and Tam basked in the sound of it. When he quieted, she tipped up on her toes and kissed him again. "I love you, Blaine Chappell. I've loved you as a friend for decades, and I love you as the man I want to spend the rest of my life with now."

He rested his forehead against hers and said, "Thank you, Tam. I'm hopelessly in love with you too."

"No car mats for my birthday this year?" she murmured.

"Definitely not." He kissed her again, pulling away only seconds later. "Let's go look at rings tomorrow. What do you think?"

"I think I'd go right now if any of the shops were open."

Blaine grinned, his eyes so bright. Tam released the reins on the hope she'd been holding back, because she didn't need to cage it any longer.

Blaine Chappell loved her, but best of all, Blaine Chappell *wanted* her.

"DO YOU THINK YOU HAVE SOMETHING LIKE THAT?" TAM asked, hopefully looking up into the face of the salesman who'd met her and Blaine at the door.

He grinned down at her. "I have exactly what you want." The salesman, named Matt, glanced at Blaine. "Do you two have a budget?"

Tam turned to look at Blaine too, and he just shook his head. "Show her what she wants, and we'll see what it costs."

Tam's giddiness refused to be caged. She was engagement ring shopping with Blaine Chappell. She got to be giddy. Overjoyed. Ecstatic.

"This way," Matt said, and he led them to a case against the far wall. "To me, it sounded like you wanted a round cut, with plenty of sparkle, and lots of charm." He reached into the case and pulled out a display that had six rings nestled in it.

"This one is what you described. Solid gold band, with plenty of sparkle. It's a round cut, brilliant cut—that's what gives it the shine." He picked up the third ring from the edge and handed it to Tam.

She couldn't look away from the glinting diamond, and she felt the cost of this gem. She slipped it onto her finger and held out her hand, cocking her head to the side to admire it. Matt continued to detail something about the ring, as it had a curving piece of gold that curled around the diamond, almost like a flower.

"Do you like it?" Blaine asked, and Tam looked up at the soft touch of his hand on her waist.

"Yes," she said, the word grinding through her throat. "But I'm not getting the first one." She took it off, took a deep breath, and handed the ring back to Matt. "What else?"

"This one is the same cut and brilliance. It's white gold, as you can see. That's not silver. There's more flair with this one with the bands around the diamond. There are an additional sixteen diamonds circling the main one, and it's quite a bit larger than the one you just had on." Matt passed the engagement ring to Tam, who slid it on her finger.

It was larger, and heavier, and Tam liked it a lot in the display, but not on her hand. She took it off without holding her hand out. "It's a very nice ring," she said.

"Not the one," Matt said with a chuckle. "Okay." He looked up from the display. "But you like this one?"

"Yes," Tam said. "I liked that one."

"Let me scan that tag, so we can come back to it in case

you don't see something else you like." He picked up the ring and used his phone to scan the barcode on the tag. "This will tell us the price too."

"Hold onto it," Blaine said. "I only want to know for the one she likes the most."

Tam almost rolled her eyes, but she didn't. Blaine had more money than most people, and he could certainly afford a dozen rings from this shop. Probably more. She linked her arm through his and enjoyed the kiss he placed against her hairline as they moved down to the next cabinet.

Matt got out another display with six rings, and Tam tried on three of them before she said, "I like gold more than white gold. And I like simplicity *and* charm, I suppose, because I don't like the ones with tons of gems or strange settings."

"We'll find you the right one, ma'am," Matt said, though Tam was probably only a couple of years older than him. "Let's try this case back here. We have a few that I think will fit your criteria."

He led them to the very back counter, right in the middle. He rounded the case and removed a display with only three rings on it. All three were gold, with two of them the round cut she liked. The third had a square gem that Matt called a princess cut.

Tam hadn't gotten out her wedding ideas folders yet, because Blaine hadn't proposed yet. He'd made it *very* clear on the way to the jewelry store that morning that he was *not* buying the ring that day. They were just *looking*. There would not be a proposal in the shop.

She tried on the princess cut ring, and immediately rejected it. "That's a no." She gave it back, and Matt handed her a ring with a thicker band, the round, sparkly diamond perched right on top, in a casing that surrounded it. It was simple and beautiful, and Tam loved it.

Two smaller—almost tiny—diamonds sat on either side of the large one, complimenting it, not taking from it.

"These are a different color," she said, pointing to the diamonds on the side. The ring slipped a little on her finger, because it was too big.

"No, they're all white diamonds," Matt said. "They just have different hues on the color scale. The one in the middle is labeled a D. It's the brightest, clearest white diamond. Very rare."

Expensive, Tam thought, but no one said it.

"The other two are also white diamonds, but they're labeled an N, and they have a slightly yellow-gold glow. With the gold band, that's enhanced."

"They're beautiful," Tam said, looking at the ring again. She couldn't seem to be able to tear her eyes from it. Blaine asked a question she didn't hear, and Matt answered it. She held out her hand, imagining doing it for her mother, her sisters, and anyone else who wanted to see it.

She heard Blaine chuckle, and she looked up to find both men looking at her. "What?"

"We've only been talking to you forever," Blaine teased. "I think that's the one you want."

"I like this one a lot."

"We want you to *love* your wedding ring," Matt said. "There's this one here, and it's—"

"I *love* this one," Tam said, looking from Blaine to Matt. "You better scan it and give him the bad news." She took off the ring, and she didn't like handing it back to Matt.

Blaine put his arm around her and drew her to his side. Tam fit there, and everything in the world was right. "It's going to be expensive," Tam said. "You heard him, right? The brightest, clearest diamond. Very rare."

"I heard him," Blaine said, his mouth right against her ear. "You remember what I told you about my inheritance, right? Five billion. I think I can afford whatever he says." He pressed his lips to her earlobe. "Even if I couldn't, I'd figure out a way, because I want you to have whatever you want."

"I thought you said you weren't buying the ring today."

"I'm not," Blaine said, looking up when Matt cleared his throat. "What's the damage?"

Matt barely blinked when he said, "This one is thirty-seven."

Tam's mouth dropped open. "Okay, I don't love it that much."

"Tam," Blaine said.

"We're not buying today anyway," Tam said, panic building in her stomach. She turned into Blaine. "Now we know, and we'll have to decide."

"The first one she tried on is fourteen," Matt said. "It probably wouldn't even need to be resized, as it seemed just right at a seven and a half. This one is an eight."

"Why the difference?" Tam asked. "They seemed almost the same to me."

"This diamond is almost fifty percent bigger, with the extra ones on the side. The gold is also twice as much for the thicker band." Matt looked at Blaine, and they both paused.

It took Tam a few seconds to realize they were communicating without speaking, and she twisted to look at Blaine. "What?"

"Nothing." He drew in a breath. "You're right. Now we know. Do you want to get some lunch?"

Tam looked back at Matt, feeling bad he wasn't going to make a sale that day. Blaine would come back another time and get something from him. If Tam knew Blaine at all, he'd get her the one that cost thirty-seven thousand dollars and plan an amazing proposal.

He'd claimed this shopping trip was just to get an idea of what she liked, but Tam knew what it was really about. He wanted to know what ring she wanted, so he could buy it for her. She wasn't sure why she felt uneasy. He had a lot of money, and he rarely did what he didn't want to do.

"Lunch sounds great," she said. She turned back to Matt too. "Thank you so much for your help. Really. I learned a lot, and you have some beautiful rings here."

Blaine knocked on the glass countertop and said, "Thanks, Matt." He put his arm around Tam again and said, "I'm thinking I need a really good burger. You in?"

"Are you thinking of driving for an hour before we even get to the restaurant?"

"Yes," he said, laughing afterward. "That's why I asked if you were in."

Tam would gladly go to the moon and back with him. She grinned up at him and put her hand on his chest. "Yes, I'm in."

24

Blaine eyed the rain pounding the windshield, his annoyance at Mother Nature warranted. She'd been dumping rain on Kentucky for a solid week now. This morning, the clouds had parted for a few minutes, and Blaine had managed to drive back to the jewelry shop where Tam had found two rings she liked.

The moment he'd pulled in, though, the sky had cracked, and water had been sluicing from it for a solid ten minutes. Blaine knew rainstorms in the South, and he could wait it out. He certainly wasn't going to get soaking wet just to dash to the door of the shop. He could wait.

He checked his email on his phone and found one originally sent from Cayden about their upcoming sales season. A couple of the other brothers had already responded to it, and Blaine read quickly.

He frowned at the suggestion to change the dates of their horses-of-all-ages sale. That traditionally happened in January, and all of their buyers knew it.

Their yearling sale was happening next month, and Cayden, Blaine, and everyone else had been getting ready for it for months.

Cayden's reason for changing the sale made sense, though, and Blaine found himself agreeing by the end of the email. *Fine with me*, he tapped out and sent. *Tell me what to do, and I'll do it.*

The reason was that the bi-annual trade show put on by the Breeders Association had just been announced for the same week as their horses-of-all-ages sale. Spur had suggested they do theirs before, but Cayden wanted to do it after. Not the week after either, but the month after, pushing things into February.

Blaine didn't like that idea, but Cayden reasoned that then people would have purchased or missed out at the trade show, and they'd have some time to adjust their budget for the sale at Bluegrass Ranch.

The rain pounding against the top of the truck lessened, and Blaine looked up from his phone. Another few seconds, and the rain tapered even more. He made his move, striding quickly toward the entrance to the jewelry store.

This door did not have a bell that rang when he walked inside. A man met him there, and Blaine grinned at Matt, who reached out and shook his hand. "Good to see you again."

"Sorry I'm late," Blaine said. "The rain is ridiculous."

"Really keeps people inside," Matt said. "It's ready for you. Come on back." They chatted on the way through the store, which smelled like roses and leather at the same time. Matt opened a safe and took out a dark blue box and faced Blaine.

"We shined it up for you, and it's been resized to the seven and a half." He opened the lid and passed the box to Blaine.

Blaine looked down at the ring that would make Tam his, and joy lit his soul the same way it had brightened her face when she'd put that ring on her finger. Blaine wanted that same reaction when *he* was the one slipping the ring on.

"It really is a pretty ring," he said.

"It is," Matt said. "You know no one will have one like it either."

"Right," Blaine said, though that wasn't important to him. "Custom design." He looked up and reached into his back pocket to withdraw his credit card. He handed it to Matt and closed the box.

The transaction happened quickly, and Blaine owned the thirty-seven-thousand-dollar ring that would bind him and Tam. He smiled his way out of the shop and all the way back to the ranch.

The rain had left everything wet, but the sun had

shown her face for the first time in a week, so Blaine wasn't complaining. He would be at this time tomorrow if it rained on his plans to propose to Tam.

"I just need good weather for an afternoon," he said, tipping his head back and looking up. "Okay, Lord? Just an afternoon." His plans to decorate her porch with ribbons and tissue paper had gone up in smoke—or rather, water —a few days ago.

He'd been brainstorming with Spur, Cayden, and Trey as to what he could do instead. His plan was to show Tam his sketches to remodel her porch at her house tomorrow evening. She'd said she'd get dinner, and Blaine had somehow conned his brothers into decorating the porch and placing the diamond on the railing while they were eating.

Then, when Blaine took her outside to the porch to "show her something," it would be beautiful and romantic, and he'd ask her to marry him.

If it rained, his décor would just be soggy and limp, not glowing and romantic. Worse, the lights could short circuit and start her grandmother's house on fire.

He got out of the truck and went inside the homestead, where Spur and Olli danced in the kitchen, the music far too loud for Blaine to tolerate. He grinned at Spur's perfect rhythm, and the way Olli laughed at him warmed his heart.

Spur laughed too, completely carefree, something Blaine hadn't seen in him in such a long time. He took Olli into his arms, and they swayed together as they quieted. They were so wonderful together, and Blaine's happiness reached a new sphere.

He came down the hall, and Spur turned toward the sound of his footsteps. "There you are. Did you get it?"

Olli squealed and leapt away from Spur. "Let me see. Let me see."

"I never should've told you guys my plan."

"Are you kidding me right now?" Olli put her hands on her hips and cocked one eyebrow at him. "I came up with that amazing idea for the proposal, and you're going to smell so great she'll be saying yes before you even ask." A smile softened her face as she held out her hand. "Now. Let me see it."

Spur moved to her side, and she glanced at him. "He's worried about the weather."

"Good thing I have a back-up plan for the proposal." Olli waggled her fingers at him. "Let me see the ring, and I'll tell you Plan B."

Blaine held up the off-white bag that held the engagement ring. Olli grinned and danced the final few steps to him to take it.

"I'm so excited," she said, taking the ring to the kitchen counter and removing the box from the bag. She opened that and gasped. "Oh...dear...this is *beautiful*." She looked at Blaine and then Spur. "I wish I could be there."

"No," Blaine said with a smile. "No, I'm not doing a public proposal like Spur here."

"It was just Mom and Dad," Spur said.

"Yeah," Blaine said. "You should hear Mom tell that story. It was like she was the one getting proposed to." He rolled his eyes. "No, it's just going to be me and Tam." That way, if she said no, no one else would witness his humiliation.

"She's not going to say no," Spur said as if he could read Blaine's mind.

Blaine took a deep breath and blew it out. "I guess we'll see tomorrow night."

Olli packed up the ring again and handed it back to Blaine. "You guys are going to have the greatest wedding and life together." She flung herself at Blaine, who grunted as he caught her. "I'm so happy for you, Blaine."

"Thanks, Olli," he said, his eyes closing, the "greatest life" she'd just spoken of flashing through his mind. "I think you said something about a Plan B?"

"Right, yes." She nearly deafened him as she squealed and stepped back. "Okay, so here's what you're going to do..."

BLAINE THOUGHT HE HAD A FIFTY-FIFTY CHANCE OF PULLING off the best proposal in the world tonight. He walked steadily toward Tam's house, refusing to think about the truck full of his brothers that had followed him.

"Twenty minutes," he muttered to himself as he went

up the steps, his folder clutched in his hand. He hoped by the end of the night, they'd be looking through a lot of folders. His with the porch sketches. Hers with the wedding plans.

She'd told him she had ideas not plans, and Blaine would do his best to contribute to the planning. Really, he just wanted her to have the wedding of her dreams. He'd never thought much about the particulars of his wedding, and she had. She might as well get what she wanted.

What she wanted was for him to contribute, so he would.

He knocked on the door and waited, remembering that her doorbell needed to be fixed. "You're not changing everything about this house," he told himself as Tam opened the door.

"Hey, cowboy," she said in a flirty voice. Her eyes dropped to the folder in his hand. "Are those the sketches?"

He tightened his grip on them. "After we eat, sweetheart. I'm starving."

"You're always starving," she teased. Stepping back, she added, "Come in then."

He did, and the scent of browned and delicious meat met his nose. "Something smells good."

"It's my granny's pot roast," she said. "I know what you like."

"Yes, you do." He grinned at her and swept her into his arms. "You must know what I want now."

"Mm, I think I have an idea." She smiled up at him and kissed him, making most of Blaine's dreams come true. She didn't let him enjoy it for long, though, before she ducked her head and added, "I want to see what's in that folder."

"I'll bet you do." Blaine stepped away from her and looked toward the kitchen. "After dinner."

"Fine," she said. "I know how to get what I want." She preceded him into the kitchen and got down two plates. "Get out the forks, buddy."

Blaine did what she said, then set the folder on top of the fridge while she pulled potatoes and carrots out of the slow cooker. "We're ready for the yearling sale," he said. "In case you were going to ask."

"I was," Tam said, turning toward him. "I was just going to ask."

"Spur bought The Gambler."

"He did?"

"He couldn't stand to let him go," Blaine said. "Cayden's not super happy with him, because he'd already printed the sale order. Well." He shrugged. "He'd sent the file to the printer. He was on the phone with them all afternoon."

"I feel bad for him," Tam said. "Did you know he asked Virginia Winters to dinner?"

"He mentioned it," Blaine said. "He never went."

"She said she was really busy right now."

"Yeah, Trey looked up what was going on at the Winters' distillery, and she's up to her eyeballs."

"What do they have going on?"

"A massive fall festival from now until Halloween. They cut mazes in their wheat and barley, and it's a real riot down there."

"So he's just going to wait."

Blaine watched her move a knife through the pot roast with quick, precise movements. "He's going to wait."

"I understand waiting." Tam gave him a dry look, and Blaine's heart deflated a little bit.

"Listen, I'm really sorry about the thirtieth birthday and all the other times I was an idiot."

Tam met his eye, clearly appreciating the statement. She said, "You don't need to apologize for anything, Blaine. We each have our own path, you know?"

"I do know." He picked up a plate and handed it to her. "Did you get that shoulder bag done?"

"No," she said darkly. "It's so thick, my needles kept breaking." She flexed her hands and squeezed her fingers into fists. "I gave up, because my hands hurt and I wasn't willing to break another needle. I threw away six today as it was."

"You didn't charge enough for that thing."

"No, I did not." She moved out of the way with her dinner and went to sit at the table. Blaine loaded his plate with meat and potatoes and joined her.

"Will you cook for me when we're married?" he asked.

Tam looked up at him. "This is literally the only thing I know how to make."

He put a bite of beef in his mouth. "It's real good."

"Will you cook for me?"

"If you like boxed mac and cheese." Blaine grinned at her.

"I do," Tam said with a sparkling smile. "Don't think I don't know that you feed all your brothers on Sundays."

"They're easy to please." Blaine kept one eye on the clock and ate as slowly as he could. His phone brightened at minute twenty-three with one word from Spur.

Done.

Then a few more. *Olli says good luck.*

Blaine smiled and flipped his phone over, forced himself to wait a few more minutes, and then said a prayer that his odds would be on the side where everything was perfect when he led Tam outside. When thirty minutes had passed, he finally got up and walked over to the refrigerator.

"Okay," he said. "You want to see what I've come up with?"

"I've been dying a slow death," she said.

He returned to the table and sat beside her again as she moved their plates out of the way. "Okay," he said, his pulse beating irregularly. "If you don't like it, it's fine. I'm not married to it. If you don't want to do it at all, because you love this house as-is, that's fine too."

Tam reached up and cradled his face, her eyes moving

up to the brim of his hat and back to his eyes. "I want you to be happy living here too."

Blaine swallowed, the very idea of that so appealing to him. He opened the folder and pulled out the first sketch. "This one keeps the original stairs. It simply expands the porch from left to right, across the whole front of the house. We'd redo the roof over the whole house, because you said that needs to be done anyway, and we can add the roof over the new part of the porch at the same time."

Tam studied the sketches, her eyes wide. Blaine watched her, hoping to find a clue as to how she felt about the idea. She finally looked up at him. "This would be great," she said. "We could put a table and chairs out there and watch the sun rise."

Blaine grinned at her. "Since we're both up at the crack of dawn." He reached down and picked up the corgi that kept putting his paws up on Blaine's legs.

"Jasper," Tam admonished. "You don't have to hold him."

Blaine let the dog settle in his lap. "He likes me." He liked the corgi too, because it comforted him to stroke the animal as he laid out the second drawing. "This one expands the steps so they're twice as wide. They'll be more like a farmhouse, and I know you like that."

"I do," she said, studying the plans.

"The porch goes around the left side and connects to the back porch. We'll cover the whole thing. Then you can sit out there while it rains and listen to the thunder roll through the sky." He smiled at the thought of that, imagining him and Tam on the south side of the house, listening to the thunder and watching the sky for lightning.

"Or, we could put a hot tub there. Think of that, Tam. In the winter, we can sit in this deliciously warm water while it snows."

She lifted her gaze to his. "We can't put a hot tub on a deck."

"Sure you can," he said, his heart pounding like a drum now. "We'll just raise the foundation a little in the corner, and it'll be set down *into* the deck, baby." He reached for her hand and stood up. "Come see. I'll show you."

She put her hand in his, and Blaine set Jasper back on the ground before heading for the front door. Once there, he paused and took a deep breath.

He opened the door and scanned the porch. The lights had been hung. The flowers laced through the wires. Olli had spritzed something that smelled like love in the air. The roses sat on the tiny table Tam had on her porch now. Blaine reached for them as he went outside, and when he turned back to Tam, he held them in front of him.

"Oh, my," Tam said, sucking in a breath.

Blaine reached for the ring box sitting on the windowsill and dropped to his knees. "Tamara," he said, his voice shaking slightly. "I love you." Everything after that scrambled in his brain, and he had no idea what he was going to say next.

This was why he didn't want anyone here to see the proposal. His brain finally caught up to the uncomfortable surface beneath his kneecaps. "Will you marry me?" He opened the box and lifted it up so the white Christmas lights he'd asked his brothers to hang would illuminate the ring.

"I knew you'd go back and get that ring," she said, her voice pitching up.

Blaine had no defense for himself. He didn't even need one. "I want you to be happy," he said, pieces of his speech returning to his mind. "I don't know if I can do it all the time, but I'm willing to try. I love you, and you'd make me the luckiest and happiest man in the world if you say yes."

Tam pressed both hands to her heart, her smile wide. "Yes," she said simply, not a hitch in her voice whatsoever.

Blaine grinned at her too, got to his feet, and drew her into his arms. He kissed her beneath the twinkling lights, with the scent of love in the air, joy pouring through him. He slid the ring she loved onto her finger, and the two of them looked at it together.

Tam put her other hand on his chest and their eyes met. "I love you, Blaine."

"I love you, too, Tam."

She kissed him, and Blaine thought he could kiss her on her front porch forever. Someone honked their horn in several rapid successive beats, and a cowboy yelled, "Yeehaw! She must've said yes!" before the truck revved its engine and sped down the street.

Blaine watched it, a frown pulling at his eyebrows. "They are so annoying."

Tam laughed and put her hand in his. "You love them. Now, come on. Show me what you mean by raise the foundation a little."

"You don't have to say it like that," he said. "I know what I'm doing."

"Say it like what?" she asked as she went down the steps.

"Come on. With that sarcastic tone in your voice." He reached the sidewalk and took her around the side of the house to where she parked. The driveway was sloped, and by his calculations, they'd only need to raise the back section of the cement by three feet to accommodate a hot tub.

He explained it all to her, her hand in his back pocket.

"All right," she said when he finished. "Let's do it."

"Yeah?" He faced her and slipped his own hands into her back pockets.

"Yeah," she said. "I'm all in with you, Blaine Chappell." She tilted her head back and looked up at him, her face full of happiness and light.

"Good," he said. "Because I'm all in with you too, Tam." He kissed her again, wondering if there was a level of happiness beyond joy. If so, he was there, because he and Tam were going to spend the rest of their lives together.

Keep reading for more about Trey and Beth - the first 2 chapters of TRAINING THE COWBOY BILLIONAIRE are included.

TRAINING THE COWBOY BILLIONAIRE CHAPTER ONE:

*T*rey Chappell loved his mother's cooking, and while she'd lured him here with the promise of chicken and dumplings, he didn't entirely hate it.

It was time anyway.

The conversation had been fine. Better than fine. Good. He'd talked about the upcoming yearlings sale, as well as Blaine's engagement, and he hadn't once had to answer a question he didn't want to.

Trey didn't actually mind answering questions if he knew the answers to them. The problem was that his mother liked to ask him things he didn't know how to answer. He wasn't sure why he couldn't let go of Sarah. He wasn't sure why he'd put all the blame on God and lost his faith.

Deep down, he still believed in the loving, benevolent God his parents had taught him about. At the same time, he couldn't believe that the Lord would allow his heart to be so completely trampled on, despite Sarah's ability to make her own choices.

He didn't know why he hadn't been able to make another relationship work, though he'd tried. He didn't know why he was so drawn to Bethany Dixon, and he had no idea why he hadn't been able to give a sure answer to her proposal. She'd asked him to marry her so they could enter the Sweetheart Classic together.

Really, so she could enter her horse into the Sweetheart Classic. She hadn't gone into details, but Trey could still hear her say, "I need the money, Trey. Plain and simple."

He'd said he'd let her know when he came to clear her garden. That had been last week, and while they'd gotten the work done, when he'd gotten a moment alone with Beth, he'd told her he needed more time to come to a final decision.

Her time was running out, and Trey felt it ticking away second by second, the clicking actually loud in his ears.

They had to be married by Halloween, with his name on the horse's certificate before she could register it for the Sweetheart Classic. It wasn't October yet, but it would be in a few days, and he really needed to come to a decision.

"Are you seeing anyone new?" Mom asked, and Trey put the last bite of his chicken and dumplings in his mouth.

He took a few seconds to chew and swallow, trying to formulate the right answer. "Kind of," he said.

Mom's brow furrowed. "How can you *kind of* be seeing someone?"

"Jules," Daddy said, and his mom lifted one hand.

"Sorry," she said. "Sorry, Trey. I know how dating goes these days. You like her, and you're not sure if she likes you, and you want to be her boyfriend, but maybe you're not yet, so there's this middle ground where *kind of* exists."

Trey gaped at his mother. It was the third Sunday in a row he'd eaten with them alone, and he found all of his hard feelings softening and falling away. "Yeah," he said. "It's a little bit like that."

He looked back and forth between his mother and his father, and the interest in their eyes wasn't lost on him. He also wanted to tell someone about the things that had been tormenting him for the past two weeks, and maybe those two people were sitting right in front of him.

Part of his brain screamed at him to eat his mom's famous peach cobbler and homemade vanilla ice cream and keep his thoughts to himself. That had been working for him for the past forty-one years, and if he wanted to talk to someone, he could go back to therapy.

"If we can help," Mom said. "Let us know." She stood up. "Now, did you eat too much to have cobbler now? We can sit on the upper verandah if you'd like."

"I can take my cobbler up there, right?" he asked.

Mom smiled as she picked up his empty plate. "Of

course, baby." She bent down and pressed a kiss to his head. "I'll get it all out."

Trey nodded and watched her go into the kitchen. She sang to herself as she got out bowls and spoons, the dishes clacking against each other.

"Thanks for coming," Daddy said in a low voice. "It means a lot to your mother."

"I know," Trey said. "She's been doing really great."

"She loves you boys," he said. "We both do."

"I know that." Trey reached up and tipped his hat forward. "Listen, I did want to talk to you about something."

Daddy leaned into the table. "Go ahead."

Trey swallowed. "All right now." He took a moment to find the right words, but they weren't there. It was the same reason he hadn't said anything to Cayden or Blaine. There wasn't an adequate way to explain the situation.

"Do you know Beth Dixon?" he asked right as his mother came back to the table.

"Are we staying in here?" She set a bowl of ice cream and cobbler on the table in front of him.

"No," Trey said, getting up. "Let's go outside." Maybe then he'd know how to explain what was in his head. He carried his bowl and steadied Daddy as he went up the steps to the second half of their back porch.

He took a bite of sweet ice cream and tart peaches. "Mm, Momma, you're a genius."

She laughed and continued to help Daddy get settled,

tucking a blanket around his legs. Trey wore his jacket too, as autumn had definitely arrived in Kentucky.

"You said something about Beth Dixon," Daddy said, and Trey caught the sharpness in his mother's eyes.

"Yes," Trey said. "I've been helping her around her farm the past little bit." He shifted a little bit, because that wasn't entirely true. It was true, but that wasn't entirely altruistic. "Her son's been hangin' around the ranch, and I take him home. Then Beth hurt her hand a few weeks ago, and we've been helping."

"We know about that," Mom said. "Blaine's told us."

"Yeah." Trey took another bite of his treat. "Well, I like her. I asked her to dinner, and she said her father could watch TJ." He cleared his throat. "We haven't done it yet or anything."

"Well, why not?" Mom asked.

"Things are busy, Mom," Trey said, a touch of darkness in his tone. He didn't want to go into how Beth had told her father she wasn't ready to start dating.

"The yearlings sale is in two weeks." November first was barely beyond that, and Trey's throat closed.

"I know," Mom said. "Sorry. Go on."

Trey didn't know how to go on. "I don't want you to get upset."

"Why would I get upset?" Mom asked.

"Julie, let the man talk," Daddy said.

"Sorry, sorry."

Trey took another bite of cobbler. The breeze blew

past the white fences and through the pastures beyond. "She's been in a...tough place since her husband died, and she wants to enter one of her horses into a race."

"Mm hm," Mom said.

"There's a catch," Trey said, watching his parents out of the corner of his eye. "It's the Sweetheart Classic."

Daddy didn't understand, if his perplexed look was any indication. Mom got it though, because her eyes widened. She sucked in a breath, but to her everlasting credit, she didn't say anything.

"The deadline to enter is November first," Trey said, driving home the immediacy of the situation.

"Trey Travis Chappell," Mom said, not moving when Daddy put his hand on her leg. "Did you marry Beth Dixon?"

"Marry Beth Dixon?" Daddy asked at the same time Trey scoffed and said, "No, Mom. Come on now."

"The Sweetheart Classic requires the entrants to be married and own the horse together," Mom said, looking at Daddy. "By November first."

Daddy's eyes widened too.

"What should I do?" Trey asked.

Mom opened her mouth and promptly closed it. She looked at Daddy, but there was no help there. Trey had a feeling there wasn't help for this situation anywhere.

Unhappiness pulled through him, and he finished his dessert and set the bowl on the ground beside him.

"Well, honey," Mom finally said. "You have to do what you think is right."

"How do you know what that is?"

"Just be honest with yourself and with her. Pray and ask for help. You'll know what to do."

"Mom," Trey said with a sigh.

"I know, I know," she said. "You don't think praying will help."

"No, Mom, I don't."

"Have you tried it?"

"No, ma'am," he said quietly. He'd prayed plenty of times for the solution to his problems, and he'd never gotten an adequate answer. God didn't seem to hear him, and if he did, he just didn't care enough about Trey to respond.

"Just an idea," Mom said. "Trey, we love you no matter what. You're a good man, and I believe you'll make the right choice for you and for Beth."

Trey looked at his father. "Dad?"

"I like what your mother said," he said. "Be honest with yourself and with her. Pray about it. Do what you think is right."

"That can't be the answer," Trey said, beyond frustrated. Be honest? Pray about it?

No, he wanted a *solution*. He wanted *an answer*.

"Why not?" Daddy asked.

"It's too easy. Be honest. Pray. Do what's right?" He

scoffed. "I'm not a six-year-old. I don't need the cookie cutter answers."

"Trey," his mother started, but she cut off when Daddy put his hand on her arm. They exchanged a look with one another, and she returned her attention to him. "You do what you think is right."

Trey wanted to roll his eyes. Instead, he got up and collected all the dishes. "Thanks for dinner and dessert, Mother." He gave her a kiss. "I'm gonna head out."

"Take some cobbler," Mom called after him, and Trey said he would.

He did dish himself some cobbler, and he took it back to the homestead. "Cobbler," he called to whoever might be in the house, but it was likely just Cayden. No one answered him, so he put the container on the counter and went out onto the back deck.

Kentucky sure was a slice of heaven to Trey, and he looked up into the sky. It had rained a lot last week, but today the evening sky shone with gold and blue.

He wrestled with himself and whether he should say a prayer or not. Surely the Lord already knew what the issue was, and he'd been decidedly silent.

"Maybe you don't know how to hear," Trey muttered to himself. "What can it hurt? It'll take sixty seconds, and then you'll get nothing, and you can go find Cayden—or better, Lawrence—and ask them what to do."

Trey took a deep breath and exhaled. He did that over and over, trying to work up the courage to pray. He knew how; he'd done so as a child and teenager and even into his adulthood. It had just been quite a long time.

"Dear Lord," he finally said. "Bethany Dixon is a good woman, and I sure do like her. She needs help, and I can help her. Should I marry the woman so she can enter her horse into the Sweetheart Classic?"

The wind kicked up, and a dog barked somewhere in the distance. Trey closed his eyes and tried—really tried—to hear something. He never heard anything with his ears, but rather his heart.

The things he should and shouldn't do came as feelings, and in that moment, Trey felt like he should help Beth if he could.

"Should I?" he asked again.

There was no squirming in his stomach. The worry that had been needling his mind for weeks disappeared. The unrest in his very soul was simply not there anymore.

Part of him was disgusted, and the other part sagged in relief against the railing on the deck. The sun continued to go down, and the day died degree by degree.

"Why are you standing here?" he asked himself. "Get over to Beth's and talk to her. The clock is ticking."

He pushed away from the railing and hurried to his pickup truck. The drive to Beth's didn't take long. The longest part of the drive was getting down the dirt lane from the house to the road. Beth's was just a bit down the road, and he pulled up to the charming, white farmhouse before he knew it.

While he still had a well of courage, he got out of the truck and marched toward the porch. He made it to the door and rang the doorbell.

"C'mon in," TJ yelled, and Trey took a deep breath.

He opened the door and stepped inside the farm-house, already looking for the child. In the very next moment, a deluge of cold water hit him straight in the face.

Trey sputtered and reached up to cover his face with his hands. "What the devil?" he asked at the same time wild laughter met his ears. He cleared the water from his eyes and hair—his cowboy hat gone completely—and looked down at his soaking wet shirt. The front of his jeans looked like he'd wet himself, and water ran down his legs toward his cowboy boots.

"That's not your uncle Hugh," a man said, and Trey's eyes flew to an older gentleman whose smile faded right before Trey's eyes. Beth's father, Clyde Turner.

"Trey," TJ said, his smile staying in place. He ran toward Trey, who scooped him up despite being a wet mess. "What are you doin' here?"

"I..." He looked at Clyde, who'd found a towel somehow and was hurrying toward him too.

"Sorry," he said. "I'm real sorry about the water. We're expecting Beth's brother, and I was just showin' TJ how to set up a prank." He smiled at the child and exchanged TJ for the towel.

They shook hands too, and Trey used the towel to mop

up the water in his hair. This wasn't a good time to chat with Beth, clearly. Beth's family was here, and she obviously didn't know about this little prank lesson going on in her living room.

He didn't think she'd like the standing water on her hardwood floors, for example.

Trey turned around to find his cowboy hat. He located it sitting in a pool of water, stepped over to it, and had just picked it up when Beth said, "Trey?"

His heartbeat spiked, and he jammed the hat on his head as he straightened and turned in the same movement.

Beth wore a pale yellow tank top that flowed around her frame in a classy, sophisticated way. She made soft, loose pants look like a ballgown, and Trey promptly swept the cowboy hat off his head again.

Aware of water dripping from his ear and sliding down his face, he held his cowboy hat to his chest with one hand and wiped his forehead with the other. "I'll do it, Beth. I'll enter the Sweetheart Classic with you."

TRAINING THE COWBOY BILLIONAIRE CHAPTER TWO:

"The Sweetheart Classic?" Daddy asked, and Bethany Dixon flew into action. She strode forward and put both hands against Trey's chest, as if she could really move a man as muscular as him.

He did fall back though, and he turned and walked out onto the front porch, Beth right on his tail. She brought the door closed behind her a little harder than she meant to, and she pressed her eyes closed as she leaned into the solidness of it.

She inhaled through her nose and realized her feet were wet. She opened her eyes and looked down. "Why is my porch wet?"

"Same reason I'm soaking wet, sweetheart," Trey said in a very dry voice.

She looked up from the puddle where she stood to find Trey standing at the top of the steps, facing her. He really was wet from head to toe, and she could only stare at the sexy way his hair spiked up with water in it.

Everything about the man called to her, and she forgot for a moment why her pulse was pounding and why she'd ushered him outside before he could say anything else.

The door behind her opened, and Daddy said, "Sorry about the water, sweetie. I'll get TJ to clean it up right now."

Beth reached up and brushed her hair out of her eyes. "Thanks, Daddy."

The door closed again, and Beth wished she could lock it from the outside. Hugh should be here soon too, and of course Trey would pick now to make his decision and come tell her about it.

She took a step forward as she tucked her hands in the pockets of her sweats. "You'll do it?"

"Yes," Trey said.

Beth nodded, her throat suddenly closed. She'd admitted so much to him already, and she really didn't want to lose more of her dignity. She moved over to the railing and leaned against it, pleased when he joined her.

She didn't look at him but gazed out over the graveled driveway and down the lane, which was bordered by pastures on both sides. "Why are you wet?"

"Your son and your father set up a prank for someone named Hugh."

"My brother," Beth said. "You'll probably need to get to know all of that, so we can..." She trailed off, finally looking up at him. "You look different without your cowboy hat on."

He automatically reached up and ran his hand through his hair. "My hat's ruined now."

Beth followed the trajectory of his hand with hers, and he froze the moment she touched him. He pulled in a slow breath while she brushed water off his forehead and curled her fingertips along the curve of his ear.

With heat racing through her body, she pulled away. "Sorry."

"It's fine," he said, his voice sounding with a hallowed quality. "Can I hold your hand?"

Beth slid her fingers down his arm and into his hand, the only answer she could currently give. In the silence that descended on them, Beth heard her own heartbeat in her ears and not much else.

Her thoughts raced and then slowed as she accepted that she was holding hands with another man besides Danny Dixon.

"I was engaged once," Trey said. "Did you know?"

Beth cleared her throat. "No, I didn't."

Trey nodded, his gaze out on the pasture like it was the most fascinating thing he'd ever seen. "Her name was Sarah Samuels."

"How'd you meet her?"

"She worked in the marketing department at the printer we use," he said. "They make all our signs, fliers, even those little name tags we give to our champion horses. The ones made of gold?" He chuckled. "It's pretty ridiculous what we do for those horses."

Beth liked the sound of his voice, and she didn't want to taint the conversation with hers.

"Anyway." Trey leaned further into the railing. "She worked with Cayden a lot, because he does almost all of the PR for the ranch, and I met her once...and it was like... I don't know. Magic."

"Sounds wonderful," Beth said, her mind wandering down paths she didn't normally allow it to. "I was married once, but I think you knew that."

His fingers tightened on hers. "I did know that." He glanced at her and grinned. "How did you meet Danny?"

"Everyone in Dreamsville knows the Dixons," she said, a smile automatically curling her mouth. "Danny was my best friend's older brother. I'd seen him around their ranch from time to time, but he was gone to college before I really started hanging out with Myra."

"You must've caught his eye when he came home on a break."

"Not really," she said. "I grew up and went to college with Myra. I didn't finish and came back. I started dating other men." She lifted one shoulder. "None of them were Danny. I didn't realize it until I went to Myra's graduation party, and there he was. I guess you could say that was when we met."

Beth lost herself in good memories of Danny before he'd become her husband. He'd graduated from college too, but his engineering degree only got used for a couple of years before he realized how much he hated it. They'd gotten married and bought this beat-up farm on the outskirts of town, next to the wildly successful Bluegrass Ranch.

How hard they'd worked. Sixteen hours, from sunup to sundown. They'd built a lot of the structures on the farm from the foundation up, and Danny had built this porch where she and Trey now stood.

"You must have loved him very much," Trey said.

"I did," Beth said, pulling herself from her sadness. She drew in a deep breath, held it, and watched her brother turn off the highway. "That's Hugh."

Trey released her hand and put another two feet of distance between them. Beth felt the loss of his touch keenly, and she looked him. "They're going to find out, like you said."

"We have five weeks to get married," he said. "I think we should probably go on at least one date before then." He kept his eyes on her brother's huge black truck as it came closer. "What do you think?"

"Yes," she said, her lungs quaking a little bit.

"That's my stipulation," he said. "I should at least be able to tell my family that we're dating before I start packing my bags to move out."

Beth swallowed. "You'll move in here?"

"You have enough bedrooms," he said. "Might as well make it look real on the outside, don't you think?"

"Yes," she said again. Hugh parked beside Trey, and Beth's window to have this conversation was running out.

"What's your stipulation?" he asked. "I suppose you can have more than one."

"I just have one," she said, her throat so very dry.

"What is it?"

Hugh got out of his truck and lifted his hand in a wave. Beth did the same, and Hugh called, "I'm okay to park here?"

"Yes," Beth called back to him.

"I'm not going to stay," Trey said. "You're busy with your family." He faced her, and while his shirt and jeans were wet, he was still so handsome.

"That's why you should stay," she said. "If we're to be married in only a few weeks." She stepped toward him and reached for the buttons on his shirt. She touched one and then the other, waiting for him to take her into his arms. If he'd been engaged before, he surely understood a woman's unspoken wants.

He finally put one hand on her hip and bent his head down. Beth ran her free hand up the side of his face, enjoying his clean-shaven face and the texture of his longer hair. "I only have one stipulation too," she whispered, the crunching of Hugh's footsteps over the gravel getting dangerously close.

"What is it now?" Trey asked.

"The first time you kiss me can't be on our wedding day."

Hugh started talking as he came up the steps, and Beth kept her eyes on Trey's shocked ones as she backed up. She finally turned away when her brother arrived and embraced him. She laughed as he picked her right up off her feet.

"Who's this?" he asked as he set her down. His bright eyes focused on Trey, and Beth decided they better go for the gold from the very beginning.

"Hugh, this is Trey Chappell. We've started seeing each other." That was one hundred percent true, and neither of them could deny it.

"Well, I'll be," Hugh said, his smile a little too wide. It went well with his wide-eyed, shocked look. He stared at Beth for a moment and then back to Trey.

"Good to meet you," Trey said, stepping forward as if Beth had introduced him to dozens of her friends and family members.

"Why you all wet?"

"I think this was meant for you," Trey said. "I just got here ahead of you."

Hugh's eyes traveled down Trey's body, and he started laughing. "I guess I owe you one then."

Trey smiled, and Beth nearly fell down with how beautiful it made him. "I'd be careful going inside."

"I'll use the back door." Hugh turned back to Beth, already mouthing words. She rolled her eyes instead of trying to read his lips, because she hated that. Even worse was when he started texting her while they were in a group. She hated that; if he had something to say, he should just say it.

"Uncle Hugh?"

The front door opened, and TJ came outside at a run, headed straight for his uncle.

Hugh laughed and picked TJ right up over his head. "Were you going to prank me? Were you? Grandpa's here, isn't he?"

"Yes," their father said. "I'm here." She watched as the three of them embraced, and Hugh followed them back inside, no buckets of water in sight. She looked at Trey, and he looked at her.

"Do you have an hour or two to spend with us here?" she asked. "It's okay if you don't. I'm really good at making up reasons why someone couldn't stay." She smiled, because that was totally true. "Or rather, reasons I can't come to this, that, or the other."

Trey approached and tucked her hair behind her ear. "I can stay for a while."

"Great," she said. "Because I need to introduce you to my father."

"We've met a couple of times now," Trey said, his eyebrows drawing down in confusion. "Once...before, and just now again. I shook his hand and everything."

Of course he had. Trey wasn't awkward the way she was. He might not know what to do in a situation, but he took it by the horns and wrestled it to the ground.

"I need to introduce you as my boyfriend," she said. "Did you tell him that?"

"Now that—no." He looked at her, slight awe in his expression. "Are you going to use that word?"

"What word? Boyfriend?"

"Yeah, that one," he said.

"You don't want me to?"

"I'm just trying to figure it all out is all," he said. "Seeing each other, I get. We are seeing each other. I've been seeing you over the past several weeks." He looked toward the open front door. "Boyfriend...I don't know if that's true."

"Then I'll just say we've recently started seeing each other," Beth said, liking that a lot better. She took the first step toward the door, and Trey went with her. "What—when do you cross the line into boyfriend?"

"About the time I kiss you," he said, dipping his head closer to hers. "Does that work for you?"

She shivered, because everything about him worked for her. "Yes," she whispered, passing through the doorway. Laughter came from the back of the house, where the kitchen sat, and Beth continued that way, determined to get the word out that she had started seeing someone again.

Trey would be the very first man she'd dated since Danny's death, and she hoped no one would find it odd that she married him in only a few weeks. She'd just say she didn't want to wait. She'd been alone long enough, and when she met Trey, she'd just...known.

Like magic, she thought, wondering what had happened to damped the magic on his and Sarah's relationship.

She couldn't help wondering if such magic really existed, and she glanced up at him, searching for something she wouldn't find on his face.

"Daddy," she said once they'd reached the kitchen. "I wanted to properly introduce you to Trey." She put a bright smile on her face. "We've started seeing each other." She beamed at Trey and then her father.

Her dad didn't miss a beat. "Yeah, I saw you holdin' his hand out there on the porch." He grinned at Beth and cocked his eyebrows at Trey.

"Come on now," Trey said, a grin on his face too. "I think *I* was holdin' *her* hand."

BLUEGRASS RANCH ROMANCE

Book 1: Winning the Cowboy Billionaire: She'll do anything to secure the funding she needs to take her perfumery to the next level...even date the boy next door.

Book 2: Roping the Cowboy Billionaire: She'll do anything to show her ex she's not still hung up on him...even date her best friend.

Book 3: Training the Cowboy Billionaire: She'll do anything to save her ranch...even marry a cowboy just so they can enter a race together.

Book 4: Parading the Cowboy Billionaire: She'll do anything to spite her mother and find her own happiness...even keep her cowboy billionaire boyfriend a secret.

Book 5: Promoting the Cowboy Billionaire: She'll do anything to keep her job...even date a client to stay on her boss's good side.

Book 6: Acquiring the Cowboy Billionaire: She'll do anything to keep her father's stud farm in the family...even marry the maddening cowboy billionaire she's never gotten along with.

Book 7: Saving the Cowboy Billionaire: She'll do anything to prove to her friends that she's over her ex...even date the cowboy she once went with in high school.

Book 8: Convincing the Cowboy Billionaire: She'll do anything to keep her dignity...even convincing the saltiest cowboy billionaire at the ranch to be her boyfriend.

CHESTNUT RANCH ROMANCE

Book 1: A Cowboy and his Neighbor: Best friends and neighbors shouldn't share a kiss...

Book 2: A Cowboy and his Mistletoe Kiss: He wasn't supposed to kiss her. Can Travis and Millie find a way to turn their mistletoe kiss into true love?

Book 3: A Cowboy and his Christmas Crush: Can a Christmas crush and their mutual love of rescuing dogs bring them back together?

Book 4: A Cowboy and his Daughter: They were married for a few months. She lost their baby...or so he thought.

Book 5: A Cowboy and his Boss: She's his boss. He's had a crush on her for a couple of summers now. Can Toni and Griffin mix business and pleasure while making sure the teens they're in charge of stay in line?

Book 6: A Cowboy and his Fake Marriage: She needs a husband to keep her ranch...can she convince the cowboy next-door to marry her?

Book 7: A Cowboy and his Secret Kiss: He likes the pretty adventure guide next door, but she wants to keep their relationship off the grid. Can he kiss her in secret and keep his heart intact?

Book 8: A Cowboy and his Skipped Christmas: He's been in love with her forever. She's told him no more times than either of them can count. Can Theo and Sorrell find their way through past pain to a happy future together?

ABOUT EMMY

Emmy is a Midwest mom who loves dogs, cowboys, and Texas. She's been writing for years and loves weaving stories of love, hope, and second chances. Learn more about her and her books at www.emmyeugene.com.

Made in the USA
Las Vegas, NV
17 March 2022